HA'

2

THE NOTORIOUS COALE BROTHERS

They are the talk of the Ton!

Twin brothers Dominic and Jasper Coale
set Society's tongues wagging
with their disreputable behaviour.

Get to know the real men behind the
scandalous reputations in this deliciously
wicked duet from Sarah Mallory!

Major Dominic Coale

He's locked away in his castle in the woods,
with only his tormenting memories for
company, until governess Zelah Pentewan
crosses the threshold…

BENEATH THE MAJOR'S SCARS

Jasper Coale, Viscount Markham

Used to having his own way where women
are concerned, Jasper would bet his fortune
on being able to seduce beautiful
Susannah Prentess—but she proves
stubbornly resistant to his charms!

BEHIND THE RAKE'S WICKED WAGER

AUTHOR NOTE

Identical twins—fascinating, aren't they? And they have been used very often in plots—by Shakespeare and Georgette Heyer, amongst others.

I have identical twin boys myself, and they came as a bit of a shock. It was only after the birth that I learned there were twins on my mother's side of the family, and as she and I were both born under the star sign of Gemini—the twins—perhaps I should have been more prepared! However, I know from experience that twins are individuals, so when I decided to write about Jasper and Dominic Coale I wanted to give them very different stories. I began with Dominic, the younger brother. This is his story.

It was common practice amongst the English aristocracy for younger sons to join the army, and so it is with Dominic. He goes off to fight in the Peninsula War, but after suffering terrible injuries he finds his life takes a very different turn from that of his twin.

When Zelah (and the reader) first meets Dominic he has retired to Rooks Tower, an isolated house on Exmoor. He is irascible and a confirmed recluse, but Zelah's young nephew Nicky has seen beyond his defensive shell and considers Dominic a firm friend. It is through Nicky that Zelah and Dominic meet and discover a mutual attraction, although they are both reluctant to acknowledge it. Zelah has been hurt before, and is determined upon an independent life, while Dominic believes his scarred face and body must repel every woman. They both have lessons to learn if they are to achieve happiness.

Some time ago I wrote a Christmas story—SNOWBOUND WITH THE NOTORIOUS RAKE—which is set on Exmoor, the beautiful wild moors in the south-west of England. Ever since I have wanted to use Exmoor again, so this is where Dominic buys his property, Rooks Tower, and it is here that Zelah falls in love with the proud man behind the horrific scars.

I really enjoyed writing Dominic and Zelah's story, and I hope you have as much pleasure reading it.

BENEATH THE MAJOR'S SCARS

Sarah Mallory

First published in Great Britain 2012
by Mills & Boon, an imprint of Harlequin (UK) Limited.
Large Print edition 2013
Harlequin (UK) Limited, Eton House, 18-24 Paradise Road,
Richmond, Surrey TW9 1SR

ISBN: 978 0 263 23261 5

Harlequin (UK) policy is to use papers that are natural, renewable and recyclable products and made from wood grown in sustainable forests. The logging and manufacturing process conform to the legal environmental regulations of the country of origin.

Printed and bound in Great Britain
by CPI Antony Rowe, Chippenham, Wiltshire

Sarah Mallory was born in Bristol, and now lives in an old farmhouse on the edge of the Pennines with her husband and family. She left grammar school at sixteen to work in companies as varied as stockbrokers, marine engineers, insurance brokers, biscuit manufacturers and even a quarrying company. Her first book was published shortly after the birth of her daughter. She has published more than a dozen books under the pen-name of Melinda Hammond, winning the Reviewers' Choice Award in 2005 from Singletitles.com for *Dance for a Diamond* and the Historical Novel Society's Editors' Choice in November 2006 for *Gentlemen in Question*.

Previous novels by the same author:
THE WICKED BARON
MORE THAN A GOVERNESS
  (part of *On Mothering Sunday*)
WICKED CAPTAIN, WAYWARD WIFE
THE EARL'S RUNAWAY BRIDE
DISGRACE AND DESIRE
TO CATCH A HUSBAND…
SNOWBOUND WITH THE NOTORIOUS RAKE
  (part of *An Improper Regency Christmas*)
THE DANGEROUS LORD DARRINGTON

Look for Sarah Mallory's
THE ILLEGITIMATE MONTAGUE
part of *Castonbury Park* Regency mini-series
Available now

For P and S, my own twin heroes.

Prologue

Cornwall—1808

The room was very quiet. The screams and cries, the frantic exertions of the past twelve hours were over. The bloodied cloths and the tiny, lifeless body had been removed and the girl lay between clean sheets, only the glow of firelight illuminating the room. Through the window a single star twinkled in the night sky. She did not seek it out, she had no energy for such conscious effort, but it was in her line of vision and it was easier to fix her eyes on that single point of light than to move her head.

Her body felt like a dead weight, exhausted by the struggle she had endured. Part of her wondered why she was still alive, when it would be so much better for everyone if she had been allowed to die with her baby.

She heard the soft click of the opening door and

closed her eyes, not wishing to hear the midwife's brisk advice or her aunt's heart-wrenching sympathy.

'Poor lamb.' Aunt Wilson's voice was hardly more than a sigh. 'Will she survive, do you think?'

'Ah, she'll live, she's a strong 'un.' From beneath her lashes the girl could see the midwife standing at the foot of the bed, wiping her hands on her bloody apron. 'Although it might be better if she didn't.'

'Ah, don't say that!' Aunt Wilson's voice cracked. 'She is still God's creature, even though she has sinned.'

The midwife sniffed.

'Then the Lord had better look out for her, poor dearie, for her life is proper blighted and that's for sure. No man will want her to wife now.'

'She must find some way to support herself. I cannot keep her indefinitely, and my poor brother and his wife have little enough: the parish of Cardinham is one of the poorest in Cornwall.'

There was a pause, then the midwife said, 'She ain't cut out to be a bal maiden.'

'To work in the mines? Never! She is too well bred for that.'

'Not too well bred to open her legs for a man—'

Aunt Wilson gasped in outrage.

'You have said quite enough, Mrs Nore. Your

work is finished here, I will look after my niece from now on. Come downstairs and I will pay you for your trouble…'

The rustle of skirts, a soft click of the door and silence. She was alone again.

It was useless to wish she had died with her baby. She had not, and the future seemed very bleak, nothing but hard work and drudgery. That was her punishment for falling in love. She would face that, and she would survive, but she would never put her trust in any man again. She opened her eyes and looked at that tiny, twinkling orb.

'You shall be my witness,' she whispered, her lips painfully dry and her throat aching with the effort. 'No man shall ever do this to me again.'

Her eyes began to close and she knew now that whenever she saw that star in the evening sky, she would remember the child she had lost.

Chapter One

Exmoor—1811

'Nicky, Nicky! wait for me—oh!'

Zelah gave a little cry of frustration as her skirts caught on the thorny branches of an encroaching bush. She was obliged to give up her pursuit of her little nephew while she disentangled herself. How she wished now that she had put on her old dimity robe, but she had been expecting to amuse Nicky in the garden, not to be chasing him through the woods; only Nurse had come out to tell them that they must not make too much noise since the mistress was trying to get some sleep before Baby woke again and demanded to be fed.

As she carefully eased the primrose muslin off the ensnaring thorns, Zelah pondered on her sister's determination to feed the new baby herself. She could quite understand it, of course: Reginald's first wife had died in childbirth and a number of wet nurses had been employed for Nicky, but each one had proved more unreliable than the last so it was a wonder that the little boy had survived at all. The thought of her sister's stepson made Zelah smile. He had not only survived, but grown into a very lively eight-year-old, who was even now leading her in a merry dance.

She had allowed him to take her 'exploring' in the wildly neglected woodland on the northern boundary of West Barton and now realised her mistake. Not only was Nicky familiar with the overgrown tracks that led through the woods, he was unhampered by *skirts*. Free at last, she pulled the folds of muslin close as she set off in search of her nephew. She had only gone a few steps when she heard him cry out, such distress and alarm in his voice that she set off at a run in the direction of his call, all concerns for snagging her gown forgotten.

The light through the trees indicated that there was a clearing ahead. She pushed her way through the remaining low tree branches and found herself standing on the lip of a steep slope. The land dropped away to form a natural bowl and the ground between the trees was dotted with early spring flowers, but it was not the beauty of the scene that made Zelah catch her breath, it was the sight of Nicky's lifeless body stretched out at the very bottom of the dell, a red stain spreading over one leg of his nankeen pantaloons and a menacing figure bending over him.

Her first, wild thought was that it was some kind of animal attacking Nicky, but as her vision cleared she realised it was a man. A thick black beard covered his face and his shaggy hair reached to the shoulders of his dark coat. A long-handled axe lay on the ground beside him, its blade glinting wickedly in the spring sunlight.

Zelah did not hesitate. She scrambled down the bank.

'Leave him alone!' The man straightened. As he turned towards her she saw that beneath the shaggy mane of hair surrounding his face he had an ugly scar cutting through his left eyebrow and cheek. She picked up a stick. 'Get away from him, you beast!'

'Beast, is it?' he growled.

'Zelah—'

'Don't worry, Nicky, he won't hurt you again.' She kept her gaze fixed on the menacing figure. 'How dare you attack an innocent boy, you monster!'

'Beast, monster—' His teeth flashed white through the beard as he stepped over the boy and came towards her, his halting, ungainly stride adding to the menace.

Zelah raised the stick. With a savage laugh he reached out and twisted the bough effortlessly out of her grasp, then caught her wrists as she launched herself at him. She struggled against his iron grip and her assailant hissed as she kicked his shin. 'For heaven's sake, I am not your villain. The boy tripped and fell.' With a muttered oath he forced her hands down and behind her, so that she found herself pressed against his hard body. The rough wool of his jacket rubbed her cheek and her senses reeled as she breathed in the smell of him. It was not the sour odour of sweat and dirt she was expecting, but a mixture of wool and sandalwood and lemony spices combined with the earthy, masculine scent of the man himself. It was intoxicating.

He spoke again, his voice a deep rumble on her skin, for he was still holding her tight against his broad chest. 'He tripped and fell. Do you understand me?'

He is speaking as if to an imbecile! was Zelah's first thought, then the meaning of his words registered in her brain and she raised her head to meet his fierce eyes. She stopped struggling.

'That's better.' He released his iron grip but kept his hard eyes fixed upon her. 'Now, shall we take a look at the boy?'

Zelah stepped away, not sure if she trusted the

man enough to turn her back on him, but a groan from Nicky decided it. Everything else was forgotten as she fell to her knees beside him.

'Oh, love, what have you done?'

She put her hand on his forehead, avoiding the angry red mark on his temple. His skin was very hot and his eyes had a glazed, wild look in them.

The man dropped down beside her.

'We've been clearing the land, so there are several ragged tree stumps. He must have caught his leg on one when he tumbled down the bank. It's a nasty cut, but I don't think the bone is broken.'

'How would you know?' demanded Zelah, carefully lifting away the torn material and gazing in horror at the bloody mess beneath.

'My time in the army has given me considerable experience of injuries.' He untied his neckcloth. 'I have sent my keeper to fetch help. I'll bind up his leg, then we will carry him back to the house on a hurdle.'

'Whose house?' she asked suspiciously. 'He should be taken to West Barton.'

'Pray allow me to know what is best to be done!'

'Please do not talk to me as if I were a child,' she retorted. 'I am quite capable of making a decision.'

He frowned, making the scar on his forehead even more ragged. He looked positively ferocious, but she refused to be intimidated and met his gaze squarely. He seemed to be struggling to contain his anger and after a moment he raised his hand to point towards a narrow path leading away through the trees. He said curtly, 'Rooks Tower is half a mile in that direction; West Barton is at least five miles by carriage, maybe two if you go back on the foot-path, the way you came.'

Zelah bit her lip. It would be impossible to carry Nicky through the dense undergrowth of the forest without causing him a great deal of pain. The boy stirred and she took his hand.

'I d-don't like it, it hurts!'

The plaintive cry tore at her heart.

'Then it must be Rooks Tower,' she said. 'Let us hope your people get here soon.'

'They will be here as soon as they can.' He pulled the muslin cravat from his neck. 'In the meantime I must stop the bleeding.' His hard eyes flickered over her. 'It will mean moving his leg.'

She nodded and squeezed Nicky's hand.

'You must be very brave, love, while we bind you up. Can you do that?'

'I'll try, Aunty.'

'Your aunt, Nicky? She's more of an Amazon, I think!'

'Well, she is not really my aunt, sir,' explained Nicky gravely. 'She is my stepmama's sister.'

Zelah stared, momentarily diverted.

'You know each other?'

The man flicked a sardonic look towards her.

'Of course, do you think I allow strange brats to run wild in my woods? Introduce us, Nicky.'

'This is Major Coale.' The boy's voice wavered a little and his lip trembled as the major deftly wrapped the neckcloth around his leg. 'And this, sir, is my aunt, Zelah.'

'Celia?'

'Zee-lah,' she corrected him haughtily. 'Miss Pentewan to you.'

'Dear me, Nicholas, you should have warned me that your aunt is a veritable dragon.'

The scar cutting through his eyebrow gave him a permanent frown, but she heard the amusement in his voice. Nicky, clinging to Zelah's hand and trying hard not to cry, managed a little chuckle.

'There, all done.' The major sat back, putting his hand on Nicky's shoulder. 'You were very brave, my boy.'

'As brave as a soldier, sir?'

'Braver. I've known men go to pieces over the veriest scratch.'

Zelah stared at the untidy, shaggy-haired figure

in front of her. His tone was that of a man used to command, but beneath that faded jacket and all that hair, could he really be a soldier? She realised he was watching her and quickly returned her attention to her nephew.

'What happened, love? How did you fall?'

'I t-tripped at the top of the bank. There's a lot of loose branches lying around.'

'Aye. I've left them. Firewood for the villagers,' explained the major. 'We have been clearing the undergrowth.'

'And about time too,' she responded. 'These woods have been seriously neglected.'

'My apologies, madam, if they are not to your liking.'

Was he laughing at her? His face—the little she could see that was not covered by hair—was impassive.

'My criticism is not aimed at you, Major. I believe Rooks Tower was only sold last winter.'

'Yes, and I have not had time yet to make all the improvements I would wish.'

'You are the *owner*?'

Zelah could not keep the astonishment out of her voice. Surely this ragged individual could not be rich enough to buy such a property?

'I am. Appearances can be deceptive, Miss Pentewan.'

She flushed, knowing she deserved the coldness of his response.

'I beg your pardon, that is, I—I am sure there is a vast amount to be done.'

'There is, and one of my first tasks is to improve the road to the house and make it suitable for carriages again. I have men working on it now, but until that is done everything has to come in and out by packhorse.'

'Major Coale's books had to be brought here by pack-pony,' put in Nicky. 'Dozens of boxes of them. She likes books,' he explained to the major, whose right eyebrow had risen in enquiry.

'We have an extensive library at home,' added Zelah.

'And where is that?'

'Cornwall.'

'I guessed that much from your name. *Where* in Cornwall?'

A smile tugged at her mouth, but she responded seriously.

'My father is rector at Cardinham, near Bodmin.'

Zelah looked up as a number of men arrived carrying a willow hurdle.

She scrambled to her feet and stepped back. The major handed his axe to one of the men before directing the delicate operation of lifting Nicky on to the hurdle. When they were ready to move off she fell into step beside the major, aware of his ungainly, limping stride as they followed the hurdle and its precious burden through the woods.

'I can see you have some experience of command, Major.'

'I was several years in the army.'

Zelah glanced at him. He had been careful to keep to the left of the path so only the right side of his face was visible to her. Whether he was protecting her sensibilities or his own she did not know.

'And now you plan to settle at Rooks Tower?'

'Yes.'

'It is a little isolated,' she remarked. 'Even more so than West Barton.'

'That is why I bought it. I have no wish for company.'

Zelah lapsed into silence. His curt tone made the meaning of his words quite clear. He might as well have said *I have no wish for conversation.* Very well, she had no desire to intrude upon his privacy. She would not speak again unless it was absolutely necessary.

Finally they emerged from the trees and Zelah had her first glimpse of Rooks Tower. There was a great sweep of lawn at the front of the house, enclosed by a weed-strewn drive. At the far side of the lawn stood a small orangery, but years of neglect had dulled the white lime-wash and many of its windows were broken. Zelah turned away from this forlorn object to study the main house. At its centre was an ancient stone building with an imposing arched entrance, but it had obviously been extended over the centuries and two brick-and-stone wings had been added. Everything was arranged over two floors save for a square stone tower on the south-eastern corner that soared above the main buildings.

'Monstrosity, isn't it?' drawled the major. 'The house was remodelled in Tudor times, when the owner added the tower that gives the house its name, so that his guests could watch the hunt. It has a viewing platform on the roof, but we never use it now.'

She looked again at the house. There had been many alterations over the years, but it retained its leaded lights and stone mullions. Rooks Tower fell short of the current fashion for order and symmetry, but its very awkwardness held a certain charm.

'The views from the tower must be magnificent.' She cast an anxious look at him. 'You will not change it?'

He gave a savage laugh.

'Of course not. It is as deformed as I!'

She heard the bitterness in his tone, but could not think of a suitable response. The path had widened and she moved forwards to walk beside Nicky, reaching out to take his hand. It was hot and clammy. Zelah hid her dismay beneath a reassuring smile.

'Nearly there, love. We shall soon make you more comfortable.'

The major strode on ahead, his lameness barely noticeable as he led the way into the great hall where an iron-haired woman in a black-stuff gown was waiting for them. She bobbed a curtsy.

'I have prepared the yellow room for the young master, sir, and popped a warm brick between the sheets.'

'Thank you, Mrs Graddon.' He did not break his stride as he answered her, crossing the hall and taking the stairs two at a time, only pausing to turn on the half-landing. 'This way, but be careful not to tilt the litter!'

Dominic waited only to see the boy laid on the bed that had been prepared for him before striding off to his own apartments to change out of his working clothes. It was a damnable nuisance, having strangers in the house, but the boy was hurt, what else could he do? He did not object to having Nicky in the house. He was fond of the boy and would do all he could to help him, but it would mean having doctors and servants running to and fro. He could leave everything to Graddon and his wife, of course, and the aunt would look after the boy until Buckland could send someone.

The thought of Miss Zelah Pentewan made him pause. A reluctant smile touched his lips and dragged at the scarred tissue of his cheek. She was not conventionally pretty, too small and thin, with mousy brown hair and brown eyes. She reminded him of a sparrow, nothing like the voluptuous beauties he had known. When he thought of her standing up to him, prepared to fight him to protect her nephew... by God she had spirit, for she barely came up to his shoulder!

He washed and dried his face, his fingers aware of the rough, pitted skin on his left cheek through the soft linen cloth. He remembered how she had glared at him, neither flinching nor averting her eyes once she had seen his scarred face. He gave her credit for that, but he would not subject her to the gruesome sight again. There was plenty for him to do that would keep him well away from the house for a few days.

* * *

'Well, I have cleaned and bandaged the leg. Now we must wait. I have given him a sleeping draught which should see him through to the morning and after that it will be up to you to keep him still while the leg heals. He will be as good as new in a few weeks.'

'Thank you, Doctor.'

Zelah stared down at the motionless little figure in the middle of the bed. Nicky had fainted away when the doctor began to work on his leg and now he looked so fragile and uncharacteristically still that tears started to her eyes.

'Now, now, Miss Pentewan, no need for this. The boy has a strong constitution—by heaven, no one knows that better than I, for I have been calling at West Barton since he was a sickly little scrap of a baby that no one expected to survive. I'm hoping that bruise on his head is nothing serious. I haven't bled him, but if he begins to show a fever then I will do so tomorrow. For now keep him calm and rested and I will call again in the morning.'

The doctor's gruff kindness made her swallow hard.

'Thank you, Dr Pannell. And if he wakes in pain…?'

'A little laudanum and water will do him no harm.'

There was a knock at the door and the house-keeper peeped in.

'Here's the little lad's papa come to see him, Doctor.' She flattened herself against the door as Reginald Buckland swept in, hat, gloves and riding whip clutched in one hand and an anxious look upon his jovial features.

'I came as soon as I heard. How is he?'

Zelah allowed the doctor to repeat his prognosis.

'Can he be moved?' asked Reginald, staring at his son. 'Can I take him home?'

'I would not advise it. The wound is quite deep and any jolting at this stage could start it bleeding again.'

'But he cannot stay here, in the house of a man I hardly know!'

Doctor Pannell's bushy eyebrows drew together.

'I understood the major was some sort of relative of yours, Mr Buckland.'

Reginald shrugged.

'Very distant. Oh, I admit it was through my letters to a cousin that he heard about Rooks Tower being vacant, but I had never met him until he moved here, and since then we have exchanged barely a dozen words. He has never once come to West Barton.'

A grim little smile hovered on the doctor's lips.

'No, Major Coale has not gone out of his way to make himself known to his neighbours.'

'I think Nicky must stay here, Reginald.' Zelah touched his arm. 'Major Coale has put his house and servants at our disposal.'

'Aye, he must, at least until the wound begins to heal,' averred Dr Pannell, picking up his hat. 'Now, I shall be away and will return tomorrow to see how my patient does.'

Reginald remained by the bed, staring down at his son and heir. He rubbed his chin. 'If only I knew what to do. If only his mama could be with him!'

'Impossible, when she is confined with little Reginald.'

'Or Nurse.'

'Yes, she would be ideal, but my sister and the new baby need her skill and attentions,' said Zelah. 'I have considered all these possibilities, Reginald, and I think there is only one solution. You must leave Nicky to my care.'

'But that's just it,' exclaimed Reginald. 'I cannot leave you here.'

'And *I* cannot leave Nicky.'

'Then I had best stay, too.'

Zelah laughed.

'Now why should you do that? You know nothing about nursing. And besides, what will poor Maria do if both you and I are away from home? I know how my sister suffers with her nerves when she is alone for too long.'

'Aye, she does.' Reginald took a turn about the room, torn by indecision.

Nicky stirred and muttered something in his sleep.

'Go home, Reginald. These fidgets will disturb Nicky.'

'But this is a bachelor household.'

'That is unfortunate, of course, but it cannot be helped.' She dipped a cloth in the bowl of lavender water and gently wiped the boy's brow. 'If it is any comfort, Reginald, Major Coale has informed me— via his housekeeper—that he will not come into this wing of the house while we are here. Indeed, once he had seen Nicky safely into bed he disappeared, giving his housekeeper orders to supply us with everything necessary. I shall sleep in the anteroom here, so that I may be on hand should Nicky wake in the night, and I will take my meals here. So you see there can be no danger of impropriety.'

Reginald did not look completely reassured.

'Would you like me to send over our maid?'

'Unnecessary, and it would give offence to Mrs Graddon.' Zelah smiled at him. 'We shall go on very comfortably, believe me, if you will arrange for some clothes to be sent over for us. And perhaps you will come again tomorrow and bring some games for Nicky. Then we shall do very well.'

'But it will not do! You are a gently bred young lady—'

'I am soon to be a governess and must learn to deal with situations such as this.' She squeezed his arm. 'Trust me, Reginald. Nicky must stay here and I shall remain to look after him until he can be moved to West Barton. Now go and reassure Maria that all is well here.'

He took his leave at last and Zelah found herself alone in the sickroom for the first time. Nicky was still sleeping soundly, which she knew was a good thing, but it left her with little to do, except rearrange the room to her satisfaction.

Zelah took dinner in the room, but the soup the housekeeper brought up for Nicky remained untouched, for he showed no signs of waking.

'Poor little lamb, sleep's the best thing for him,' said Mrs Graddon when she came to remove the dishes. 'Tomorrow I shall make some lemon jelly, to tempt his appetite. I know he's very fond of that.'

'Oh?' Zelah looked up. 'Is my nephew in the habit of calling here?'

'Aye, bless his heart. If he finds an injured animal or bird in the woods he often brings it here for the master to mend, and afore he goes he always comes down to the kitchens to find me.'

Zelah put her hands to her cheeks, mortified.

'Oh dear, he really should not be bothering Major Coale with such things, or you.'

'Lord love 'ee, mistress, the boy ain't doin' no 'arm,' exclaimed Mrs Graddon. 'In fact, I think 'e does the master good.' She paused, slanting a sidelong glance at Zelah. 'You've probably noticed that the major shuns company, but that's because o' this.' She rubbed her finger over her left temple. 'Right across his chest, it goes, though thankfully it never touched his vital organs. Took a cut to his thigh, too, but the sawbones stitched him up before he ever came home, so his leg's as good as new.'

'But when he walks…'

The housekeeper tutted, smoothing down her apron.

'He's had the very finest doctors look at 'im and they can find nothing wrong with his leg. They say 'tis all in his head. For the master don't always limp, as I've noticed, often and often.' She sighed. 'Before he went off to war and got that nasty scar he was a great one for society—him and his brother both. Twins they are and such handsome young men, they captured so many hearts I can't tell you!'

'You've known the family for a long time?'

'Aye, miss, I started as a housemaid at Markham, that's the family home, where the master's brother, the viscount, now lives. Then when the master decided to set up his own house here, Graddon and I was only too pleased to come with him. But he don't go into company, nor does he invite anyone here, and I can understand that. I've seen 'em— when people meets the master, they look everywhere but at his face and that do hurt him, you see. But Master Nick, well, he treats the major no different from the rest.'

Zelah was silent. In her mind she was running over her meeting with Major Coale. Had she avoided looking at his terrible scarred face? She thought not, but when she had first seen him she believed he was attacking Nicky and she had been in no mood for polite evasions.

The housekeeper went off and Zelah settled down to keep watch upon her patient.

As the hours passed the house grew silent. She had a sudden yearning for company and was tempted to go down to the kitchen in the hope of meeting the housekeeper, or even a kitchen maid. She would do no such thing, of course, and was just wondering how she could occupy herself when there was a knock at the door. It was Mrs Graddon.

'The major asked me to bring you these, since you likes reading.' She held out a basket full of books. 'He says to apologise, but they's all he has at the moment, most of his books being still in the crates they arrived in, but he hopes you'll find something here to suit.'

'Thank you.' Zelah took the basket and retreated to her chair by the fire, picking up the books one by one from the basket. Richardson, Smollett, Defoe, even Mrs Radcliffe. She smiled. If she could not amuse herself with these, then she did not deserve to be pleased. She was comforted by the major's thoughtfulness. Feeling much less lonely, she settled down, surrounded by books.

It was after midnight when Nicky began to grow restless. Zelah was stretched out on the bed prepared for her when she heard him mutter. Immediately she was at his side, feeling his brow, trying to squeeze a little water through his parched lips. He batted aside her hand and turned his head away, muttering angrily. Zelah checked the bandages. They were still in place, but if he continued to toss and turn he might well open the wound and set it bleeding again.

She wished she had not refused Mrs Graddon's offer to have a truckle bed made up in the room for a maid, but rather than wring her hands in an agony of regret she picked up her bedroom candle and set off to find some help.

Zelah had not ventured from the yellow bedroom since she had followed Nicky there earlier in the day. She retraced her steps back to the great hall, too anxious about her nephew to feel menaced by the flickering shadows that danced around her. There was a thin strip of light showing beneath one of the doors off the hall and she did not hesitate. She crossed to the door and knocked softly before entering.

She was in Major Coale's study, and the man himself was sitting before the dying fire, reading by the light of a branched candelabra on the table beside him.

'I beg your pardon, I need to find Mrs Graddon. It's Nicky...'

He had put down his book and was out of the chair even as she spoke. He was not wearing his coat and the billowing shirt-sleeves made him look even bigger than she remembered.

'What is wrong with him?'

'He is feverish and I c-cannot hold him….'

'Let me see.' He added, observing her hesitation, 'I have some knowledge of these matters.'

Zelah nodded, impatient to return to Nicky. They hurried upstairs, the major's dragging leg causing his shoe to scuff at each step. It was no louder than a whisper, but it echoed through the darkness. Nicky's fretful crying could be heard even as they entered the anteroom. Zelah flew to his side.

'Hush now, Nicky. Keep still, love, or you will hurt your leg again.'

'It hurts now! I want Mama!'

The major put a gentle hand on his forehead.

'She is looking after your little brother, sir. You have your aunt and me to take care of you.' He inspected the bottles ranged on the side table and quickly mixed a few drops of laudanum into a glass of water.

The calm, male voice had its effect. Nicky blinked and fixed his eyes on Zelah, who smiled at him.

'You are a guest in the major's house, Nicky.'

'Oh.' The little fingers curled around her hand. 'And are you staying here too, Aunt Zelah?'

'She is,' said the major, 'for as long as you need her. Now, sir, let me help you sit up a little and you must take your medicine.'

'No, no, it hurts when I move.'

'We will lift you very carefully,' Zelah assured him.

'I don't want to…'

'Come, sir, it is only a little drink and it will take the pain away.'

The major slipped an arm about the boy's shoulders and held the glass to his lips. Nicky took a little sip and shuddered.

'It is best taken in one go,' the major advised him.

The little boy's mouth twisted in distaste.

'Did you take this when you were wounded?'

'Gallons of it,' said the major cheerfully. 'Now, one, two, three.' He ruthlessly tipped the mixture down the boy's throat. Nicky swallowed, shuddered and his lip trembled. 'There, it is done and you were very brave. Miss Pentewan will turn your pillows and you will soon feel much more comfortable.'

'Will you stay, 'til I go to sleep again?'

'You have your aunt here.'

'*Please.*'

Zelah responded with a nod to the major's quick glance of enquiry.

'Very well.' He sat down at the side of the bed and took the little hand that reached out for him.

'Would you like me to tell you a story?' asked

Zelah, but Nicky ignored her. He fixed his eyes upon the major.

'Will you tell me how you got your scar?'

Zelah stopped breathing. She glanced at the major. He did not look to be offended.

'I have told you that a dozen times. You cannot want to hear it again.'

'Yes, I do, if you please, sir. *All* of it.'

'Very well.'

He pulled his chair closer to the bed and Zelah drew back into the shadows.

'New Year's Day '09 and we were struggling through the mountains back towards Corunna, with the French hot on our heels. The weather was appalling. During the day the roads were rivers of mud and by night they were frozen solid. When we reached Cacabelos—'

'You missed something,' Nicky interrupted him. 'The man with the pigtail.'

'Ah, yes.' Major Coale's eyes softened in amusement. In the shadows Zelah smiled. She had read Nicky enough stories to know he expected the same tale, word for word, each time. The major continued. 'One Highlander woke to find he couldn't get up because his powdered pigtail was frozen to the ground. A couple of days later we reached the village of Cacabelos and the little stone bridge over the River Cua. Unfortunately discipline had become a problem during that long retreat to Corunna and General Edward Paget was obliged to make an example of those guilty of robbery. He was about to execute two of the men when he heard that the French were upon us. The general was extremely vexed at this, and after cursing roundly he turned to his men. "If I spare the lives of these men," he said, "do I have your word of honour as soldiers that you will reform?" The men shouted "Yes!" and the convicted men were cut down.'

'Huzza!' Nicky gave a sleepy cheer.

Major Coale continued, his voice soft and low.

'And just in time, for the enemy were already in sight. They were upon us in an instant, the French 15th Chasseurs and the 3rd Hussars, all thundering down to the bridge. All was confusion—our men could not withdraw because the way was blocked with fighting men and horses. Fortunately the chasseurs were in disarray and drew back to regroup, giving us time to get back across the bridge. We fixed bayonets and waited below the six guns of the horse artillery, which opened fire as the French charged again. The 52nd and the 95th delivered a furious crossfire on their flanks, killing two generals and I don't know how many men, but still they came on and fell upon us.'

He paused, his brow darkening. Nicky stirred and the major drew a breath before going on.

'I found myself caught between two chasseurs. I wounded one of them, but the other closed in. His sabre slashed down across my face and chest. I managed to unseat him and he crashed to the ground. He made another wild slash and caught my leg, but I had the satisfaction of knowing he was taken prisoner and his comrades were in full retreat before I lost consciousness.'

'Don't stop, sir. What happened then?' Nicky's eyes were beginning to close.

'I was patched up and put on to a baggage wagon. Luckily I had no serious internal injuries, for I fear it would have been fatal to be so shaken and jarred as we continued to Villafranca. I remember very little after that until we reached England. Someone had sent word to Markham, and my brother came to collect me from Falmouth and take me home. There I received the best treatment available, but alas, even money cannot buy me a new face.'

He lapsed into silence. Nicky was at last in a deep sleep, his little hand still clasped in the major's long lean fingers. Silence enveloped them. At length the major became aware of Zelah's presence and turned to look at her. She realised then her cheeks were wet with tears.

'I—I beg your pardon.' Quickly she turned away, pulling out her handkerchief. 'You have been most obliging, Major Coale, more than we had any right to expect.' She wiped her eyes, trying to speak normally. 'Nicky is sleeping now. We do not need to trouble you any longer.'

'And what will you do?'

'I shall sit with him...'

He shook his head.

'You cannot sit up all night. I will watch over him for a few hours while you get some sleep.'

Zelah wavered. She was bone-weary, but she was loath to put herself even deeper in this man's debt. He gave an exasperated sigh.

'Go and lie down,' he ordered her. 'You will not be fit to look after the boy in the morning if you do not get some sleep.'

He was right. Zelah retired to the little anteroom. She did not undress, merely removed her shoes and stretched out on the bed, pulling a single blanket over her. Her last waking thought was that it would be impossible to sleep with Major Coale sitting in the next room.

Zelah was awoken by a cock crowing. It was light, but the sun had not yet risen. She stared at the unfamiliar surroundings, then, as memory returned, she slipped off the bed and crept into the next room. Nicky was still sleeping soundly and the major was slumped forwards over the bed, his shaggy dark head on his arms.

The fire had died and the morning air was very chill. Noiselessly Zelah crossed the room and knelt down by the hearth.

'What are you doing?'

The major's deep voice made her jump.

'I am going to rescue the fire.'

'Oh, no, you are not. I will send up a servant to see to that.'

He towered over her, hand outstretched. She allowed him to help her up, trying to ignore the tingle that shot through her at his touch. It frightened her. His presence filled the room, it was disturbing, suffocating, and she stepped away, searching for something to break the uneasy silence.

'I—um—the story you told Nicky, about your wound. It was very…violent for a little boy. He seemed quite familiar with it.'

'Yes. He asked me about my face the very first time he saw me and has wanted me to recount the story regularly ever since.' He was watching the sleeping boy, the smile tugging at his lips just visible through the black beard. 'I was working in the woods and he came up, offered to help me finish off the game pie Mrs Graddon had packed into my bag to sustain me through the day.'

'You must have thought him very impertinent.'

'Not at all. His honesty was very refreshing. Most people look away, embarrassed by my disfigurement.'

'Oh, I beg your pardon. I hope you did not think that *I*—'

The smile turned into a grin.

'You, madam, seemed intent upon inflicting even more damage upon me.'

The amusement in his eyes drew a reluctant smile from Zelah.

'You did—do—look rather savage. Although I know now that you are very kind,' she added in a rush. She felt herself blushing. 'You have been sitting here all night and must be desperate for sleep. I can manage now, thank you, Major. You had best go…'

'I should, of course. I will send someone up to see to the fire and order Mrs Graddon to bring your breakfast to you.'

'Thank you.' He gave her a clipped little bow and turned to leave.

'Major! The chasseur—the one who injured you—was he really taken prisoner?'

He stopped and looked back.

'Yes, he was.' His eyes narrowed. 'I may *look* like a monster, Miss Pentewan, but I assure you I am not.'

Chapter Two

Nicky was drowsy and fretful when he eventually woke up, but Dr Pannell was able to reassure Zelah that he was recovering well.

'A little fever is to be expected, but he seems to be in fine form now. I think keeping him still is going to be your biggest problem.'

Zelah had thought so too and she was relieved when Reginald arrived with a selection of toys and games for his son.

'Goodness!' She laughed when she saw the large basket that Reginald placed on the bed. 'Major Coale will think we plan to stay for a month.'

Reginald grinned.

'I let Nurse choose what to send. I fear she was over-generous to make up for not being able to come herself.'

'And what did our host say, when you came in with such a large basket?'

'I have not seen him. His man informed me that he is busy with his keeper and likely to be out all day.' He glanced at Nicky, happily sorting through the basket, and led Zelah into the anteroom. 'I had the feeling he was ordered to say that and to make sure I knew that he had given instructions for a maid to sit up with the boy during the night. Setting my mind at rest that he would not be imposing himself upon you while you are here.'

'Major Coale is very obliging.'

'Dashed ragged fellow though, with all that hair, but I suppose that's to cover the scar on his face.' He paused. 'Maria asked me to drop a word in your ear, but for my part I don't think there's anything to worry about.'

'What did she wish you to say to me?'

He chewed his lip for a moment.

'She was concerned. Coale was well known as something of a, er, a rake before the war. His name was forever in the society pages. Well, stands to reason, doesn't it, younger son of a viscount, and old Lord Markham had some scandals to his name, I can tell you! Coale's brother's inherited the title now, of course, and from what I have read he's just as wild as the rest of 'em.' He added quickly, 'Only hearsay, of course. I've never had much to do with that side of the family—far too high and mighty for one thing. The Bucklands are a very distant branch. But that's neither here nor there. We were worried the major might try to ingratiate himself with you—after all, we are mighty obliged to him—and Maria thought you might have...stirrings.'

'Stirrings, Reginald?'

He flushed.

'Aye. Maria says that sometimes a woman's sympathy for an injured man can stir her—that she can find him far too...attractive.'

Zelah laughed.

'Then you may set Maria's mind at rest. The only *stirring* I have when I think of Major Coale is to comb his hair!'

Reginald stayed for an hour or more and after that Hannah, the chambermaid appointed to help Zelah look after Nicky, came up to introduce herself. By the time dinner was brought up it was clear that she was more than capable of nursing Nicky and keeping him amused, and Zelah realised a trifle ruefully that it was not Nicky's boredom but her own that might be a problem.

* * *

Zelah and Hannah had taken it in turns to sit up with Nicky through the night, but there was no recurrence of the fever and when Dr Pannell called the following morning he declared himself satisfied that the boy would be able to go home at the end of the week.

'I will call again on Friday, Miss Pentewan, and providing there has been no more bleeding we will make arrangements to return you both to West Barton. You will be the first to use the major's new carriageway.'

'Oh, is it finished?' asked Zelah. 'I have been watching them repair the drive, but I cannot see what is going on beyond the gates.'

'I spoke to the workmen on the way here and they told me the road will be passable by tomorrow. The road-building has been a godsend for Lesserton, providing work for so many of the men. The problems with grazing rights is making it difficult for some of them to feed their families.'

'Is this the dispute with the new owner of Lydcombe Park? My brother-in-law mentioned something about this before I came away.'

'Aye, Sir Oswald Evanshaw moved in on Lady Day and he is claiming land that the villagers believe belongs to them.' The doctor shook his head.

'Of course, he has a point: the house has changed hands several times in recent years, but no one has actually lived there, so the villagers have been in the habit of treating everything round about as their own. The boundaries between Lydcombe land and that belonging to the villagers have become confused. He's stopped them going into Prickett Wood, too, so they cannot collect the firewood as they were used to do and Sir Oswald's bailiff is prepared to use violence against anyone who tries to enter the wood. He's driven out all the deer, so that they are now competing with the villagers' stock for fodder.' He was silent for a moment, frowning over the predicament, then he shook off his melancholy thoughts and gave her a smile. 'Thankfully Major Coale is of a completely different stamp. He is happy for the local people to gather firewood from his forest. It is good fortune that Nicky chose to injure himself on the major's land rather that at Lydcombe.'

Zelah had agreed, but as the day wore on she began to wonder if she would have the opportunity to thank her host for his hospitality. With Hannah to share the nursing Zelah was growing heartily bored with being confined to the sickroom.

* * *

When the maid came up the following morning she asked her casually if the major was in the house.

'Oh, no, miss. He left early. Mr Graddon said not to expect him back much before dinner.'

She bobbed a curtsy and settled down to a game of spillikins with Nicky. Left to amuse herself, Zelah carried her work basket to the cushioned window seat and took out her embroidery. It was a beautiful spring day and she could hear the faint call of the cuckoo in the woods.

The sun climbed higher. Zelah put away her sewing and read to Nicky while Hannah quietly tidied the room around them. The book was one of Nicky's favourites, *Robinson Crusoe,* but as the afternoon wore on his eyelids began to droop, and soon he was sleeping peacefully.

'Best thing for'n. Little mite.' Hannah looked down fondly at the sleeping boy. 'Why don't you go and get yourself some rest, too, miss? I'll sit here and watch'n for 'ee.'

Zelah sighed, her eyes on the open window.

'What I would really like to do is to go outside.'

'Then why don't 'ee? No one'll bother you. You could walk in the gardens. I can always call you from the window, if the boy wakes up.'

Zelah hesitated, but only for a moment. The

spring day was just too beautiful to miss. With a final word to Hannah to be sure to call her if she was needed, she slipped down the stairs and out of the house.

The lawns had been scythed, but weeds now inhabited the flowerbeds and the shrubs were straggling and overgrown. After planning how she would restock the borders and perhaps add a statue or two, she moved on and discovered the kitchen garden, where some attempt was being made to improve it.

The hedge separating the grounds from the track that led to the stables had been hacked down to waist height, beds had been dug and cold frames repaired. Heartened by these signs of industry, Zelah was about to retrace her steps when she heard the clip-clop of an approaching horse. Major Coale was riding towards the stables on a huge grey horse. She picked up her skirts and flew across to the hedge, calling out to him.

He stopped, looking around in surprise.

'Should you not be with the boy?'

She stared up at him.

'You have shaved off your beard.'

'Very observant. But you have not answered my question.'

'Hannah is sitting with him. It was such a beautiful day I had to come out of doors.'

She answered calmly, refusing to be offended by his curt tone and was rewarded when he asked in a much milder way how the boy went on.

'He is doing very well, thank you. Dr Pannell is coming in the morning to examine Nicky. All being well, I hope to take him back to West Barton tomorrow.' He inclined his head and made to move on. She put up her hand. 'Please, don't go yet! I wanted to thank you for all you have done for us.'

'That is not necessary.'

'I think it is.' She smiled. 'I believe if I had not caught you now I should not have seen you again before we left.'

He looked down at her, unsmiling. His grey eyes were as hard as granite.

'My staff have orders to look after you. You have no need to see me.'

'But I want to.' She glanced away, suddenly feeling a little shy. 'You have been very kind to us. I wanted to thank you.'

She could feel his eyes boring into her and kept her own fixed on the toe of his muddy boot.

'Very well,' he said at last. 'You have thanked me. That is an end to it.'

He touched his heels to the horse's flanks and moved on.

'I wish I had said nothing,' she muttered, embarrassment making her irritable. 'Did I expect him to thaw a little, merely because I expressed my gratitude? The man is nothing but a boor.'

Even as she spoke the words she came to a halt as another, more uncomfortable thought occurred. Perhaps Major Coale was lonely.

What was it Mrs Graddon had said? *He was a great one for society.* That did not sit well with his assertion that he had no wish for company. His curt manner, the long hair and the shaggy beard that had covered his face until today—perhaps it was all designed to keep the world at bay.

'Well, if that is so, it is no concern of mine,' she addressed the rosemary bush beside her. 'We all have our crosses to bear and some of us do not have the means to shut ourselves away and wallow in our misery!'

When Dr Pannell called the next day he gave Nicky a thorough examination, at the end of which Zelah asked him anxiously if he might go home now.

'I think not, my dear.'

'But his mama is so anxious for him,' said Zelah, disappointed. 'And you said he might be moved today…'

'I know, but that was when I thought the major's

new road would be finished. Now they tell me it will not be open properly until tomorrow. Be patient, my dear. Major Coale has told me his people will be working into the night to make the road passable for you.'

With that she had to be satisfied. Nick appeared quite untroubled by the news that he was to remain at Rooks Tower. His complaisance was much greater than Zelah's. She hated to admit it, but she was finding the constant attendance on an eight-year-old boy and the company of an amiable but childish chambermaid a little dull.

After sharing a light luncheon with Nicky, Zelah left the boy reading with Hannah and went off in search of Mrs Graddon, to offer her help, only to find that the good lady had gone into Lesserton for supplies. Unwilling to return to the sickroom just yet, Zelah picked up her shawl and went out to explore more of the grounds.

Having seen enough of the formal gardens, she walked around to the front of the house and headed for the orangery. A chill wind was blowing down from the moors and she wrapped her shawl about her as she crossed the lawn. The orangery was built in the classical style. Huge sash windows were separated by graceful pillars that supported an elegant pediment. Between the two central columns were glazed double doors. The stone was in good order, if in need of a little repair, but the woodwork looked sadly worn and several panes of glass were broken.

Zelah was surprised to find the doors unlocked. They opened easily and she stepped inside, glad to be out of the wind. The interior was bare, save for a few dried leaves on the floor, but there were niches in the walls which were clearly designed to hold statues. A shadow fell across her and she swung around.

'Oh.'

Major Coale was standing in the doorway. She guessed he had just returned from riding, for his boots were spattered with mud and there was a liberal coating of dust on his brown coat. His broad-brimmed hat was jammed on his head and its shadow made it impossible to read his expression. She waved her hand ineffectually.

'I—um—I hope you do not mind…'

'Why should I?' He stepped inside, suddenly making the space seem much smaller. 'I saw the open doors and came across to see who was here. What do you think of it?'

'It is in need of a little repair,' she began carefully.

'I was thinking of tearing it down—'

'No!' She put her hand to her mouth. 'I beg your

pardon,' she said stiffly. 'It is of course up to you what you do here.'

'It is indeed, but I am curious, Miss Pentewan. What would *you* do with it?'

'New windows and doors,' she said immediately. 'Then I would furnish it with chairs for the summer and in the winter I would use it as it was intended, to shelter orange trees.'

'But I have no orange trees.'

'You might buy some. I understand oranges are extremely good for one.'

He grunted.

'You are never at a loss for an answer, are you, ma'am?'

Yes, she thought, *I am at a loss now.*

She gave a little shrug and looked away.

'I should get back.'

'I will accompany you.'

She hurried out into the sunlight and set off for the house. Major Coale fell into step beside her.

'So you will be leaving us tomorrow. I met Dr Pannell on the road,' he explained, answering her unspoken question. 'You will be glad to return to West Barton.'

'Yes.' He drew in a harsh breath, as if she had touched a raw wound and she hurried to explain. 'It is not—you have been all kindness, and your staff have done everything required…'

'But?'

She drew her shawl a little tighter.

'I shall be glad to have a little adult company once more.'

There. She had said it. But as soon as the words were uttered she regretted them. 'Please do not think I am complaining—I am devoted to Nicky and could not have left him here alone.'

'But you have missed intelligent conversation?'

'Yes,' she responded, grateful that he understood. 'When I lived at home, in Cardinham, Papa and I would talk for hours.'

'Of what?'

'Oh, anything! Politics, music, books. At West Barton it is the same, although my sister is a little preoccupied at the moment with her baby. But when Reginald is at home we enjoy some lively debates.' She flushed a little. 'Forgive me, I am of course extremely grateful to you for all you have done—'

'I know, you told me as much yesterday. Yet it appears I am failing as a host.' They had reached the front door and he stopped. 'Perhaps you would join me for dinner this evening.' The request was so unexpected that she could only stare at him. 'No, of course that is not possible. Forget I—'

'Of course it is possible.' She spoke quickly, while an inner voice screamed its warnings at her. To dine alone with a man, was she mad? But in that instant when he had issued his invitation she had seen something in his eyes, a haunting desolation that burned her soul. It was gone in a moment, replaced by his habitual cold, shuttered look. But that brief connection had wrenched at the core of loss and loneliness buried deep within her, and Zelah found the combination was just too strong to withstand. 'I would be delighted to join you.'

His brows rose.

'There will be no chaperone.'

'Nicky will be in the house and your housekeeper.'

His hard eyes searched her face for a moment.

'Very well, Miss Pentewan. Until dinner!'

With that he touched his hat, turned on his heel and marched off towards the stables.

Zelah looked at the scant assortment of clothes laid out on the bed. Whoever had packed her bag had clearly assumed she would spend all her time in the sickroom. Neither her serviceable grey gown nor the dimity day dress was suitable for dining with the major. However, there was a green sash and matching stole that she could wear with her yellow muslin. Mrs Graddon had washed it for her and there were only a few drawn threads from her escapade in the woods. Once she had tied the sash around her waist and draped the stole over her arms she thought it would serve her well enough as an evening dress.

In the few hours since the major had invited her to dine, Zelah had pondered upon his reasons for doing so, and had come to the conclusion that it was twofold: he was being kind to her, but also he was lonely. If she thought for a moment that he was attracted to her she would have declined his invitation, but Zelah had no illusions about herself. Her mirror showed her a very nondescript figure, too thin for beauty and with soft brown hair that was neither fashionably dark nor attractively blond. And at two-and-twenty she was practically an old maid.

Sometimes she thought back to the happy girl she had been at eighteen, with a ready laugh and a sparkle in her eyes. Her figure had been better then, too, but at eighteen she had been in love and could see only happiness ahead. A year later everything had changed. She had lost her love, her happy future and her zest for life. Looking in her mirror now, she saw nothing to attract any man. And that could only be to her benefit, she reminded herself, if she was going to make her own way in the world.

* * *

Hannah had found her a length of yellow ribbon for her hair and five minutes before the appointed hour she presented herself to her nephew.

'Well, will I do?'

Nicky wrinkled his nose.

'I wish I could come with you, Aunty.'

'So, too, do I, love,' said Zelah earnestly. She had been growing increasingly anxious about meeting the major as the dinner hour approached.

'Ah, well, after I've given Master Nicky his supper we are going to finish our puzzle,' said Hannah, beaming happily. 'Now you go on and enjoy your dinner, miss, and don't 'ee worry about us, we shall have a fine time!'

Zelah made her way down to the great hall, where the evening sun created a golden glow. She had no idea where the drawing room might be and was just wondering what to do when Graddon appeared.

'This way, madam, if you please.'

He directed her to a door beside the major's study and opened it for her.

After the dazzling brightness of the hall, the room seemed very dark, but when her eyes grew accustomed she saw that she was alone and she relaxed a little, looking about her with interest. It was a long room with a lofty ceiling, ornately plastered.

The crimson walls were covered with large paint-
ings, mostly of men and women in grey wigs and
the fashions of the last century, but there was one
painting beside the fireplace of a young lady with
her hair tumbling like dark, polished mahogany
over her shoulders. She wore a high-waisted gown
and the artist had cleverly painted the skirts as if
they had just been caught by a soft breeze. Zelah
stepped closer. There was a direct, fearless stare in
the girl's dark eyes and a firm set to those sculpted
lips. She looked strangely familiar.

'My sister, Serena.'

She jumped and turned to find the major standing behind her.

'Oh, I did not hear you—' She almost said she
had not heard the scuffing of his dragging foot.
Flustered, she turned back to the painting. 'She is
very like you, I think.'

He gave a bark of laughter.

'Not in looks, I hope! Nor in temperament. She
was not the least serene, which is why Jasper and I
renamed her Sally! Very wild and headstrong. At
least she was until she married. Now she is a model
of respectability.'

'And is she happy?'

'Extremely.'

She took a last look at the painting, then turned

to her host. Although she had seen him without his beard that afternoon, his clean-shaven appearance still surprised her. He had brushed his thick, dark hair and tied it back with a ribbon. The ragged scar was now visible, stretching from his left temple, down through his eyebrow and left cheekbone to his chin, dragging down the left side of his mouth.

The look in his eyes was guarded with just a touch of defiance. Zelah realised he expected her to look away, revolted by the sight of his scarred face. She was determined not to do that and, not knowing quite what to do, she smiled at him.

'You look very smart, sir.'

The wary look disappeared.

'Thank you, ma'am.' He gave a little bow. 'I believe this is still the standard wear for dinner.'

They both knew she was not referring to the black evening coat and snowy waistcoat and knee breeches, but her smile grew.

'Your dress is very different from the first time I saw you.'

'I keep that old coat for when I am working in the woods. It is loose across the shoulders and allows me to swing the axe.' He paused. 'Graddon informs me that there has been a slight upset in the kitchen and dinner is not quite ready.' A faint smile lifted the good side of his mouth. 'Mrs Graddon is an estimable creature, but I understand my telling her I would be entertaining a guest caused the sauce to curdle.'

'Sauces are notoriously difficult,' she said carefully.

He held out his arm to her.

'Perhaps you would care to step out on to the terrace while we wait?'

Zelah nodded her assent and took his proffered arm. He walked her across the room to the door set between the long windows.

'You see the house has been sadly neglected,' he said as he led her out of doors. He bent to pluck a straggling weed from between the paving slabs and tossed it aside.

'The rose garden has survived quite well,' she observed. 'It needs only a little work to bring it into some sort of order.'

'Really? When I last looked the plants were quite out of control.'

'They need pruning, that is all. And even the shrubbery is not, I think, beyond saving. Cut the plants back hard and they will grow better than ever next year.'

'Pity the same thing does not apply to people.'

She had been happily imagining how the gardens might look, but his bitter words brought her back to reality. She might be able to forget her companion's disfigurement, but he could not. A sudden little breeze made her shiver.

'I beg your pardon. It is too early in the year to be out of doors.'

The major put his hand out to help her arrange her stole. Did it rest on her shoulder a moment longer than was necessary, or was that her imagination? He was standing very close, looming over her. A sense of his physical power enveloped her.

This is all nonsense, she told herself sternly, but the sensation persisted. *Run, Zelah, go now!*

'Perhaps, ma'am, we should go back inside.'

He put his hand beneath her arm and she almost jumped away, her nerves jangling. Immediately he released her, standing back so that she could precede him into the room. He had turned slightly, so that he presented only the uninjured side of his face to her and silently Zelah berated herself. Major Coale was acting as a gentleman, while she was displaying the sort of ill-mannered self-consciousness that she despised. That was no way to repay her host's kindness. She must try harder.

He escorted her to the dining room, where Zelah's stretched nerves tightened even more. A place was set at the head of the table and another on its right hand. It was far too intimate. She cleared her throat.

'Major, would—would you object if I made slight adjustment to the setting?'

She flushed under his questioning gaze, but he merely shrugged.

'As you wish.'

She squared her shoulders. The setting at the head of the table was soon moved to the left hand, so that they would be facing each other. She had to steel herself to turn back to the major.

The silence as he observed her work was unnerving, but Zelah comforted herself that the worst he could do was order her to go back to her room and eat alone. At last those piercing eyes moved to her face.

'Do you think you will be safer with five foot of mahogany between us?'

'It is more…seemly.'

'Seemly! If that is your worry, perhaps we should ask Mrs Graddon to join us.'

Zelah's anger flared.

'I agreed to dine with you, sir, but to sit so close—'

'Yes, yes, it would be *unseemly*! So be it. For God's sake let us sit down before the food arrives.'

He stalked to her chair and held it out. She sat down. He took his own seat in silence.

'I beg your pardon,' said Zelah. 'I did not mean to put you to all this trouble.'

It was a poor enough olive branch, but it worked. Major Coale gave her a rueful look.

'And I beg your pardon for losing my temper. My manners have lost their polish.'

The door opened and the footmen came in with the first dishes.

After such an unpromising start Zelah feared that conversation might be difficult, but she was wrong. The major proved an excellent host, exerting himself to entertain. He persuaded her to take a little from every dish on the table and kept her glass filled while regaling her with amusing anecdotes. She forgot her nerves and began to enjoy herself. They discussed music and art, the theatre and politics, neither noticing when the footmen came in to light the candles, and by the time they finished their meal Zelah was exchanging opinions with the major as if they were old friends. When the covers were removed the major asked her about Nicky and she found herself chatting away, telling him how they filled their days.

'Hannah is so good with him, too,' she ended. 'Thank you for sending her to help me.'

'It was Mrs Graddon who suggested it, knowing the girl comes from a large family.'

'Nicky adores her and would much rather play spillikins with her than attend to his lessons.'

His brows rose. 'Don't tell me you are making him work while he is laid up sick?'

She laughed.

'No, no, but I like him to read to me a little each day and to write a short note to his mama. He is reluctant to apply himself, but I find that with a little encouragement he is willing enough. And it is very good practice for me.'

'Practice?'

'Yes, for when I become a governess.'

She selected a sweetmeat as the butler came up to refill her glass. The major waved him away.

'Thank you, Graddon, that will be all. Leave the Madeira and I will serve Miss Pentewan.' He waited until they were alone before he spoke again.

'Forgive my impertinence, ma'am, but you do not look old enough to be a governess.'

She sat up very straight.

'I am two-and-twenty, Major Coale. Not that it is any of your business!' She bit her lip. 'I beg you pardon. I am a guest in your house—'

'Guest be damned,' he interrupted roughly. 'That is no reason you should endure my incivility. Being a guest here should not put you under any obligation.'

Zelah chuckled, her spurt of anger dying as quickly as it had come.

'Of course I am under an obligation to you, Major. You have gone to great lengths to accommodate us. And how could I not forgive you for paying me such a handsome compliment?'

He gave a short laugh and filled their glasses.

'So why *are* you intent on becoming a governess? Can Buckland not support you?'

'Why should he do so, if I can earn my own living?'

'I should not allow *my* sister to become a governess.'

'But your father was a viscount. Reginald is only a brother by marriage, and besides, he has a family of his own to support.' She picked up the glass he had filled for her and tasted it carefully. She had never had Madeira before, but she found she enjoyed the warm, nutty flavour. 'I would not add to his burdens.'

He reached out, his hand hovering over the sweetmeats as he said lightly, 'Perhaps you should look for a husband.'

'No!'

The vehemence brought his head up immediately and she was subjected to a piercing gaze. She decided to be flippant.

'As I am penniless, and notoriously difficult to please, I think that might be far too difficult. I do like this wine—is it usual for gentlemen to drink it at the end of a meal? I know Reginald prefers brandy.'

To her relief he followed her lead and their conversation moved back to safer waters. She took another glass of Madeira and decided it must be her last. She was in danger of becoming light-headed. Darkness closed around them. The butler came in silently to light more candles in the room and draw the curtains against the night, but they made no move to leave the table, there was still so much to say.

The major turned to speak to Graddon and Zelah studied his profile. How handsome he must have been before his face was sliced open by a French sabre. It was a momentary thought, banished as soon as it occurred, but it filled her with sadness.

'You are very quiet, Miss Pentewan.'

His words brought her back to the present and she blushed, not knowing how to respond. In the end she decided upon the truth.

'I was thinking about your face.'

Immediately he seemed to withdraw from her.

'That is why I wanted you upon my right hand, to spare you that revulsion.'

She shook her head.

'It does not revolt me.'

'I should not have shaved off my beard!'

'Yes, you should, you look so much better, only—'

'Yes, madam? Only what?' The hard note in his voice warned her not to continue, but she ignored it.

'Your hair,' she said breathlessly. 'I am surprised your valet does not wish to cut it.'

'I have no valet. Graddon does all I need.'

'But I thought he was a butler…'

'He does what is necessary. He was with me in Spain and brought me back to England. He stayed with me, helped me to come to terms with my new life.'

'And Mrs Graddon?'

'She was housemaid at Markham and decided to marry Graddon and come with him when I moved here.' He raised his glass, his lip curling into something very like a sneer. 'You see, my misfortune is their gain.'

She frowned.

'Please do not belittle them. They are devoted to you.'

'I stand corrected,' he said stiffly. 'I beg your pardon and theirs.'

'I think you would look much better with your

hair cut short. It is very much the fashion now, you know.'

He leaned closer, a belligerent, challenging look in his eye. It took all her courage not to turn away.

'I need it long,' he said savagely. 'Then I can bring it down, thus, and hide this monstrous deformation.' He pulled the ribbon from his hair and shook the dark curtain down over his face. 'Surely that is better? I would not want to alarm the ladies and children!'

He was glaring at her, eyes narrowed, his mouth a thin, taut line, one side pulled lower by the dragging scar.

'Nicky is not afraid of you,' she said softly. 'Nor do you frighten me.'

For a long, interminable time she held his eyes, hoping he would read not pity but sympathy and understanding in her gaze. He was a proud man and she was dismayed to think he was hiding from the world. To her relief, his angry look faded.

'So would you have me trust myself to a country barber?' he growled. 'I think not, Miss Pentewan. Perhaps next time I go to London—'

'I could cut it for you.' She sat back, shocked by her own temerity. 'I am quite adept at cutting hair, although I have no idea where the skill comes from. I was always used to trim my father's hair, and since I have been at West Barton I have cut Nicky's. I am sure no one could tell it was not professionally done.'

He was frowning at her now. She had gone too far. The wine had made her reckless and her wretched tongue had let her down. Major Coale jumped up and strode to tug at the bell pull. He was summoning a footman to escort her to her room.

'Graddon, fetch scissors and my comb, if you please.' He caught her eye, a glint in his own. 'Very well, Miss Pentewan, let us put you to the test.'

'What? I—' She swallowed. 'Are you sure it is what you want?'

'Are you losing your nerve, madam?'

Zelah quite thought that she was. Two voices warred within her: one told her that to dine alone with a gentleman who was not related to her was improper enough, but to cut the man's hair would put her beyond the pale. The other whispered that it was her Christian duty to help him quit his self-imposed exile.

The glint in his eyes turned into a gleam. He was laughing at her and her courage rose.

'Not at all. Let us do it!'

'Major, are you quite sure you want me to do this?'

He was sitting on a chair by the table and Zelah

was standing behind him, comb in hand. They had rearranged the candelabra to give the best light possible and the dark locks gleamed, thick and glossy around his head, spreading out like ebony across his shoulders. The enormity of what she was about to do made her hesitate.

The major waved his hand.

'Yes. I may change my mind when I am sober, but for now I want you to cut it.'

Zelah took a deep breath. It was too late to go back now, they had agreed. Besides, argued that wickedly seductive voice in her head, no one need ever know. She picked up the scissors and moved closer until her skirts were brushing his shoulder. It felt strange, uncomfortable, like standing over a sleeping tiger. Thrusting aside such fanciful thoughts, she took a secure grip of the scissors and began. His hair was like silk beneath her fingers. She lifted one dark lock and applied the scissors. They cut through it with a whisper. As she continued her confidence grew, as did the pile of black tresses on the floor.

His hair was naturally curly and she had seen enough pencil drawings of gentlemen with their hair *à la Brutus* since she had arrived at West Barton to recreate the style from memory—Reginald and Maria might live in a remote area of Exmoor, but they were both avid followers of the *ton*, receiving a constant stream of periodicals and letters from friends in London advising them of the latest fashions. She cut, combed and coaxed the major's hair into place. It needed no pomade or grease to make it curl around his collar and his ears. She brushed the tendrils forwards around his face, as she had seen in the fashion plates. Her fingers touched the scar and he flinched. Immediately she drew back.

'Did I hurt you?'

'No. Carry on.'

Carefully she finished her work, combing and snipping off a few straggling ends until she was satisfied with the result. It was not strictly necessary, but she could not resist running her fingers though his glossy, thick hair one final time.

'There.' She brushed the loose hair from his shoulders. 'It is finished.'

'Very well, Delilah, let us see what you have done to me.'

He picked up one of the candelabra and walked over to a mirror.

Zelah held her breath as he regarded his image. In the candlelight the ugly gash down his face was still visible, but it seemed diminished by the new hairstyle. The sleek black locks were brushed forwards to curl about his wide brow, accentuating the strong lines of his face.

'Well, Miss Pentewan, I congratulate you. Perhaps you should not be looking for a post as a governess, after all. You should offer your services as a *coiffeuse*.'

Relief made her laugh out loud. She said daringly, 'You look very handsome, Major.'

He turned away from the mirror and made a noise between a growl and a cough.

'Aye, well, enough of that. It is time I sent you back to the sick room, madam. You will need to be up betimes.'

'Yes, of course.' She cast a conscience-stricken look at the clock. 'Poor Hannah has been alone with Nicky for hours.' She held out her hand to him. 'Goodnight, sir. I hope we shall see you in the morning before we leave?'

Again that clearing of the throat and he would not meet her eyes.

'Perhaps. Goodnight, Miss Pentewan.' He took her hand, his grip tightening for a second. 'And thank you.'

Chapter Three

The following morning Reginald drove over in his travelling chaise, which Maria had filled with feather bolsters and pillows to protect Nicky during the long journey home. Nicky looked around as his father carried him tenderly out of the house.

'Is Major Coale not here, Papa?'

'He sends his apologies, Master Nick,' said Graddon in a fatherly way. 'He went off early today to the long meadow to oversee the hedge-laying.'

'But I wanted to say goodbye to him!'

Nicky's disappointed wail touched a chord in Zelah: she too would have liked to see the major. However, she was heartened by Reginald's response.

'Your mama has already penned a note to Major Coale. She has not only given him permission to call at any time, but she has also invited him to dinner. And once we have you home, Nicholas, you may write to him yourself, thanking him for his care of you.'

'Yes, and I can ask him to call and see me,' agreed Nicky. He frowned, suddenly unsure. 'He will come, won't he? If I ask him 'specially.'

'I do not see how he can refuse.' Reginald grinned at Zelah. 'But I might have to instruct the staff not to send him round to the kitchens—when I saw him last he looked so ragged one might easily mistake him for a beggar.'

'I think you might be surprised,' murmured Zelah, smiling to herself.

The five miles to West Barton were covered with ease and they were greeted with great joy by the household. Maria clasped her stepson and wept copiously, bewailing the fact that she had been unable to visit him, while Nurse promised him all sorts of treats to make up for his ordeal.

'I only hope being in That Man's house hasn't given you nightmares,' said Nurse, tucking Nicky into his bed. 'I believe he is truly hideous to look at.'

Anger welled up in Zelah, but she fought it down and said quietly, 'Nonsense. Major Coale has a scar on his face, nothing more.'

'Yes, and I don't care for *that*,' exclaimed Nicky. 'He's a great gun.'

'Of course he is, my pet. Now, you need to rest after your long journey.'

Obedient to her unspoken wishes the others left Nicky to Nurse's care and made their way back downstairs to the morning room.

'I don't like to think that he has been making a nuisance of himself.' Reginald frowned. 'When Coale told me he has been running free at Rooks Tower—'

'Major Coale and his people are very happy to see him,' said Zelah. 'With everyone here so busy with the new baby, Nicky has been left too much to his own devices.'

Her words were met with a short silence. Then Maria sighed.

'It is very true. Nurse has been giving all her attention to me and little Reginald and we were only too happy to think that Nicky was amusing himself in the garden.' Her softly reproachful eyes moved to her husband. 'And you have been out of the house so much recently…'

'Trying to gather evidence for the villagers,' he replied defensively. 'I could hardly take the boy with me! I never thought—Nicky seemed quite happy.' He gave Zelah a rueful smile. 'No wonder he took to you so well, although looking after Nicky was not the reason you came to us. My poor sister, you have been with us for only a few weeks and we have turned you into a nursemaid.'

'I am pleased to help, you know that, but Nicky needs companions of his own age,' she said gently. 'Or at the very least a tutor…'

'But he is so young!' Maria clasped her hands together. 'I suppose I must stop thinking of him as a baby now.' She brightened. 'You are looking for a post as a governess, Zelah—perhaps you should start with Nicky. We could pay you—'

'Dear sister, that is a kind thought, but that is not what I meant. And I could not take a salary off you; I have no wish to be an added drain upon your resources.'

Reginald shook his head.

'No, it would not do at all. I believe Mr Netherby gives lessons to a few boys in the vicarage. I will make enquiries when I go into Lesserton this afternoon.'

Maria stretched out her hands to him. 'Oh, must you go, with Nicky just come home…?'

He squeezed her fingers.

'I'm afraid I must.'

'What is this business that takes you there so often, Reginald?' asked Zelah. 'Is it something to do with Lydcombe Park? I remember you saying the new owner was causing difficulties.'

'Aye. He is planning to open mines on his land.'

'But surely that is a good thing,' exclaimed Maria. 'It will provide work—'

'Not much. Evanshaw will be bringing in engineers and miners of his own. But the land he wants to mine is in dispute. The villagers believe it is theirs by ancient charter and have been using the land for years, grazing their animals on the hill as well as hunting in Prickett Wood. Sir Oswald claims it for his own and he has employed a bailiff, William Miller. A nasty piece of work who patrols the land with his henchmen.'

'And is there nothing they can do?'

'Those he has evicted are too poor to do anything themselves, but I have been organising the villagers. We have petitioned the Crown and put together a fund to pay for a lawyer to come to Lesserton and settle this once and for all.'

'But can you not talk to Sir Oswald?' said Zelah. 'Surely he does not want to be on bad terms with his neighbours.'

Reginald shrugged. 'I called upon him as soon as he took possession of the house on Lady Day, but he was not at all hospitable. I do not think he intends to live at Lydcombe. The house is merely a shell; everything of value in it has been sold. He told me he means to sell off the timber from his land and then sink his mine. He has no interest at all in the people.'

'Then of course you must fight this,' exclaimed Zelah. 'I quite understand now why you are so busy. And please do not worry about Nicky, at least for the moment. I am very happy to help you look after him.'

Zelah went upstairs to relieve Nurse, satisfied that Maria and Reginald would find a solution to Nicky's loneliness. Taking lessons at the vicarage would go a long way towards filling his days and would also provide him with the companionship of other boys. For the present, her concern was to keep him entertained while the deep gash on his leg healed.

The fine spring weather continued but Zelah was too busy to go out, dividing her day between Nicky and Maria, who was delighted to have her back and insisted that Zelah should sit with her whenever she could. It was therefore a full three days before she could find the time to enjoy the sunshine. She tied a straw bonnet over her brown curls, but declined her sister's offer of a parasol, declaring that her complexion was past praying for.

Leaving the house by a side door, she set off across the grass at a very unladylike pace. It was good to be out in the fresh air again and she lifted her face up to the sun, revelling in its warmth. She walked briskly, enjoying the opportunity for a little quiet reflection.

She had been at West Barton for a month now and had made no progress in finding a position. She could make excuses, of course. Maria had told her how helpful it was to have her there, looking after Nicky, but deep in her heart Zelah knew she did not want to dwindle into the role of favourite aunt, at everyone's beck and call and willing to perform any little task in gratitude for being allowed to live with the family.

'You are being very ungrateful,' she said aloud. 'A position as governess would be far from comfortable. Here you could more than earn your keep.' She climbed over a stile and jumped lightly down. 'But as a governess I would be *paid*!'

She strode on. What she wanted, she realised, was independence. If she was fortunate enough to find a good position, then it might be possible to save a little of her salary each year until she had enough to retire. That, of course, would take many, many years, but what else had she to look forward to?

Perhaps you should look for a husband.

Major Coale's words came into her mind. She could almost hear his deep voice saying them.

A husband. That was the ambition of most young ladies, but it was not hers. Besides, no man would want her if he knew her past—and she could not consider marrying a man without telling him everything.

No, thought Zelah practically, she had only two choices: she could remain at West Barton, loved and valued at the present, but destined to become nothing more than a burdensome old maid, or she could make a bid for independence.

'I choose independence,' she said to a cow, regarding her balefully from the next field. 'I shall go back now and write out an advertisement for the newspaper.'

She crossed the field and scrambled over the stile on to the lane that led up to West Barton and as she did so she saw a rider approaching from the direction of Lesserton. Major Coale. In a panic she considered jumping back over the stile and hiding until he had gone by, but it was too late; he had already seen her.

'Good morning, Miss Pentewan.' He raised his hat to her. She felt a little rush of pride when she saw his short hair. His cheeks were still free of a beard, too. There was no sign that he planned to revert to his former shaggy appearance. 'I am on my way to enquire after young Master Buckland.'

'He is doing very well, Major, thank you. The doctor says he may leave his bed tomorrow.'

He professes to dislike society, she thought. *Perhaps he will be satisfied with that report. He will touch his hat, turn and ride away again.*

'I am glad to hear it.' He kicked his feet free from the stirrups and jumped down. 'Are you walking back to the house now? May I join you?'

'I…yes, of course.'

She waited until he was beside her and began to walk on, very slowly, the grey mare clopping lazily along behind them. After a few yards the major stopped.

'Is this how you usually walk, Miss Pentewan? I am surprised you ever get anywhere.'

'Yes—no, I…' She trailed off, her gaze dropping to his booted feet. 'I thought, your leg…'

'I am not a cripple, madam.'

Mrs Graddon's words flashed into her mind and she recalled when she had offered to cut his hair and he had got up from the table to summon his servant. There had been no dragging step, no sign of a limp then.

'Does the wound not pain you?' she asked him.

'Not at all, unlike this dawdling pace.'

She gave a little huff of irritation.

'I beg your pardon. I was trying to be considerate.'

His hard look informed her quite clearly that he did not appreciate her efforts. She put up her chin.

'If the wound has healed and there is no pain, why, then, does it affect your step?'

'Habit, I suppose. What does it matter? I do not go into society.'

'But that might change.'

'I think not.'

She gave up the argument and walked on at her normal pace. The major matched her stride for stride and Zelah hid a smile. A little furrow of concentration creased his brow, but he was no longer limping.

'Your journey back was not too tiring, Nicky did not suffer overmuch?'

'Not at all. The new road is very smooth.' She waved her hand at the lane. 'It puts our own track to shame.'

'My engineer used a new method of road-building: smaller stones, tightly packed. It seems very good, but we shall see how well it wears.' His glance shifted to her skirts and the band of damp around the hem. 'You have not been keeping to the roads, I think?'

She laughed. 'No, I have crossed a couple of very muddy fields. It was such a lovely day I could not bear to remain indoors a moment longer.'

'I suppose Nicky requires a great deal of attention. Your time cannot be your own.'

She was surprised by his concern.

'You are not to be thinking I begrudge him a moment of it, nor Maria, but sometimes one likes a little time alone—but I have had that now,' she said quickly, sensing his hesitation. She added shyly, 'This last stretch is the least interesting, and I am always glad of company for it.'

The house was in sight. She called to the gardener's boy to take the major's horse to the stables and led him in through the front door, sending a footman running to fetch Maria.

'Please come into the morning room, Major. My brother-in-law is out and will be sorry to have missed you, but my sister will be here directly.'

'Must I see her? I would rather you took me directly to see the boy.'

'You know I cannot do that. Besides, my sister will want to give you her thanks in person.'

He gave a little pout of distaste but the scar at the left side of his mouth distorted it into a full grimace. He muttered irritably that he wanted no thanks. Zelah felt a smile tugging her lips.

'You sound very much like a sulky schoolboy, Major.' She heard the door open and turned. 'Ah, Maria, here is Major Coale come to visit Nicky, if you will allow it.'

Maria hesitated at the door, then smiled and came forward.

'Major Coale, I am so delighted to meet you at last. I have heard so much about you from my son and I have been longing to thank you in person for taking such care of him.'

Watching him take her outstretched hand and bow over it gracefully, Zelah was aware of a little stab of jealousy that he had never saluted her in that way.

'My husband is in Lesserton at present, Major, and I am sure he will regret that he is not here to greet you. However, he is looking forward to seeing you next week at dinner—you received my note, I hope?'

'I did, ma'am, and I am delighted to accept.'

'Reginald is at a meeting,' said Zelah. 'There is a dispute over the boundary between the villagers' land and that belonging to Lydcombe Park. Have you heard about it?'

'Yes,' he said indifferently. 'I recall Netherby telling me something of it when he came to call.'

'Did he not tell you of the meeting?'

'He did, but it's no business of mine.'

His tone was final and Maria was quick to change the subject.

'Goodness, how the morning is flying! I am sure Nicky is anxious to see you, sir. Zelah, my love, perhaps you would escort Major Coale upstairs?'

'Oh—but I was about to retire to change my gown. It became sadly muddied during my walk....'

'Well, the major has already seen it and Nicky will not notice.' Maria laughed aside her objections. 'I must go and relieve Nurse—little Reginald will be waking up soon and demanding to be fed.' She turned to smile at the major. 'I shall say good-day to you now, sir, and look forward to seeing you here for dinner next week.'

Silently Zelah led the major away. The slight hesitation in his step had returned, but whether it was due to the exercise or the awkwardness of meeting his hostess she did not know and would not ask. Nicky's face lit up when the major walked in.

'I knew you would come!' Nicky greeted him enthusiastically.

'Did you doubt it, after you wrote me such a very polite letter?'

'It was Zelah's idea. She helped me write it.'

'But the sentiments were all Nicky's,' she said quickly.

The major turned towards her, amusement warming his hard eyes.

'Including the invitation to call? I am quite cast down.'

Zelah flushed scarlet, but she was saved from finding a response by her nephew, who had spotted a packet protruding from the major's coat pocket.

'Is that a present for me, Major?'

'It is, sir. It is the travel backgammon set from Rooks Tower. Hannah told me how much you enjoyed using it so I thought you might like to have it. She sends you her best wishes, by the bye.'

Nicky gave a little crow of delight and immediately challenged the major to a game.

'Oh now, Nicky, I am sure Major Coale is far too busy—'

'Major Coale has a little time to spare,' Dominic interrupted her. 'And my honour is at stake here—I cannot refuse a challenge!' He nodded at her. 'You may safely leave the boy with me for an hour, Miss Pentewan, if you wish to go and change your gown.'

'…and he stayed for a full two hours playing backgammon with Nicky. It was most good-natured of him. It left me free to look after baby and Zelah went off to write her letters.'

The family were at dinner and Maria was telling her husband about Major Coale's visit.

'Yes, I must say he struck me as very gentlemanly when I passed him on the road,' said Reginald. 'Quite a change from when I first made his acquaintance. *Then* he was looking very wild, but he is very much altered.' He cast an amused glance at Zelah. 'Having you in the house was a civilising influence, my dear.'

'Not that civilising,' she responded. 'I told him about your opposition to Sir Oswald's plans for Prickett Wood and he was not at all interested in supporting you.'

Maria was inclined to be sympathetic.

'One can hardly blame him, poor man. He is so hideously disfigured it must be a trial for him to go into society at all.'

Reginald paused, considering.

'Do you really think him so repulsive, my love? I can't say I really noticed his scar the last time I saw him.'

This response earned him a warm smile from his sister-in-law.

'Well, of course, it *was* the first time I had seen him,' said Maria. 'But his manners are so polished and he *is* the son of a viscount. Once he has been to dinner and I have seen him a little more, I am sure I shall grow accustomed.'

A week went by and Zelah waited hopefully each day for a response to her advertisement for a position as governess. She had written it out in her best copperplate and sent it to the newspaper offices in Barnstaple and Taunton, but no replies were forthcoming.

'Oh, my dear, perhaps it is not meant to be,' said Maria, when Zelah explained this to her. 'Can you not content yourself with living here? You know we are very happy to keep you with us.'

'Thank you, Maria, and I love being here as a guest, but it was never my intention to become your pensioner.'

Maria cried out at that, protesting that she would always be a guest, never a burden, but Zelah had seen Reginald poring over his accounts, she had heard him discussing with Maria the possibility of selling off some of their land to pay for Nicky to attend Mr Netherby's school. Zelah did not mention it, merely saying cheerfully, 'I do not despair—tomorrow I shall write another notice and send it off to the newspapers in Bristol and Bath. I am sure someone there must require a governess.'

'I am sure they do, love, but for now let us forget this plan of yours and look forward to this evening. Major Coale is coming to dinner, had you forgotten?'

Zelah had not forgotten, but for some reason she did not want to admit it and she was glad when her sister continued.

'What will you wear, Zelah, the green robe you had made up last summer?'

'I thought I might put on my grey gown.'

'What?' Maria sat up, scandalised. 'That gown has done service for several years now and is very severe. You should save it to wear when you are interviewed by a prospective employer. No,' she said decisively, 'you will wear the green and I shall fetch out my Norwich shawl for you to drape over your arms, should the evening turn chilly.' Maria sighed loudly. 'There is certainly no reason for you to save your best silk any longer. If you are set upon finding work, then it is not at all suitable for a governess.'

Zelah hugged her.

'Pray do not be sad for me, dearest sister. I think it is quite exciting, and if I find the children are just too abominable, I shall give it all up and come running home to you!'

When the dinner hour approached, Zelah ran lightly down to the drawing room, her silk skirts whispering as she moved. She had to admit there was something very uplifting about putting on a pretty dress. Maria had even sent her own maid to put up Zelah's hair, restraining it by a matching green bandeau and leaving just a few loose curls tumbling artlessly to her shoulders. To complete the picture Zelah threaded a small jade cross on a green ribbon and tied it around her neck.

'There,' she told her reflection, 'a picture of simple elegance. What does one need with diamonds and emeralds?'

The approving looks of her sister and brother-in-law raised her spirits even more and when Major Coale arrived she turned towards the door, her eyes sparkling and a smile of genuine welcome parting her lips.

Dominic entered the room ready to bow and say all that duty required, but when his eyes alighted upon Zelah Pentewan he stopped, his brain refusing to function. In a matter of seconds he regained his composure, bowing to his host and greeting Mrs Buckland with the usual polite phrases, but all the time his brain was in turmoil.

He had not been looking forward to the evening. He remembered his first meeting with his hostess, recalled her hesitation and the way her eyes travelled everywhere save to his face. He hoped she would soon recover from the habit, but it did not surprise him. It was always thus with a new acquaintance.

Except Zelah, who had never shown any reluctance to look at him, save when he teased her or paid her compliments and made her blush. Gazing at her now, he wanted to shower her with compliments, for she looked quite charming. Her gown, which was the colour of new leaves, brought out the green flecks in those expressive eyes that now met his own and a delicate flush mantled her cheeks. She looked genuinely pleased to see him and for a moment his spirits soared.

It had been a long time since any young woman had smiled at him in quite such a welcoming way, save those he had paid on rare occasions to spend the evening with him in a vain attempt to relieve his loneliness. Dominic quickly damped down his pleasure. Her smiles were nothing more than natural friendliness. No woman could ever be attracted to him now.

So he retreated into the safety of his perfect society manners and quelled the impulse to hold her fingers an instant longer than was required, or even—as he really wanted—to kiss her hand.

* * *

Dinner should have been a relaxed affair. Maria and Reginald were at pains to put their guest at ease and the major responded with perfect civility. There was very little for Zelah to do other than eat her food and enjoy the sound of his deep, well-modulated voice, yet she could not be easy. Every nerve end ached, her skin was so sensitive she wondered if it was perhaps some kind of fever, but when she touched her own cheek the skin was not unnaturally warm. Zelah wondered at her reaction and finally concluded she had lived retired for too long and had forgotten how to behave amongst strangers.

At last Maria gave the signal to withdraw and the ladies left the men to their brandy.

'I think it is going exceedingly well,' said Maria, sinking into a chair and disposing her skirts elegantly around her. 'Major Coale is very well read and Reginald was right, now that we have been in his company for a while I hardly notice his poor face at all. But you have been very quiet, Zelah my love. I would have thought the major's knowledge of art and literature would have made him an interesting guest for you.'

'He is—that is, the conversation was flowing so

well I didn't like to—I mean, I could find nothing to add.'

'That is most unlike you, little sister.' Maria patted her cheek. 'I do believe you are a little shy of the major, but there is no need. Indeed, you should know him better than any of us. You must try to be a little more sociable. I assure you, Zelah, you have nothing to fear. He is perfectly harmless.'

But Major Coale did not *feel* perfectly harmless. Zelah could not explain it. Part of her wanted to stay near him, to engage him in conversation and at the same time she wanted to run away. It was most confusing.

When the gentlemen came in she was prepared to make an effort to join in, but they were getting on so well that the conversation flowed quite easily without any contribution from herself and she remained beside her sister, a relieved and silent observer. Maria, however, was determined that she should participate more and when the tea tray was brought in she handed two cups to Zelah, instructing her to carry one to their guest.

Bracing herself, Zelah moved across the room. Major Coale accepted the cup with a word of thanks, adding, as Reginald lounged away and they were left alone, 'Buckland tells me Nicky is to go to school.'

'Yes. Mr Netherby teaches a small group of boys for a few hours each day and he has agreed to take him. It is as much for the company as anything.'

'And when does he start?'

'As soon as he is walking again, which should not be long now, he is making good progress.'

She sipped at her tea, trying to think of something to say. She wanted to tell him how handsome he looked, but that would be most improper, and unfortunately, everything else that came to mind was connected to their having dined together, a fact that must remain secret.

'You are very quiet this evening, Miss Pentewan. Why is that? I know you are not afraid of me.'

The glinting smile in his eyes drew an answering gleam from her.

'Not when I was on your land, certainly. But here...' she glanced around '...I fear I am less at ease with you in these more formal surroundings.'

'That is singular—if anything you should feel safer here, with your family.'

She smiled. 'You must think me very foolish.'

'Not at all. Have you found a suitable post yet, as a governess?'

'No, and it is very lowering. Maria ascribes it to my lack of experience.'

'She may well be right.'

'But I am very well qualified! Papa himself took charge of my education. He taught me French and mathematics and the use of globes—and he allowed me free access to his extensive library.' She sighed. 'But of course, apart from my nephew I have little experience of children.' She turned her eyes upon him as a thought occurred to her. 'I wonder perhaps if you have a young relative in need of a governess?'

He threw back his head and laughed at that. Zelah smiled, surprised at the little curl of pleasure it gave her, to have amused him so.

'No, Miss Pentewan, I do not. I have only one sister, you saw her portrait. She is now married, but when she was younger she was such a minx that I have the greatest sympathy with every one of the poor ladies employed to instruct her.'

'Oh dear, was she so bad?'

'A perfect hoyden. She ran through at least a dozen governesses. Do not look so dismayed, ma'am, the Coales are renowned for being wild to a fault. Not all families will be as bad.'

'No-o.' Zelah was not convinced. She gave herself a little shake. 'I have not given up hope, Major.

I have already sent off more advertisements. I am sure something will turn up.'

'Of course it will.' He put down his cup. 'It is growing late and I must get back.'

He rose and crossed the room to take his leave of his hostess. Zelah felt a deep sense of disappointment that he was going so soon, which was irrational, since she had avoided his company most of the evening.

Nicky was making good progress. By the end of the week he was hobbling around the garden, showing off his heavily bandaged leg to all the servants.

Zelah watched him from her bedroom window. He was in the garden, talking to the aged retainer employed to cut the lawn. She was too far away to hear what was being said, but she could imagine him recounting the tale of how he hurt his leg. The old man was leaning on his scythe and giving the boy his full attention, even though she was sure he would have heard the story several times over. She put her chin on her hands, smiling. Nicky had such a natural charm, no wonder everyone loved him. Reginald was taking him to join the vicar's little school next week and she hoped the other boys would take to him.

There was a knock at the door.

'If you please, miss, Major Coale is here to see you.'

'Is my sister not available?'

The maid bobbed another curtsy. 'He asked to speak to you, ma'am.'

'Oh.'

She turned to the mirror and picked up her brush, then put it down again. Without removing all the pins, brushing out her curls and pinning it all back up again, which would take far too long, there was not really much improvement she could make, save to tuck an escaping tendril behind her ear.

Zelah pulled the neckline of her gown a little straighter, smoothed out her skirts and, after a final look in the mirror, made her way downstairs to the morning room.

The major was standing by the window, his back to the room and his hands clasped behind him.

'Good morning, Major Coale.' He turned to face her, but with his back to the light Zelah could not read his expression. She said quickly, 'Nicky is in the garden, sir, if you wish to see—'

'No, it is you I came to see,' he interrupted her, his tone more clipped and curt than ever.

She sank on to a chair. He ignored her invitation to sit down and took a turn about the room. Zelah waited in silence, watching him. His right leg was dragging and he was frowning, the crease of his brow making the scar running down his face even more noticeable. Zelah clasped her hands tightly together and waited.

'Miss Pentewan.' His shadow enveloped her as he stopped before her chair. Then, with a slight shake of his head, he took another turn about the room, saying as he walked, 'You may think I should have spoken first to Buckland or perhaps to your sister, to sound them out on the matter, but you are of age, and knowing how you value your independence I decided to address you directly.'

Zelah dropped her gaze. There was a slight crease in her own brow now. Her heart was hammering so hard against her ribs she thought it might burst free at any moment. She hoped he would not expect her to speak, for her throat felt so tight she could hardly breathe. He approached, his steps thudding a soft, uneven tattoo on the carpet and soon she was staring at the highly polished toes of his topboots, yet still she could not look up.

He cleared his throat again. 'Miss Pentewan, I have a proposal for you.'

Chapter Four

Zelah closed her eyes, waiting for the world to stop spinning. After a few deep breaths she opened her eyes, but could not bring herself to look up into the major's face. Instead she fixed her gaze on the rather poor landscape painting on the wall.

'A p-proposal, sir?' Her voice was little more than a croak.

'Yes.'

She jumped up and went to the window, her hands on her burning cheeks. What was she to say? Could this really be happening? She kept her back to him as he began to speak again.

'You have honoured me with your confidence and informed me that you are seeking employment as a governess. I want to ask—that is, would you consider a rather...*different* form of employment?'

The heat and colour fled from her cheeks as swiftly as it had come. She wheeled around, this time firmly fixing her eyes upon his face. Her heart was still hammering but there was such a confusion of thoughts in her head that she felt sick. She swallowed, hard.

'Just what are you offering me, Major?'

He looked uncomfortable. She found herself praying.

Please do not let him say it. I cannot bear to think he would even ask...

'Miss Pentewan, you will know I am alone at Rooks Tower.' Her heart sank even lower. She clenched her hands together, closed her eyes and prepared her answer even as he continued. 'I have been struggling for some weeks now but—madam, would you consider working as my archivist?'

'Sir, thank you, but I could not possibly—*what?*'

He shrugged. 'Archivist, librarian, I am not sure what title you would use, but I need someone to put my books in order. Rooks Tower has a large library and I intend to make use of it. I have had the room decorated, but have done nothing about unpacking the books I brought with me from Markham. I have collected a great number of volumes over the years and transported them all here, but they are in no particular order. It is the devil of a job and with the summer coming on I need to be supervising the work outside as much as possible. I just haven't the time…'

She blinked at him.

'You…you want me to, to *arrange your books*?'

'Yes. Oh, I know it is not the type of work you were looking for, but from our discussions I received the impression that you were intent upon becoming a governess because that is the only respectable occupation available to a young woman.'

'Respectable, yes, and…I know nothing about organising a library!'

A smile tugged at the corner of his mouth.

'You told me you knew nothing about children, but that has not stopped you advertising yourself as a governess. I need someone to sort out all those damn—dashed volumes.'

'But surely you should employ a scholar to do this, someone who understands the value of your collection—'

Again that grimace distorted his features.

'I am not interested in its value, only that the books are recorded in some sort of order and that they are on the shelves and to hand when I want them. They are, in the main, useful books that I have collected.' He took a turn about the room. 'Besides, I do not wish to have a stranger in my house. No, madam, I want the library organised and all the books catalogued during the next few months. I see no reason why you could not walk over there every day and continue to live with your brother and sister.'

'I—I am not sure…'

He waved an impatient hand.

'You need fear no impropriety. Mrs Graddon and the housemaids will be present and I spend most of my time out of doors. I am willing to pay you a total of fifty guineas for the work: twenty-five when you begin, and the rest once the library is complete. It should not take too long, two months, perhaps three at the most.'

'Then the remuneration you offer is far too generous.'

He shrugged. 'I want it to be done, and soon. The cost is not important.'

Zelah shook her head, trying to think clearly. In the space of a few minutes her spirits had experienced ecstatic heights, deep despair and a fury of indignation, and all for nothing. He was offering her nothing more or less than a job of work.

The major picked up his hat.

'Perhaps you would like to consider it. Talk it over with your sister.'

'No,' she answered him quickly. 'No, I have made my decision.'

If she discussed this with Maria or Reginald they might well try to dissuade her, but here was an opportunity to earn her keep, albeit for a short time, and remain with her family. She squared her shoulders, raised her head and met his gaze.

'I accept your offer, Major Coale.'

For a long, breath-stopping moment his eyes searched her face, then he smiled and she found herself responding, until he looked away from her.

'Thank you, that is excellent news,' he said crisply. 'I see no reason for delay. Report to Rooks Tower on Monday morning!'

'My dear sister, have you lost your wits?'

Zelah gazed up at her brother-in-law, a laugh hovering on her lips. 'Why should you think that? I have merely accepted a very lucrative engagement.'

She had kept the news of the major's proposal until they were sitting together in the drawing room after dinner. She had hoped that a good meal would put Reginald in a more mellow mood, but her announcement was still met with a mixture of indignation and amazement.

'You cannot accept,' declared Maria. 'It would be most improper.'

'But I *have* accepted and there will be nothing improper about the arrangement. Major Coale has already informed me that he spends his days out of doors.'

'For an unmarried lady to be alone in his house—'

'I shall not be alone, Reginald, I shall be surrounded by servants. Besides, who will know of it?'

'The whole of Lesserton by the end of the week,' replied Reginald drily.

'But it is a job of work. I shall continue to advertise for a position as a governess, but until then it will give me a measure of independence, and if the task takes only three months then I should be able to save a good proportion of my money against hard times.' Zelah looked at her sister, begging her to understand. 'I have been here long enough, Maria. I told you when I came I would not be your pensioner. Major Coale has promised to give me half my fee in advance. I intend to give some of it to you, to pay Nicky's school fees.'

'But there is no need of that, Reginald and I have already agreed—'

'To sell the seven-acre field, I know.' Zelah interrupted her. 'I would much rather you took my money.'

'Never,' cried Maria, pulling out her handkerchief. 'I would not dream of taking your wages—'

Reginald held up his hand.

'I think Zelah has a point,' he said slowly. 'To sell

off the field would mean less return at harvest. If we keep it, we may well be able to repay your sister by the end of the year.'

Maria did not look convinced. She reached across and took Zelah's hands.

'Oh, my dear, for any young lady to take such a position, in the house of a man like Major Coale, would be to risk her reputation, but in your case—'

'In my case I have no reputation to risk.'

An uncomfortable silence followed Zelah's bald statement. She withdrew her hands from her sister's grasp and rose.

'I made up my mind when I left Cardinham that I would support myself. I have caused my family enough sorrow and will not compound my guilt by allowing you to keep me.'

'But you might marry—'

'You know I have set my mind against marriage.'

'Oh, sister, pray do not say that—'

Reginald put up his hand to silence his wife's protest.

'My dear, Zelah is right,' he said heavily. 'Any man who formed an attachment would have to be told of her…unfortunate past.'

Zelah winced.

'But if a man truly loved her—' cried Maria, looking beseechingly at her husband.

Zelah shook her head.

'Of all the requirements a man may have when looking for a wife three things are paramount: good birth, good fortune and a spotless character. I am afraid I have only the first of those requirements. So you see, it is much better that I should learn to make my own way in the world.' She smiled at them, knowing tears were not far away. 'If you will only allow me to continue living here while I work at Rooks Tower, then I shall consider myself truly blessed.'

'Of course you may.' Reginald came forwards to kiss her cheek. 'We could not countenance you living anywhere else.'

'Good day to you, Miss Pentewan. The master said you was coming. I am to show you to the library.'

Despite having told herself that she did not expect the major to be at Rooks Tower to greet her, Zelah was disappointed. She followed the housekeeper through the hall, heading away from the main staircase and towards a pair of ornate double doors. Zelah expected to pass through into a grand reception chamber, but she was surprised to find herself enveloped in shadows. When her eyes grew accustomed to the gloom she could see that it was indeed a large room with a magnificent marble fireplace and intricate linenfold panelling on the walls, but each of the long windows was shuttered to within a few inches of the top, allowing in only enough light to see one's way between the furniture.

'The master instructed that these shutters should remain closed,' explained the housekeeper. 'This is the yellow salon and everything here is just as it was when Major Coale bought it, but he never uses it. One soon gets used to walking through the gloom.' There was a tiny note of regret in the older woman's voice. She had reached the far end of the room and threw open the doors. 'This is where you will be working.'

The library was identical in size to the yellow salon, but here the morning light shone in through a series of long windows that filled one wall. The other three walls were lined with open bookcases in rich mahogany, their ranks broken only by the doors and the ornate chimney breast. A large desk and chair stood at one end of the room and a wing chair had been placed near the hearth, but the remaining floor space was taken up with a multitude of crates and boxes.

'Goodness,' murmured Zelah, her eyes widening. She felt a little tremor of excitement as she thought of all the books packed in the boxes. Who knew what treasures lay in store!

'It is indeed a sorry mess,' said Mrs Graddon, misinterpreting her reaction. 'I'm sure you'll soon begin to set it all in order. The master has left you new ledgers in the desk drawer and there's pens, paper and ink, too. Graddon will send someone to help you with the boxes.'

She went away and Zelah stood for a few moments, wondering just where to start.

She began by exploring the room, running her fingers along the smooth polished wood of the empty shelves and then over the cold marble of the fireplace. She moved across the room. The long windows with their low sills looked out on to a wide terrace where little tufts of grass sprouted between the paving. Beyond the stone balustrade the grounds sloped down to the river before the land rose again, the park giving way to woodland that stretched away as far as the distant hills.

An idyllic setting, she thought, drinking in the peaceful tranquillity of the scene. Then setting her shoulders, she turned again to face the task ahead of her.

When the clock on the mantelpiece chimed four o'clock Zelah looked up, surprised. She had no idea where the day had gone. Books were piled haphazardly on the shelves and several opened crates littered the floor. The volumes had been packed in no particular order, novels and religious tracts jostling with books on wild flowers and a furniture directory. She would have to go through them all before she could begin to catalogue them. The room looked even more chaotic now than when she had started, but it could not be helped.

She tidied her desk and glanced around the room, mentally deciding just where she would begin tomorrow. Her eyes fell upon the small door in the far corner. The housekeeper had told her it led to the tower. Zelah stood for a moment, indecisive. Perhaps, while no one was about, she would take a quick peep at the tower.

The door opened on to a small lobby where a steep, wooden stairway wound its way upwards. There was an air of neglect about the plain painted walls and worn treads, but the banister was firm enough and Zelah began to climb the stairs. A door on the first landing opened on to a storage room which was filled with old furniture. Zelah gave it only a cursory glance before moving on to the second floor. She found herself at last on a small landing. The wooden stairs gave way to a narrow stone spiral staircase at the side of which was a single door. Grasping the door handle, Zelah turned it, half-expecting it to be locked. It opened easily and she stepped into a room filled with sunlight. At first glance it seemed there were no walls, only windows from breast-height to ceiling, the leaded lights divided by thin stone mullions and giving an extensive view of the country in all directions.

The only solid wall was behind her, surrounding the door through which she had entered and housing a small fireplace. There were just three pieces of furniture in the room: a mahogany pedestal desk and chair and a much older court cupboard pushed under one window, its well-worn top level with the sill. Zelah knew that such pieces had been designed to display the owner's plate, a visible indication of wealth and status, but this cupboard was as empty as the desktop. There was nothing in the room to detract from the magnificent views. Zelah moved to the windows. From the first she could see right over the forest and vales towards Devon, from the next the road curled off towards Lesserton and the densely packed trees of Prickett Wood, while from a third she looked out across the park and woods of Rooks Tower to the uplands of Exmoor. She put her hands on the window ledge, drinking in the views.

'There are no books up here, Miss Pentewan.'

Zelah jumped. Major Coale was standing in the doorway, his hat and riding crop in one hand.

'Oh, I did not hear you come upstairs.' She noted idly that his broad shoulders almost brushed the door frame on each side and was glad when he moved into the room and his size did not appear so daunting. She waved towards the window. 'I was entranced by the view.'

'Obviously.'

'I hope you do not mind,' she hurried on, her eyes searching his face for some softening of his expression. 'I have done all I can in the library today and wanted to look at the tower and did not wish to disturb the servants…'

He placed his hat and crop on the cupboard.

'And is this what you expected?' he asked, drawing off his gloves.

Her smile was spontaneous, any nervousness forgotten.

'Not at all. I had not imagined the views would be so extensive. You can see all the way into the next county! It is such a lovely room. Imagine how wonderful to sit at this desk—why, in the summer you could work all day and never need to light a candle.' She looked up at him. 'Is this your desk, sir? Do you use this room?'

He shook his head.

'This room is as it was when I bought Rooks Tower and so far this year I have been too busy putting the estate in order to worry overmuch about the interior.'

'I would like to use it.' Zelah clasped her hands together, hoping her eagerness did not sound foolish. 'I could bring the books up here to catalogue them. That way, once the library is tidy, you would be able to use it for your guests—'

'There are no guests,' he said shortly.

'But one day—'

'It is not my intention to invite anyone here. Ever.'

She felt the last word was added for her benefit. It was uttered with such finality that it gave her pause, but not for long.

'Is… Would that be because of…?' She touched her own cheek and saw him flinch. He turned slightly, presenting his undamaged side to her, his profile reminding her of how dangerously attractive he must once have been.

'I did not move to Rooks Tower to be sociable,' he said curtly. 'My years as a soldier have left me impatient of society. Its values and petty tyrannies disgust me.'

'But you have family and friends, sir. Surely you will not cut yourself off from them so completely?'

'Damn you, madam, we are not here to discuss how I choose to run my life!'

Zelah recoiled from his angry retort. She bit her lip against further argument, but was not daunted enough to forget her original idea.

'I beg your pardon, Major. Of course it is no business of mine. But I would like to make use of this room, if you will allow me.' She waited for a moment, then added coaxingly, 'I promise I will not let the view distract me from my work.'

His brow cleared.

'The view is even better from the roof, especially on a fine day like this.'

She waited expectantly. His hard eyes glinted and she knew he had read her mind.

'Would you like to see it?'

Zelah followed him out to the landing and on to the spiral stair. It was only just wide enough for one person and she was obliged to hold up her skirts as she climbed the steep steps. A series of tiny windows sent shafts of dazzling sunlight across her path, making it difficult to see the next step.

When they reached the top he threw open the door and the light flooded in.

'Do you not keep it locked?'

'No need. My servants never come up here.' He

turned and reached down for her. 'Give me your hand. There is no handrail and these last few stairs are uneven.'

His fingers curled around her hand, warm and secure as he guided her up the final steps to the roof. She found herself on a flat roof, paved over with stone slabs and surrounded by a crenellated parapet.

'Oh,' she breathed. 'I feel I am on top of the world.'

She became aware that the major was still holding her hand and looked up at him warily. Immediately he released her. She gazed out across the hills, her hands clutched against her breastbone.

'Magnificent, isn't it?' He stood beside her, the rough wool of his jacket rubbing against her bare arm. 'Do not go too near the edge and do not lean against the battlements,' he warned her. 'The stonework is in poor condition.'

'But you will repair it, won't you, Major? I cannot bear to think that this view would be lost.' She swung round and peeped up at him, trying and failing to suppress a smile. 'Even though you are adamant you will not be having any guests here.'

The answering gleam in his eyes made her own smile grow and she gazed up at him quite unselfconsciously, thinking how much better he looked when he was not scowling at everyone and everything. In fact, she did not even notice his scarred face when he looked at her in just that way.

The playful breeze tugged a lock of hair free from her sensible topknot and whipped it across her face. She was going to sweep it away, but Dominic's hand came up first and his fingers caught the errant curl.

Zelah held her breath. Their eyes were still locked, and instead of removing his hand after tucking the curl behind her ear, he allowed it to slip to her neck while he ran his thumb lightly along her jaw. Her heart began to pound against her ribs and she kept her hands clenched across her breast as if to prevent it breaking free. Her mouth dried. There was an almost forgotten ache curling inside her. Anxiety? Excitement?

With his hand on her neck he held her as surely as if she was in chains. She could not move. Indeed, she did not want to move, she wanted him to lower his head and kiss her. She wanted to feel his hands undressing her, exploring her body.

Oh dear heaven, where had such wanton ideas come from?

Something of her thoughts flickered in her eyes and immediately he released her. Zelah switched her gaze to the view, trying to recall what they were saying. Ah, yes. She had been teasing him. Well, that was clearly a very dangerous thing to do.

The major cleared his throat. 'If you have seen enough, perhaps we should go back downstairs.'

'Yes.' She was anxious to get away from his disturbing presence. 'Yes, of course.'

She went carefully down the steep spiral, one hand on the wall. Her legs were shaking and she was very conscious of Major Coale following her down. When they reached the landing she hurried on to the wooden stairs, halting only when she heard the major's voice behind her.

'I have to collect my hat and whip. Feel free to make use of the room if you wish, Miss Pentewan. I have no objection.'

'Thank you.' She forced the words out and glanced back at him. He was standing once again in the doorway, blocking the light and enveloping her in his shadow. Binding her to him by some force beyond her comprehension.

Zelah gave herself a mental shake. Fanciful nonsense. She must not give in to it. She nodded, trying to sound businesslike. 'If there is nothing else, sir, I shall go home now.'

'No, nothing.'

Dominic watched her hasten away. Her hand looked unsteady on the banister, but she descended the stairs without mishap and disappeared from sight.

He exhaled, his breath hissing through his clenched teeth. He had not meant to frighten her, but when they were up on the roof and she stood before him, her eyes shining with excitement, he had felt the desire slam through him. He should have known better. He could have moved away, turned his back on her, but the craving to touch her was so strong that he had given in to it. Even now he could feel her skin beneath his thumb, soft as a flower petal. And she had not moved away. Petrified, he thought sourly, for an instant later he had seen the horror in her face.

What if he had frightened her so much that she did not return tomorrow? Perhaps that would be for the best. She unsettled him, with her teasing and her challenging questions. He squared his shoulders. He was a soldier. He would not be beaten by this slip of a girl! They had an agreement and *he* would not be the one to break it. Let her come to Rooks Tower and organise his library. But perhaps it would be wise if he kept out of her way.

The walk back to West Barton did much to calm Zelah's disordered nerves. She had allowed herself to relax in Major Coale's company. After all, one did not tease a gentleman, unless he was a relative, or a very close friend. Certainly one did not tease an employer. She must be more careful. No one knew better than she the consequences of becoming too familiar with a gentleman!

Each evening at dinner Maria and Reginald asked Zelah about her day at Rooks Tower. They were naturally interested in her progress, but even more concerned about the behaviour of her employer. Each time Zelah was able to reply with complete sincerity that she had not seen Major Coale. For the first few days after the incident on the tower roof she was relieved that they did not meet, but gradually his elusiveness began to frustrate her. She had many questions to ask him and was obliged to leave notes, asking where he wanted certain books and how he would like them arranged. His answer, via the butler or Mrs Graddon, was always the same, 'The master says to do as you think best and he will discuss it with you later.'

It was nearly two weeks before she saw Major Coale again. By that time she had removed all the books from their crates and was working on making a record of every title, bringing small piles of books to the large mahogany desk to list in one of the ledgers provided.

It was a particularly sunny day and the room was uncomfortably warm, so Zelah had removed the fine muslin scarf from her shoulders and tossed it aside while she worked. She heard footsteps approaching and looked up, expecting to see Graddon or one of the footmen bringing refreshments, and she was taken by surprise when Major Coale strode in. He looked as if he had come direct from the stables; his hat was tucked under his arm and in one hand he carried his gloves and riding crop. His riding jacket hung open, displaying an embroidered waistcoat that fitted across his broad chest as snugly as the tight buckskins that covered his thighs. There was only the slightest drag on his right leg and his step was firm, brisk. He exuded energy.

Nonplussed, Zelah reached for her scarf and quickly knotted it across her shoulders as she rose and came around the desk to greet him.

His brows twitched together, the slight movement accentuating the ragged scar and deepening the unsmiling look into something resembling a scowl as they approached each other. Zelah tried not to feel intimidated.

'Have you come to see how I progress?' She summoned up a smile. 'The rooms looks much better without all the boxes, I think.' She waved her hand towards the bookshelves. 'Of course, they are not yet in any great order, but this way it is easier to see just what books we have.' She became more natural as she warmed to her theme. 'I need you to tell me how you want them arranged. Are you happy to have sermons and music ranked alongside books on ratcatching, shoeing horses and draining bogs?'

She observed a definite glint of humour in his eyes, albeit reluctant.

'I doubt if that is how you would place them. I think the last three should be grouped with estate management.'

'And your novels, Major? I thought to put them on these shelves, near your chair by the fire. They would be at hand then when you wish to sit in here and read.'

'That seems a good idea. You are not using the tower room?'

'No, not at present.'

The room held unsettling memories of the feelings he had roused in her. He tapped the riding crop against the palm of his hand as he glanced around the room, his expression unreadable.

'I came to tell you that you will soon have more books arriving. A few months back I purchased the contents of Lydcombe Park Library. The books have been in storage with my man of business since the sale. They are in a number of large crates, too big for the pack ponies, but now the road is finished they can be brought here by wagon, as soon as I can spare the men to fetch them.'

'Oh. Well then, it is a good thing I have not yet put everything in order.' She bent an enquiring gaze upon him. 'Are these *useful* books, sir, or might we find more classical texts in this consignment?'

'I have no idea. I have never seen them.'

'So we may well have more than one copy of some titles, sir.'

'If that is the case then I shall leave it to you to decide which one to keep.' His tone was cold, indifferent, and Zelah wondered if he was perhaps displeased with her way of working. She was framing the question in her mind when he reached out and flicked the edge of the muslin scarf. 'If you covered up your charms for my benefit then you were wasting your time, Miss Pentewan. I have no interest in hired staff.'

His words hit Zelah with the shock of cold water. She was rendered speechless, but thankfully she was not expected to respond. The major turned on his heel and marched out.

Zelah retreated to the desk and sank down on the chair, shaking. He had seen her put the scarf about her, was that the reason for his brusque manner? Had he taken her action as an insult? She shook her head. It had been a defensive gesture to cover her bare neck and shoulders, because she did not want him to think she was flaunting herself. He had taken it as a personal slight, as if she thought he had designs upon her virtue. She could have laughed, if she had not been so angry. Slowly, with trembling hands, she began to pack up. She would do no more today.

Chapter Five

Zelah set off across the grass, heading for the woodland path that led directly to West Barton. She had not gone far before she heard the major calling her name. She stopped and turned to see him striding towards her.

'Where are you going?'

'Home.' She waited for him to come up to her.

'It is still early.'

She looked away from his hard, searching gaze.

'I have done enough for today.'

'You are angry with me.'

'Yes.'

'Because I accused you of covering your… charms?'

'It was uncalled for, uncivil and unnecessary.' She added more quietly, 'I thought you knew me better than that.'

He was her employer, he could dismiss her if he

objected to her comments, but she did not regret her words.

'You are quite right. I was very rude. What can I do to make amends?'

She did not hesitate.

'I would like you to show a little more interest in your library. I have no idea if you are happy with my work so far, if it meets with your approval. You have not been near the library until today.'

'On the contrary, I visit the library every evening.'

'Oh.'

'Yes, Miss Pentewan. I am taking a close interest in your progress, but I visited West Barton last week, to enquire after Nicky. Your brother-in-law considers your employment at Rooks Tower nothing short of scandalous. I thought by taking myself out of the house every day it would mitigate the impropriety.'

'Some would still consider it improper if you were to take yourself out of the *country* while I am working for you! It is unfortunate that my brother-in-law does not approve but he understands my desire for independence. The fact that he has not thrown me out of the house shows he is prepared to put up with my "scandalous" behaviour, even if he cannot condone it.' She had hoped he might smile at this, but when he did not she added impatiently, 'For heaven's sake, you have some rare books in your collection. Pine's *Horace*, for example, and Hooke's *Micrographia*.' She exhaled through clenched teeth. 'You have engaged me to work for you, Major, and I would much rather discuss matters directly with you than be forever passing messages via Mrs Graddon.'

At last his forbidding frown was lightened. There was a glimmer of understanding in his hard eyes.

'Very well, Miss Pentewan. I will make efforts to be available. Starting tomorrow.'

'Thank you. I will bid you good day, sir.'

'You are still going?'

'Of course.'

'Then I will walk with you.' One side of his mouth quirked at her look of surprise. 'I know what you are thinking: I am now taking too great an interest in my hired staff. You would like to throw my earlier comments in my face.'

'I am not so impolite.'

'Unlike me?'

'Yes, I thought you impolite.'

'Pray do not let yourself be constrained by your good breeding, Miss Pentewan. Rip up at me, if you wish, you have my permission!'

A smile tugged at her mouth.

'It would be no more than you deserve.'

'I am aware of that. So let me make amends now by walking to the edge of my land with you.'

She gave in, nodding her assent, and he fell into step beside her.

'You walk this way every day?'

'Yes. It is much the quickest route.'

'Then you have seen the changes. I have cleared the paths and thinned out the trees—that was what I was doing when I first met you and Nicky in the woods.'

She remembered her first sight of him. A bearded woodsman, his hair long and wild and with a fearsome axe at his side. It was a powerful image that remained with her, even if the major looked so much more civilised now.

'You have done much of the work yourself, I think.'

'Yes. I like to keep active.'

'And it sets your people a good example.'

'There is that, too.'

They were walking through the woods now and Zelah could see the signs of clearance everywhere, but new growth was already appearing, bright splashes of green pushing up from the ground. The Major raised his hand to acknowledge a woman and her children coming through the trees. The woman dipped a slight curtsy, then she murmured a word to the children, who tugged at their forelocks.

'You do not mind the villagers coming here to collect their firewood?'

He shrugged.

'Once we have cut up the logs and taken them away they are welcome to anything that is left, although Phillips, my keeper, tells me there has been a marked increase in the number of people coming into the woods of late.'

'The villagers no longer have access to Prickett Wood,' explained Zelah. 'Reginald tells me the new owner is going to fence it off. Do you know Sir Oswald?'

'A nodding acquaintance only.'

'But I thought his land borders your own.'

'Not quite, so I have had no reason to make contact with Sir Oswald. I told you, I do not socialise, Miss Pentewan.'

'Perhaps you should.' She screwed up her courage. 'People would soon grow accustomed to your… to your scars.'

His short bark of laughter held more than a touch of bitterness.

'I would be accused of frightening the children.'

'No! Think of Nicky.'

'A lonely child, desperate for company. When he

is with his new school friends I doubt he will be as keen to acknowledge me.'

'That is not true, he is proud to be acquainted with you.'

'Kind words, ma'am, but I fear you know very little of human nature. But it is not just that.' He paused, and, glancing up, she saw him gazing into the distance, as if looking into another world. 'Spain was a very sobering experience for me, Miss Pentewan. There is no glory in war, in all the death and carnage that takes place, but I found the life infinitely preferable to what I had been before—a rake, a fop, whose only interest was to wear a fashionable coat and flirt with all the prettiest women. That is what society expects of a gentleman, madam, and I want none of it now.'

'But the people here are not fashionably idle, Major Coale. There are many good, hard-working men who want nothing more than to better themselves and their families.'

'Then good luck to them, but they shall not do so on my coat-tails.'

'That is not what I meant—'

'Enough!' They had reached the lane that separated Major Coale's land from the gardens of West Barton. Dominic stopped. 'I am a lost cause, Miss Pentewan. I will live my own life, in my own way.

I have no wish to consort with my neighbours, and there's an end to it.' He looked up. 'We part here.'

She said impulsively, 'Even so, there is no reason why you should not treat your wounds. There is a cream, a herbal remedy, it is excellent for softening the skin—'

'I want none of your potions, madam!'

'It is not a potion, but it might help.'

'I hired you as my librarian, not my doctor.' He glowered at her. 'Do not push me too far.'

The implacable look in his eyes told her she must accept defeat. For the moment. As a child she had accompanied her father when he visited his parishioners. They had met with pride and stubbornness many times, but her father's message had always been the same. Where Zelah had been inclined to argue, he would stop her, saying gently, 'Let the matter lie for now, but never give up.' She therefore swallowed any retort and merely inclined her head.

'Thank you, sir, for your company.'

He bowed.

'It was a pleasure. Until tomorrow.'

It was only a step across the lane to the little wicket gate leading to the gardens, but when Zelah turned to latch the gate there was no sign of the major. He had disappeared back into the woods.

* * *

Zelah always enjoyed her days at Rooks Tower, but when she awoke the following morning she felt an added sense of anticipation. A blustery wind was blowing the grey clouds across the sky when she set out. It tugged at her skirts and threatened to whip away her bonnet. She arrived at last, windswept but exhilarated, and made her way through the darkened salon to the library. She looked around her with satisfaction. Most of the books were on the shelves now and in a rough order. She had dusted and cleaned each one, putting aside any that required repair. She was engaged in writing the details in the ledgers, in her neat copperplate hand, when the major came in.

'No, no, do not get up.' He waved her back into her seat. 'Carry on with your laborious task. I would not give you an excuse to shirk your duties.'

He perched himself upon the edge of the desk and turned the ledger to inspect the latest entries. She was pleased that he no longer attempted to present only his right side to her and she laughed up at him, barely noticing the jagged line running down his face.

'I am obliged to break off now and again to rest my eyes, so I consider your interruption very timely.'

'If this were my job I would welcome any inter-ruption. It would irk me beyond bearing to sit here all day.' He pushed the ledger back towards her. 'Do you not long to be out of doors?'

A spatter of rain hit the windows and she chuck-led.

'Not when the weather is like this! When the sun is shining I admit it is very tempting to go out, but then I open the windows, and I have my walk home to look forward to.'

'There is that, of course. Now, is there anything you want of me today?'

'Only to look at the books I have set aside, sir, and tell me if you want them repaired or thrown away...'

She directed his attention to the books piled on a side table. The major went through them with the same decisiveness he gave to every other task she had seen him perform.

'So, these are to go to the bookbinder for new covers and the rest...' Zelah paused, picking up a dilapidated copy of Newton's *Principia*. 'Are you quite sure you want me to throw these away?'

'Perfectly. The book you are holding has been ruined by damp and misuse, it is beyond repair.' Reluctantly Zelah put the book down and he gave an impatient sigh. 'Pray do not get sentimental over such an object, madam. There may well be another copy amongst the books from Lydcombe Park. If not, then you can order a new one for me.'

'Yes, sir. May I pass the old ones on to Mr Netherby? Some of his pupils might make use of them.'

'If that is what you wish.' He picked up a small earthenware jar hidden behind a pile of books. 'What is this?'

'That?' Zelah ran her tongue over her lips. 'It is the cream I mentioned to you.' His brows snapped together and she hurried on. 'I, um, I was going to give it to Graddon. I thought he might apply it for you...'

'Did you now? Graddon is no nursemaid.'

She sighed. 'Pity. I am sure it would help—'

He interrupted her with a growl.

'I have told you before, Miss Pentewan, confine yourself to your library duties!'

The jar hit the table top with a thud and he strode off, closing the door behind him with a decided snap.

The jar remained on the side table for three days. It was studiously ignored by the major, although Zelah was sure he knew it was there. Then, just when she was beginning to wonder if she should ask Graddon to try to persuade his master, Major Coale made reference to it.

He had come in for his daily report on her progress and when she had finished he walked over to the side table and picked up the jar.

'What is in this witch's potion of yours?'

'It is no witchcraft, Major, only flowers. Marigold petals, mixed with oil and wax to make a salve. It will help repair the skin and soften the scar tissue. My mother used to prepare it for our parishioners.' She added coaxingly, 'I assure you it will not hurt, sir. I helped Mama to apply it often, once to a group of miners injured in a pit collapse. Their injuries were severe and they said it did not cause any pain, but on the contrary, it was quite soothing.'

His inscrutable gaze rested on her for a moment. 'Very well.' He handed her the pot. 'Let us see.'

She blinked. 'I beg your pardon?'

He perched himself on the edge of the desk.

'Apply your magic potion, and we will see how well it works.'

'Apply it here? Now?' Zelah swallowed. 'I am not sure…'

'Damnation, Delilah, I let you be my barber, surely you do not balk at touching my face—or is the scar too abhorrent?'

'Not at all, sir.'

She opened the jar and scooped a little of the ointment on to her fingers. She remembered how she had felt when she had cut his hair, standing so close, aware of his latent strength. She felt again as if he was some wild beast allowing her to come near, but at any minute he might turn and savage her. After a very slight hesitation she applied the cream gently to his cheek.

She smoothed it across the skin, working between the hard ridges of his cheekbone and his jaw.

'There, does that feel better?' He grunted and she chuckled. 'Pray do not be ashamed to admit it. A mixture such as this soothes the damaged skin and makes it flexible again, in the same way that wax will soften leather.'

'Are you comparing my face to a boot, madam?'

Zelah laughed as she massaged the ointment into his cheek. 'I would not dare be so impertinent!'

She felt him smile beneath her fingers.

'Oh, I think you would.'

She did not reply, but continued to work her fingers over his skin until all signs of the cream had disappeared.

'The sabre did not only cut my face. It slashed open my body, too.'

Zelah stopped. She said gently, 'May I look?'

He untied his neckcloth and tugged it off, leaving

his shirt open at the neck. Zelah pushed aside the material to expose his left shoulder. The skin was golden brown, tanned, she guessed, from working shirtless on the land. It was marred by a wide, uneven white line across his collarbone and cutting down his chest, where it carved a path through the covering of crisp black hair. Her heart lurched at the thought of the pain he must have endured. She forced back a cry of sympathy, knowing it would not be welcome. Instead she tried to be matter-of-fact, scooping up more cream and spreading it gently across the ragged furrow of the wound.

'It is a pity you did not rub something in this sooner,' she said, absorbed in her task, 'but it is not too late. If you apply this regularly, it will soften the skin and help the scarred tissue to stretch.'

She worked the ointment into his skin, moving over the collarbone and down to his breast. A smattering of black hair curled around her fingers as she stroked the finely toned muscle.

Zelah could not say exactly when the change in the atmosphere occurred, but suddenly the air around her was charged with tension and she realised just what a perilous situation she was in. Not merely the impropriety of being alone with a man who was not her husband, but the dangerous sensations within her own body. She concentrated on the skin that she was covering with ointment, forcing herself to think of that small area of scarring and not the whole body. Not the man. It was impossible. She should stop, move away, but she could not. Of their own accord her fingers followed the scar across the solid breastbone and on, down.

Dominic's hand clamped over hers.

'That will do.' His voice was unsteady. 'Perhaps I should finish this myself. Later.'

Zelah blushed, consumed from head to toe with fiery embarrassment.

'I…um…' She had to take a couple of breaths before she could continue. 'It is best applied every day, and directly after bathing.'

She tried to look up, but could only lift her eyes as far as his mouth. The faint, upward curve of his lips was some comfort.

He released her hand. 'You are far too innocent to be Delilah, aren't you?'

She dare not meet his eyes. Her cheeks were still burning. She put the lid back on the jar and handed it to him.

'It was never my wish to be such a woman.'

'No, of course not. You are far too bookish.' He pushed himself off the desk and picked up his neckcloth. 'I must go. I want to see Phillips today about restocking the coverts.'

Zelah glanced towards the window as another shower of rain pattered against the glass.

'Should you not wait until the storm passes?'

'Why? It will not harm me. In fact, I think I would welcome a cold shower of rain!'

With a brief nod he strode out of the room and as his hasty footsteps disappeared so the calm and silence settled over the library again.

Zelah sat down at the desk and dropped her head on to her hands. So she was 'too bookish' to be Delilah, the beautiful temptress. She should be pleased that Dominic did not think of her in those terms, and she *was* pleased, wasn't she?

With a sinking heart Zelah realised that she was just a little disappointed.

Zelah's working days had developed a regular pattern. Major Coale would visit the library every morning to discuss the day's tasks. Whenever he was obliged to be out early he would leave her instructions and call in to see her as soon as he had returned to Rooks Tower. Their meetings were brief and businesslike, but Zelah looked forward to them and when, two weeks later, the major left word that he was gone to Exeter and would not be back until the following day, she was surprised at the depth of her dissatisfaction.

* * *

The following day saw the delivery of the books from Lydcombe Park. She was reluctant to spoil the space and tidiness of the library and ordered some of the crates to be taken up to the tower room. Unpacking all the new books and arranging for the empty crates to be taken away kept Zelah occupied for most of the day. She was buttoning her pelisse when she heard a familiar step approaching the library and she turned towards the door, her spirits rising. Major Coale came in, his boots still muddy from the journey, and she was unable to keep the smile of welcome from her face.

His first words were not encouraging. 'What, Miss Pentewan, going already? I heard that the books from Lydcombe Park had been delivered. Surely that is a case for working longer.'

'And so I would, sir, but I am walking to Lesserton today, to collect Nicky from his lessons.'

'Then I shall take you there in the curricle.'

'But you have just this minute come in…'

'From riding, madam, a very different exercise. You may show me just what you have done with the books while we wait for my carriage.'

Unable to muster her arguments, Zelah consented and ten minutes later she was sitting beside the major in his sleek, low-slung racing curricle and marvelling at the smooth new road he had built. They had to slow their pace when they joined the Lesserton road, but they still made good time and soon reached the village. They were heading for the main street and, seeing how busy it was, Zelah glanced at the major. He was wearing a wide-brimmed hat, tilted to shadow the left side of his face, so that his scarred cheek and chin were barely visible. She was pleased to note that the majority of the men touched their caps and the women dropped a curtsy as they bowled past. Some children and one or two of the adults stopped to stare, but she decided this was due to the unusual sight of a fashionable carriage with a diminutive groom perched upon the rumble seat.

'Where shall I drop you?' enquired the major.

'Here, if you please. I am still a little early, so I shall indulge myself by looking in the shops on Market Street before I collect Nicky. You have no need to hand me out, I can easily jump down.' She suited the action to the words as the curricle drew to a stop and gave a friendly little wave as Major Coale set his team in motion again.

The morning clouds had given way to a warm, sunny afternoon and when Nicky came running out from the vicar's rambling house she persuaded him to take a detour before they made their way home. They were just setting off when Nicky gave a delighted cry.

'Major Coale!'

Zelah looked up to see the major approaching. She noted with no little satisfaction that there was now only the faintest irregularity in his purposeful stride.

'Good day to you, Master Nicholas! How do you go on, how is your leg?'

'Much better now, Major. Zelah wants to see the bluebell woods, so I am going to take her. Will you come with us?'

'Nicky!'

Her admonition went unheeded. Nicky gazed hopefully at the major, who replied gravely, 'I would be delighted.'

Zelah shook her head vehemently. 'No, no, I am sure you must have more important things to do.'

'As a matter of fact I don't. Sawley noticed that one of the horses has a shoe loose and he is now at the smithy, so I was coming to say if you do not mind waiting a half-hour or so I would take you back to West Barton.'

'You would take us up in your curricle?' demanded Nicky, his eyes wide. 'In your *racing* curricle?'

'I only have the one, I'm afraid, but it is perfectly safe, as your aunt will testify.'

'That is very kind of you, I'm sure, Major Coale,' said Zelah, realising it would be cruel to withhold such a treat from Nicky. 'However, there is no need for you to accompany us on our walk.'

'But Major Coale *wants* to come with us, don't you, sir?'

'I do indeed.'

Zelah looked helplessly from one to the other. Major Coale held out his arm to her.

'Shall we proceed?'

There was no help for it. She laid her hand on the major's sleeve.

'Maria told me about the woods,' she explained as they followed Nicky along the lane that led out of the village. 'She said the bluebells are a picture, but for only a short time each year. I do hope we won't be too late, we are well into May now.'

'We shall soon find out.'

Nicky had scrambled over a stile and the major followed, turning back to help Zelah.

'Careful, there is a ditch on this side and it is a little muddy.'

As Zelah stepped over he reached out and lifted her, putting her down well away from the muddy puddle at the foot of the stile. A hot, fiery blush spread through her, from her head right down to her toes. Whether it was his hands on her waist, or the feeling of helplessness as he held her she did not know and, what was worse, she instinctively gripped his arms, so that when he had placed her on the ground he could not immediately release her, but stood looking down at her with a smile lurking in his grey eyes.

'Are you ready to go on, Miss Pentewan?'

She swallowed. So many new and shocking sensations were coursing through her that she could not think. Her hands were still clutching at his sleeves and, instead of letting go, she wanted to hold on even tighter. It took all her willpower to release him and to step back.

'Y-you startled me,' she stammered. 'I could quite easily have climbed over by myself...'

'I'm sure you could, but my way was much more pleasurable, don't you think?'

His self-possession annoyed her.

'Are you trying to flirt with me, Major Coale?'

'Do you know, I think I am.' He laughed. 'How strange. I used to do it all the time before that damned chasseur tried to cut my face off. I beg your pardon, it was unwittingly done.'

Disarmed by his response, her anger melted away and she chuckled.

'That has pricked the bubble of my self-esteem! What an abominable thing to say.'

'Not at all. It was, in a way, a compliment. I have not felt so at ease in anyone's company since I came back to England.'

'Then I will take it as such, sir.'

She met his eyes, responding to the warm smile in his own and forgetful of everything else until he looked away.

'Nicky is almost out of sight. Shall we continue? Else I fear he will abandon us and we will be left to wander these woods all night.'

Zelah moved on, ignoring his proffered arm. She was shocked to realise just how much she would like to be wandering here all night with Major Coale.

Nicky had stopped at a turn in the path to wait for them and as they reached him Zelah gave a little gasp of pleasure. The woodland stretched before them, the sun filtering through the lacy canopy of leaves onto the floor, which was covered in a thick carpet of bluebells and wild garlic.

'Oh, how beautiful!' She sank down, putting out her hands to brush the delicately nodding bluebells. 'They are at the very peak of their bloom. I think we should pick some for you to take back to your mama, Nicky—make sure you pick them at the bottom of the stem, love.'

She began to collect the tallest flowers and within minutes had a large bunch, then Nicky handed her his contribution.

'Goodness, that was quick!' She rested the delicate blooms more securely on one arm and looked towards the major, who was still standing on the path. 'What do you think, Major, are they not beautiful?' He did not respond, merely stared at her across the dell. 'Oh, I beg your pardon. Perhaps you are wishing to turn back, it must be growing late.'

'We don't have to turn back,' said Nicky. 'The path curves round by Prickett Wood and goes back to the village. It's not far.'

The major cleared his throat.

'Let us go on, then.'

Nicky ran on ahead, but when the major began to stride out Zelah had to hurry to keep up with him.

'I am sorry if we have delayed you, Major.'

'It is not important.'

She frowned at his harsh tone, but said no more, concentrating her energies on hurrying along beside him. They left the wood and found themselves on a wide track running between the trees.

'I remember this,' declared Zelah. 'The road leads into Lesserton and the trees to our left lead into

Prickett Wood, so you can be back at the smithy very soon now, sir.'

He did not reply and she gave a mental shrug. The easy camaraderie with which they had started out had gone and she tried to be glad about it, for when Major Coale chose to be charming she found him very hard to resist. She turned her attention to Nicky, running ahead of them, darting in and out of the trees, fighting imaginary foes. He seemed much happier now that he was spending some of his time at Mr Netherby's school. He did not appear to miss her company at all.

Nicky plunged into the undergrowth at the side of the road and she waited for him to reappear, but he had not done so by the time they reached the point where he had dashed off the path. She was about to remark upon this to her companion when they heard a man shouting, as if in anger.

'What the devil—?'

The major followed the narrow overgrown track into the wood and Zelah went after him, a chill of anxiety running down her spine. They heard the man's voice again.

'What in damnation do ye think you're doing here? Trespassin', that's what! I'll give 'ee what for!'

'Take your hands off the boy!'

The major barked out the command as they came

into a small clearing. Nicky was wriggling help-lessly while a burly man in a brown jacket and buckskins held his collar. The man had raised his fist but he did not strike, instead he glared at them.

'And who the devil might you be?'

'Never mind that. Unhand the boy. Now.'

'That I won't. He's trespassin'. This is Sir Os-wald's land and no one's allowed in here.'

'The boy strayed a few yards off the path. He's done no harm.' The major's cool authority had some effect. The man lowered his fist, but he kept a tight grip on Nicky's collar. He said stubbornly, 'He's still trespassin' and so are you. I have me orders, thrash any brats that comes into the wood—'

The major advanced. 'Then you will have to thrash me first.'

The man scowled, his harsh features becoming even more brutish.

'Aye, well, then that's what I'll do.'

'No, please!' Neither man heard Zelah's cry.

There was another shout and a tall, thick-set man pushed through the bushes towards them. He was carrying a shotgun, but Zelah was relieved that he was not threatening anyone with it.

'What is going on here? Miller? Who the devil are these people?'

'Trespassers, Sir Oswald. They—'

The major interrupted him. 'I am Coale, from Rooks Tower. If this is your man, then I'd be pleased if he'd unhand my young friend.'

'Major Coale, aye, of course. Let the boy go, William.'

Reluctantly the man released his grip and Nicky tore himself free and ran over to Zelah, clutching at her skirts. Sir Oswald watched him, then looked at Zelah, giving her a rueful smile.

'I beg your pardon if my bailiff frightened your boy, ma'am, but I have been having a great deal of trouble from the village children running in and out of the woods at all times, causing havoc.'

'Mayhap they dispute your ownership of these woods,' put in Dominic.

'These are ignorant folk, Major. Just because they have been allowed to use the land in the past they think they have a right to it, but it ain't so. I have to keep 'em out.'

'By beating small boys who wander inadvertently onto your land?' The major's lip curled. 'Your methods are a little extreme.'

'But what can I do?' Sir Oswald shrugged. 'We are culling the deer and I would not want to risk shooting anyone.' He looked back at his bailiff. 'It's all right, Miller, you may go back to your work, I'll escort these good people back to the lane.' Sir Oswald stretched out his arm, as if shepherding them along. Zelah took Nicky's hand and led him away. Behind her she could hear Sir Oswald's voice.

'I do not say I like appearing the ogre, Major, but I have to protect my own, and these people are very stubborn. Is it any wonder that Miller has become a little…hardened? But he knows his territory. Believe me, no one will come to any harm as long as they stay off my land.'

'I do believe we have been warned off,' murmured Dominic, when they were once more on the path and making their way back to the village.

'What a horrid man.' Zelah shivered. 'Heaven knows what would have happened to Nicky if we had not been there.'

'He has no right to shoot the deer,' declared Nicky, who was recovering from his ordeal. 'They have been there for ever, and it's not his land.'

'Well, that is what your papa is trying to prove.' Zelah squeezed his hand. 'I hope he is successful. I do not like to think of Sir Oswald riding roughshod over everyone.'

'There must be documents,' said Dominic. 'Papers stating what belongs to the village.'

'There are, but they are old and not very clear.'

'Robin says it's to do with the boundary stones,' said Nicky.

'Oh?' Zelah glanced down. 'And who is Robin?'

'He's my friend.'

'Another one?' The major's brows lifted. 'I thought I was your friend.'

'Robin is a *different* friend. He lives in the woods.'

'Ah, you mean the crow catcher.' Dominic turned to Zelah to explain. 'There is an old man who is paid to do odd jobs around the village, trapping crows or catching moles, helping out at lambing. In winter I believe he lives with his sister in the village, but during the better weather he has a hut on the edge of the forest. I did not know he was a friend of yours, Nicky.'

'Oh, yes. Sometimes he lets me go hunting with him, sometimes we just follow the deer, to watch them.'

'Well, you had best warn this friend to avoid Sir Oswald Evanshaw's land,' said Zelah. 'I don't think that bailiff of his would think twice about giving an old man a beating.'

'They won't catch Robin,' said Nicky confidently. 'He knows everything about the land here.'

They had reached the village and the major's groom was standing with the curricle outside the smithy, waiting for them. Nicky forgot everything save the excitement of climbing into this elegant equipage, where he sat between Zelah and the major as they drove back to West Barton. Zelah glanced at the bluebells, still cradled on her arm.

'I almost dropped them all when we ran into Sir Oswald and his horrid bailiff, but I am very glad I did not. They are beginning to droop a little, but I think they will recover, do not you, Major?'

He took his eyes off the road for a moment to look at the mass of nodding bells.

'I am sure they will. You have a knack of reviving wilting spirits, Miss Pentewan.'

It was only natural that Nicky should describe the events in Prickett Wood to his parents. Maria had been outraged at the treatment of her son and Reginald immediately called for his horse and rode off to confront Sir Oswald. The ladies waited anxiously for his return and Maria was just suggesting they should put dinner back an hour when Reginald came in, a frown darkening his usually genial features.

'Oh, my dear, I was beginning to worry that you might have come to blows.' Maria ran to her husband and took his arm, coaxing him to a chair.

'He could not have been more accommodating,

damned scoundrel. Apologised profusely, said his man, Miller, was over-zealous.'

'So it will not happen again?' Zelah enquired.

Reginald's scowl darkened. 'Damned rascal had the nerve to say he hoped I'd be able to keep my family away from his land, because he's putting mantraps in Prickett Wood!'

Chapter Six

Zelah was present when Reginald explained the situation to Nicky, impressing upon his son how important it was that he did not stray on to Sir Oswald's land.

'But Prickett Wood isn't his land, it belongs to the village,' Nicky protested vehemently. 'Robin says so!'

'And I hope it is so, but until we can prove it, you must stay away. A mantrap can take a man's leg off, Nicky, it is a barbaric device.'

'But what about Robin, Papa? What about the villagers?'

'Sir Oswald tells me he will post notices in Lesserton and at the edge of the wood. You must not worry about Robin, son, he's too wily an old bird to be caught. As to the rest, well, we have a lawyer coming down from London in a few weeks' time and he is bringing with him a copy of the royal charter. We must hope that settles the matter once and for all.'

Maria declared that if Reginald was not available to take his son to school and back then a servant should accompany him. She tried to insist that Zelah should take a servant with her to Rooks Tower each day, but the suggestion was energetically rebuffed.

'My dear sister, your people have more than enough to do without accompanying me. Besides, my way goes nowhere near Sir Oswald's land. I cross from the gardens directly into Major Coale's woods.'

'Who knows what danger may lurk there?' Maria muttered darkly.

Zelah dismissed her sister's concerns and happily made her way to Rooks Tower the following day, and she was somewhat surprised when Major Coale announced that he intended to accompany her on her homeward journey.

'I assure you there is no need, sir.'

'But I insist, Miss Pentewan.'

'This is absurd,' she challenged him. 'There can be no danger from Sir Oswald or his men on your land.'

Something akin to surprise flashed in his eyes, but it was gone in an instant.

'One never knows,' he replied glibly, falling into step beside her.

'But you are far too busy!'

'Not today. I have spent the day giving instructions for the refurbishment of the orangery. The carpenter knows what to do now and I would only be in the way. Come, Miss Pentewan. Do not look so mutinous. Can you not accept my company with good grace?'

'I suppose I must.'

He laughed. 'A grudging acceptance, ma'am.'

'But this is not treating me as an employee, an independent being who is quite capable of looking after herself.'

He did not respond to her grumbling, but strode across the park and into the woods, describing to her all the improvements he had planned. It was impossible to sulk and Zelah found herself voicing her opinion, telling him her preference for chestnut trees to be planted in the park and suggesting an avenue of limes along the length of the new drive.

'These are long-term plans, Major. Are you planning to settle here?'

'Possibly.'

'Then you should become more involved with the

village. You could support my brother-in-law in his efforts to oppose Sir Oswald.'

'I wondered when we would come back to that. I have told you before, Miss Pentewan, one of the reasons I like Rooks Tower is its isolation. I have no desire to become embroiled in local disputes.'

'But—'

He stopped. 'Enough, madam. Sir Oswald may be perfectly entitled to enclose the land, for all we know, and to cover it with mantraps. I will deal with matters that concern me, and no more.'

There was a note of finality in his voice and Zelah firmly closed her lips upon the arguments she wanted to utter.

'Well, at least you could attend the summer assembly. It is looked upon almost as an obligation, you know, to be seen there. Besides, you would become better acquainted with your neighbours.'

He looked so fierce, his lips thinning and his crooked left brow descending so low that for a moment she thought he might shout at her, but he contented himself by saying curtly, 'If I have business with my neighbours I will call upon them. I see no point in social chit-chat.'

They were in the woods now, another few minutes would bring them to the lane, so there really was no point in prolonging the argument.

There was a sudden crashing in the undergrowth and a hind shot across their path, so close it almost brushed Zelah. It was swiftly followed by a large stag. Startled, Zelah jumped back. The major pulled her into his arms, twisting around to shield her in case another creature should plunge out of the bushes.

He held her tight against him, one hand cradling her head against his chest. She could feel the thud of his heart through the rough wool of his coat. To be held thus was strange, unfamiliar, but she did not find it unpleasant.

Zelah allowed herself to savour the feeling of safety and of refuge as the silence settled around them once more, but as the shock abated she realised her situation and pushed herself away. He released her immediately.

'I beg your pardon. Did I hurt you?'

His curt tone only added to her confusion. Without his arms tight around her she felt quite…vulnerable.

'N-no. I—um—I have never seen a stag at such close quarters before. Magnificent.'

'So it is you!' Nicky's cheerful voice came from the undergrowth at the side of the path. 'We wondered what had startled the deer.'

He emerged from the bushes, followed by a

thin man in a faded brown coat and breeches who touched his hat.

'Major.'

'Good day, Robin.' Dominic nodded. 'And to you, young Master Buckland.'

'But, Nicky…' Zelah put her hand on her nephew's shoulder '…why are you out of school?'

'Mr Netherby was called away and he cancelled his classes today, so I joined Robin in the woods. Pray do not worry, Zelah. John the stable boy was in Lesserton and he carried a message back for me, telling Papa that there was no need to send the carriage to collect me. I have been having *such* a good time with Robin, following the deer. We were doing very well until you startled them.'

Zelah gave an uncertain laugh. 'I think they startled *us*.'

'Ah, beggin' yer pardon, ma'am.' Old Robin took off his hat as he nodded to her. 'The hind turned away from yer voices and found us blockin' her way, so she took off across the path and the stag followed.'

'Are they not splendid creatures, Aunt?' Nicky's upturned face glowed with excitement. 'We have been following them all day.'

'I trust you have not been near Sir Oswald's land.' Zelah frowned, concerned.

'I wouldn't take the boy there, ma'am, you may be sure o' that,' Robin assured her. He turned aside and spat on the ground. 'Not that Sir Oswald owns all the land he's laid claim to, whatever he may say.'

'You know where the boundary runs?' Zelah asked eagerly.

'Aye, that I do. Not that the deer follow boundaries of any man's making.'

Nicky scowled. 'Sir Oswald's told Robin that he'll shoot any animals he finds on his land, but they've been wandering there for years, they don't know any different.'

Dominic shrugged. 'I've no doubt Sir Oswald is trying to make his estate profitable.'

'Aye,' said Robin, rubbing his nose, 'he's cutting down timber above Lydcombe Park and that's his right, on that piece of land. What's going on at Prickett Wood is another matter.'

'If you know something, then you should tell my brother-in-law,' said Zelah. 'Or Sir Arthur, who I think is the magistrate here.'

'Aye, p'rhaps I will.'

His response was too vague to satisfy Zelah, but before she could reply Nicky addressed her.

'I am very glad we met you, Aunt, for I was coming to the Tower to see if you were ready to walk home with me. Robin has some work to do.'

The old man turned to the major, his eyes bright in his weather-beaten face.

'Thought I'd take a look at the moles in yer south lawn, sir, if you still wants 'em gone?'

'I do, Robin. If you wish, you can take yourself off to the Tower now. Tell Mrs Graddon I sent you and she'll make sure there's a meal for you tonight. I shall escort Miss Pentewan and Master Nicky to West Barton.'

It was on the tip of Zelah's tongue to say that was not necessary, but the look of delight on Nicky's face silenced her. They parted from old Robin and set off for the lane. She was not obliged to converse, because Nicky chattered away quite happily to the major, describing his lessons and his friends. The path was narrow and she was content to fall behind, listening to their conversation.

'This is where I shall bid you goodbye.' They had reached the lane and Major Coale stopped.

'Will you not come to the house, sir?' Nick gaze up at him hopefully. 'I know Mama would be happy to offer you some refreshment.'

'Thank you, but no. I have work that needs my attention.'

'But—'

'Do not press him, Nicky,' cautioned Zelah. 'The major sees no point in *social chit-chat*.'

He met her eyes, the glint in his own confirming that he understood her. 'Quite, Miss Pentewan. Good day to you.'

Chapter Seven

'What will you wear to the assembly tomorrow, Maria?'

Zelah was sitting in the drawing room with her sister. Dinner had been a quiet affair, just the two of them since Reginald had not yet returned from his meeting in Lesserton.

'I thought my bronze silk with the matching turban. It has a train, but I will not be dancing, so that will not matter. What think you, Zelah? It is not new but good enough for the summer assembly, I think. After all, it is not a special occasion.'

Zelah sighed.

'It will be very special to *me*. I do so love to dance, but it has been three years since I had the opportunity.'

'Goodness me, yes. I suppose you did not go to the assemblies near Cardinham after…I mean—'

'No, and I have added some new ribbons to my

lemon silk for the occasion,' Zelah broke in, speaking quickly to cover her sister's confusion.

'I am sure you will look charming,' agreed Maria, thankful to follow a safer line of thought. 'We will put your hair in rags in the morning to make it curl—'

'No, no, Maria, I shall be at Rooks Tower.'

'What? You cannot work on those horrid books tomorrow, you will have no time to prepare for the assembly.'

Zelah laughed at her sister's horrified look.

'I am not such a great lady, I need only enough time to change my gown.'

'No, no, that will never do. Did you not tell Major Coale about the assembly?'

'I did, but I do not think he attaches much importance to such things.'

'Well, you must send a note over in the morning, telling him you cannot come.'

Zelah shook her head.

'I have not seen him since the day Nicky came to the woods to meet me. I fear he was not best pleased with me then, so I would not wish to antagonise him further. He might turn me off.'

'Oh dear, I never thought, when you decided to earn your own living, that it would come to this. It cannot be right.'

Maria's voice wavered, she drew out her handkerchief to wipe her eyes and Zelah realised that she had scandalised her sister. In Maria's world only her duty to her husband and family would take precedence over a social event. She said gently,

'It is not so very bad, my love. If I was a governess already, I should not be able to dance at all.'

'Oh, Zelah, if only it could be otherwise.' Maria dabbed at her eyes. 'If only you had not—'

Zelah jumped up. 'Let us not think of it,' she said quickly. 'I have a lifetime to regret a moment's madness, but tomorrow I shall go to the assembly, where no one knows my past, and dance to my heart's content.'

Zelah went off to Rooks Tower the following day, promising Maria that she would return a little earlier to prepare for the assembly, but soon after she arrived Graddon came to inform her that the carter had brought more books for her.

'Seems they were missed off his last consignment.' They watched the crates being carried in and the butler shook his head. 'Looks to me as if you'll have to begin all your work again, miss.'

'Nonsense,' she replied bracingly. 'All that is required is a little reorganisation…well, perhaps rather a lot! But it is not impossible. The first thing is to empty all these boxes.'

The afternoon was well advanced when Major Coale came in to find her surrounded by books.

'You look to be in your element.'

'I am.' She smiled, relieved at his friendly tone. 'This is the remainder of the books you purchased from Lydcombe Park and they are by far the most ancient. There are many more classical texts here— including some in the original Greek and Latin.'

'Can you read them?'

'I know a little, but not enough to work out all these. I shall have to take them to Mr Netherby to translate.'

'Let me have a look…'

He pulled a chair up beside her at the desk and they began deciphering the texts. There was a great deal of hilarity when either of them made a mistake and they continued in perfect harmony until the chiming of the clock proclaimed the hour.

'Goodness, I must go!' cried Zelah. 'It is the assembly this evening. Maria will be wondering where I am.' She laughed. 'Do you know, I almost think I would prefer to stay here, working on these texts?' She added mischievously, 'Is it something about this house that turns one into a recluse? No, no, Major, pray do not fire up, I was only teasing, when I should really thank you, sir, for helping me.'

'So you will go away. You will become a lady for the night.'

She bridled at that.

'I am no less a lady for working here, Major.' She rose and began to move the books off the desk.

'Of course not. So what will you wear and who will you dance with?'

She chuckled as she collected another armful of books from the desk. 'I shall wear my lemon silk robe and as for dancing, why, I will dance with anyone who asks me!'

After Zelah left Rooks Tower the house seemed very quiet. Usually this did not worry Dominic, but for some reason this evening he was restless, unsettled. By God but the chit irked him, prattling on as she did about company, and society and his obligations to his neighbours. He grinned. She had had the nerve to tease him, too, calling him a recluse. It was impossible not to smile at her impertinence. He shut himself in his study and tried to read, but it was no good. He prowled about the room, too restless to sit down. Perhaps he should look in at the assembly. All the local people would be there, and there were a few things that needed to be discussed, small matters that could be dealt with in a moment. With his usual decisiveness he strode out of the room and soon set the household on its ears, calling for an early dinner and sending Graddon to search out his dancing pumps.

The Lesserton Assembly was crowded and good natured. Sir Oswald Evanshaw's appearance had surprised some and dismayed even more of those gathered in the long room of the White Hart. There were plenty of resentful looks, but mostly everyone ignored him, not wishing to bring their disputes into the ballroom. Zelah was going down the line with a young farmer when his stifled exclamation brought her head up and she saw Major Coale in the doorway. Although he was not wearing regimentals his upright bearing proclaimed the soldier. He was looking grim, but Zelah knew that was merely his defence against the stares of the crowd. Mr Eldridge the MC was bowing, making him welcome, and as soon as the dance ended Zelah hurried over to her brother-in-law.

'I wish you would go and greet Major Coale, Reginald,' she urged him. 'It cannot be easy for him, when he is so new to the area.'

Reginald was inclined to hang back.

'Dash it all, Zelah, I barely know the man myself.

If Coale wishes to be introduced, then Eldridge is the man to do it.'

Zelah gave him a little push.

'But you are a relative, Reginald, albeit a distant one. And you are so well acquainted with everyone here that you are much better placed to introduce the major to his neighbours. Please, Reginald. I think it cost Major Coale a great deal to come here this evening. He is not likely to put himself forwards.'

'No, with that hideous scar running down his face I suppose he is not,' Reginald mused. 'Very well, I'll go and talk to him.'

With that Zelah had to be content. She went off to dance again, but found her attention returning constantly to the major. She saw him conversing with Reginald and was relieved when they were joined by several other gentlemen. With some satisfaction she watched the whole group stroll away to the card room and she felt at liberty to give herself up to the enjoyment of the dance.

Some of the young ladies present might bemoan the lack of eligible gentlemen at the Lesserton Assembly, but Zelah was not amongst their number. She wanted only to dance and her sister numbered sufficient married gentlemen amongst her acquaintance to provide Zelah with a partner for almost every set. She was therefore happily engaged on the dance floor for the best part of the evening. She was delighted to see Major Coale take to the floor, partnering Mrs Eldrige, and when the movement of the dance brought them together she gave him a wide smile.

'You came.'

'Yes.'

She wanted to ask him if he was enjoying himself, but there was no time before she was swept off by her next partner. She watched him lead out a couple more partners, both older matrons, and realised that he was avoiding the young ladies who cast surreptitious glances at him and giggled if he went near them. Their insensitive behaviour angered her, but there was little she could do, so when her brother-in-law swept her off to dance again she tried to push the matter from her mind as he whisked her around the floor in a lively jig.

Standing at the side of the room and watching the dancers, Dominic smiled to himself. Everyone was eager to improve their acquaintance with him, but not because he was the son of a viscount, that cut little ice here. They saw him as their landlord, or a fellow land-owner or even a farmer. Phillips, his gamekeeper, would be pleased to know Abraham

Judd had trapped the fox that had been terrorising the local bird population and Giles Grundy had suggested digging out the culvert at Rooks Ford, which would benefit them both. All in all it was a successful evening. Not that he would want to make a habit of it, he had grown used to his own company, but Zelah was right, it was a good way to keep in touch with his neighbours. Sir Oswald Evanshaw came up and Dominic returned his bow with a nod.

'Evening, Coale. Surprised to see you here, what with your...' His eyes flickered over Dominic's face and shifted away to the dance floor. 'How are you enjoying the entertainment?' Sir Oswald raised his quizzing glass and surveyed the room, his lip curling slightly. 'A far cry from London, ain't it? In fact it's positively rustic, but it behoves us to make an appearance, what?'

Dominic felt the slight nudge in the ribs from Sir Oswald's elbow and he moved away a little.

'I saw you dancing, too. By Gad, but you are braver than me, Coale. I wouldn't dare to approach any of the dragons lest they devour me!'

'They are more like to refuse you,' murmured Dominic.

Sir Oswald laughed.

'You are right there, of course. It's this demmed

court case, they have set me up as the villain of the piece.'

'Can you blame them? They have grazed those fields for years.'

'I know.' Sir Oswald shook his head. 'They have got it into their heads that they can use my land, that it's their right, but it ain't, Coale, and the sooner they learn that the better. They have even paid for a London lawyer to come down to plead their cause at the hearing next week. I told 'em to save their money, but what can you do? It's ill advised, Major, and I hope you'll support me in that.'

Dominic looked at him, surprised.

'The legal wranglings over grazing rights and the ownership of Prickett Wood is none of my concern, Evanshaw.'

'Not directly, perhaps, but you never know when they might turn on you and begin claiming your land, too. It would be helpful if they knew that you supported my case.'

Dominic regarded him in silence for a long moment. Sir Oswald was smiling, but there was no warmth in his pale eyes, just a cold, calculating look.

'I know nothing of your case,' he said at last, 'and I do not see why you are so concerned, if you are sure the land is legally yours.'

Sir Oswald's eyes snapped with impatience and he chewed his lip.

'At least assure me you won't join with the villagers. It's bad enough that Buckland should lend them his support. The farmers, well, I can understand them fighting me, but Buckland—demme, he's a *gentleman*! It makes the lower sort think they have a chance.'

Dominic did not answer and with a curt nod Sir Oswald lounged away, shouldering his way through the crowd until he disappeared into the card room. An unpleasant fellow, Dominic decided as he strolled around the edge of the room. He found himself hoping that Buckland and the villagers did find some legal loophole that would stop Evanshaw claiming the disputed land.

'You are looking very serious, Major. I hope you are enjoying yourself.'

He looked down at Maria Buckland, sitting on a nearby bench, sipping at a glass of wine. Shaking off his thoughtful mood, he scooped a glass from the tray of a passing waiter and sat down beside her.

'I am, ma'am. More than I expected to do.'

'I am very glad of it. I have always found the society here most friendly. But we were surprised to see you this evening: I understood you had told Mr Eldridge you did not plan to attend.'

Dominic smiled.

'That is correct, ma'am, but I was, er, *persuaded* to change my mind. By your sister.'

'Oh dear, I hope she was not impertinent.'

With some difficulty Dominic prevented the smile from turning into a grin and he resisted the temptation to tell Mrs Buckland exactly what he thought of her sister.

'No, no. Not at all.'

'Do you know, Major, when I think of Zelah spending her life as a governess I am quite cast down.'

Dominic had heard that innocent tone in many a woman's voice, and he was immediately on the alert.

'Indeed?' He sipped his wine, determined to empty the glass and move on as quickly as possible.

'Zelah is extremely accomplished,' Maria continued, still in that thoughtful tone. 'Do you not agree, Major?'

'She certainly seems to be well educated.'

'Oh, she is and her birth is impeccable.' Maria clasped her hands around her glass and gave a huge sigh. 'It is the most tragic waste that her worth—and her charms—are not more widely appreciated. She would make some lucky gentleman the perfect wife.'

Dominic choked in the act of finishing his wine.

'Madam, that is the most blatant proposition-ing—!'

'Oh heavens, Major, you quite mistake me, I did not mean—' Maria put her hand on his arm to prevent him from rising. 'Oh, my dear sir, I do not mean that *you* should be that gentleman! I beg your pardon. It is just, well, you and Reginald are related, after all.'

'A very distant connection,' he flashed.

Her gracious smile did not falter.

'But it was thanks to Reginald that you heard Rooks Tower was for sale, did you not? So we have been of use to you, I believe.' She leaned a little closer. 'Let me be frank with you.'

He eyed her with some misgiving.

'I'm afraid you have been too frank already.'

'No, no. Pray allow me to explain. Zelah is a charming girl, but this assembly is the nearest she will get to a come-out, and much as I value the local society, you must admit there is no one here worthy of her. It is not that there are not good families living nearby, but you will never find Sir Arthur Andrews, or the Conisbys or the Lulworths attending such an assembly as this. No, what Zelah needs is a benefactor. Someone to hold a ball for her. A splendid affair attended by the best families in the area, so that they may see just what a jewel she is. And so that *Zelah* might see that there is an alternative to becoming a governess.' She gave another sigh. 'I would happily hold a ball for her, if we were in a position to do so, but you have visited West Barton, Major, you know we have no reception rooms suitable for more than a very small gathering.' She fixed her eyes, so like her sister's, upon him. 'I believe Rooks Tower has several excellent reception rooms.'

Despite himself, Dominic's lips twitched.

'Mrs Buckland, you have been very frank with me, let me be equally plain. I will happily acknowledge that your husband and I are related and that it was through our mutual relative that I heard about Rooks Tower. I am very grateful for that, but even so I have no intention of holding a ball, for Miss Pentewan or anyone else.'

She stared at him and he held her gaze unblinking, until finally she nodded.

'Reginald warned me how it would be, that you would not countenance such a thing, but Zelah thinks so highly of you, I thought I might put it to the touch.'

The music had ended and Reginald Buckland was even now bringing Zelah across to them. Dominic rose.

'Well, you have done so and you may now be easy.'

* * *

Laughing and breathless, Zelah took Reginald's arm and tripped across the room to join her sister. She immediately noticed the tall figure of the major beside Maria as they left the dance floor. He was standing with his left side turned to the wall so that he was presenting the right, uninjured side of his face to the room. Zelah found herself staring at his profile, the smooth plane of his cheek and the strong, clean line of his jaw. There was just the hint of a smile on the sculpted lips, perhaps it was something Maria had said to him. She was struck again by how handsome he was—had been.

As if aware of her attention he turned to look at her and she saw again the cruel, jagged scar that distorted the left side of his face. She kept her eyes upon him, refusing to glance away. She would not betray any sign of pity, even by a flicker of an eyelid. Whatever happy thoughts he had shared with Maria had gone. There was no hint of a smile in his hard grey eyes. Beside her she could hear Reginald's loud, cheerful banter.

'By Gad, Zelah, you have worn me out! I think I must sit and rest my old bones beside Maria for a while. What say you, will you sit down or shall I find you another partner? Eh, who would you dance with next?'

Her gaze never wavered.

'I will dance with the major, if he will have me.'

It was a bold statement. For a frightening moment she thought he would refuse. Then, unsmiling, he held out his hand. Triumphant, she put up her head and proudly accompanied him to the floor.

The musicians had decided that their audience needed some respite from the energetic dances and now began a slower, much more stately beat. Zelah had time to observe her partner and to be observed. Her own gaze dropped beneath his unwavering scrutiny and she felt herself blushing like any schoolgirl. She would have missed her step, if her partner had not been adept at leading her. His grip tightened and she gave him a little smile, grateful for his support.

'You are a very good dancer, Major.'

'Thank you. I was used to be so, but I am very much out of practice.'

'Ah, but you have been used to dancing in the grandest ballrooms. Your idea of *out of practice* is polished perfection to our little assembly.'

'You flatter me, ma'am.'

'No, I do not.' She met his look, suddenly serious. 'You are not lame when you are dancing.'

'Not when I am dancing with you.'

The sudden and unexpected heat of his glance

seared Zelah and a flame of desire threatened to engulf her. She fought it back. That way led only to disaster.

'Nonsense. You have danced several times this evening without any halting step.'

'How can you know that?'

'Because I was watching you.'

The corner of his mouth lifted slightly.

'How very gratifying.'

Too late she realised he had tricked her. Triumph danced in his eyes and drew an answering gleam from her own. She sank her teeth into her bottom lip to prevent the smile that was trying to spill out.

'I was dancing too, so you were often in my sight, I was not deliberately looking out for you.' Her lofty response resulted in a chuckle and she tried to scowl at him. 'Fie, sir, you twist my words to pander to your own vanity!'

'You are twisting your own words. I have said very little.'

'No, but you *looked*—' She laughed. 'You are making May-game of me, Major. Is this how one flirts in the highest circles? I fear I am a very unworthy opponent.'

The music came to an end and she sank into her curtsy. He reached out for her proffered hand to pull her up.

'There is nothing at all unworthy about you, Miss Pentewan,' he murmured and she watched, speechless, as he carried her fingers to his lips.

Once it was seen that Major Coale was no longer confining his attentions to the married ladies, those parents with daughters to marry off began to flock around him and he obliged them all by remaining on the floor for the rest of the night, but Zelah could not quell the little thrill of triumph when he led her out for the last dance of the evening.

'You must be well practised by now, Major.'

'You have done me a great disservice, madam. Since dancing with you I have been besieged with partners.'

'Tell me you did not enjoy it.'

His smile was genuine, softening his face, and again she felt the ache of attraction.

'I have not danced like that since…since I returned from the Peninsula.'

'Then you should do so more often, Major. You look the better for it.'

His hand tightened on her fingers and her body cried out to respond to the warm invitation in his eyes, but she shook her head at him.

'I will not allow you to flirt with me, or to tease me, Major. I have a serious point to make and will not be distracted. You see how everyone accepts you and you are much more at ease with them. I consider this a good night's work.'

'Have I become your charity? Your good cause?'

A quick glance assured her he was not offended and she smiled up at him

'Not at all. But it has done you the power of good to come into society, sir, even if it is only country society!'

Chapter Eight

The early morning sunshine poured in through the windows of the breakfast room at Rooks Tower, sending golden bars of light across the floor. Dominic pushed his plate away and sat back, going over his plans for the day. He had arranged to meet Philips in the West Wood and he knew he would enjoy riding out. Even before sitting down to breakfast he had sent word to the stables to have Cloud saddled, but as he crossed the hall his eyes were drawn to the double doors leading off, his mind flying ahead through the darkened room and into the library beyond. It was the work of a moment to turn aside and stride through the shuttered salon. He pushed open the connecting doors and stepped into the library.

Zelah was already at work, a linen apron fastened over her dark-grey gown as she carefully dusted one of the many piles of books. Her bouncing curls had been ruthlessly drawn back into a knot, exposing the slender curve of her neck and the dainty shell of her ear. She presented a demure picture, cool and elegant. Nothing like the carefree, vibrant creature he had danced with last night, but every bit as alluring. His heart lifted when he remembered Maria Buckland's words—'Zelah thinks so highly of you.'

'I hardly expected you to come today,' he said. 'And here you are, earlier than usual.'

When she turned to smile it brought the golden sunshine into the room.

'I could not sleep. Is that not nonsensical, after dancing into the early hours?' She added shyly, 'I enjoyed myself so much. I hope you did, too, sir?'

'Very much. Do they hold many such assemblies in Lesserton?'

'Oh, I do not think so.' She picked up another book to dust. 'Maria says there will not be another until the harvest.'

He tapped his riding crop idly against his boot. The rest of Mrs Buckland's conversation gnawed away at his brain.

'I do not believe governesses go to balls, Miss Pentewan.'

She looked up at him, her brows raised in surprise at his comment.

'I do not think they do, sir.'

'Then what will you do, since you love to dance?'

'I shall have to teach my charges the basic steps. Then I will skip around the nursery with them!' She finished cleaning the book and put it carefully in place on the bookshelf. 'Have you come to spoil my morning with melancholy thoughts? You will not do it. Last night's music is still running through my head.'

It was still in Dominic's head, too. He wanted to sweep her up in his arms and carry her around the room, breathing in her fresh, flowery scent, making her laugh again.

No. To flirt with a pretty girl in a crowded ballroom was acceptable, to do so with an employee here, under his own roof, would be madness. He gripped the riding crop tighter, felt the sting as it slapped hard against his leg. He said curtly, 'There is still a great deal of work to do here, Miss Pentewan. Do not let last night's amusements interfere with your duties.'

He turned on his heel and marched out, leaving Zelah to gaze after him. Well! Did he think her so inept, so petty minded that she would be distracted from her work by an evening's entertainment? She threw down her duster in disgust. The morning had been so golden, so wonderful that she had been eager to reach Rooks Tower and continue with her work. She had been enjoying herself, carefully cleaning each volume, checking it for damage and putting in its place ready for cataloguing while in her mind she relived the pleasures of the evening, but with a few cold words he had destroyed her pleasure. First he had evoked thoughts of the drudgery that awaited her as a governess, then he had reminded her—quite unnecessarily—of her duties.

With a little huff of anger she stalked across to the window. It would serve him right if she walked out now and left him to organise his own books! Hard on the heels of this mutinous thought was the realisation that Major Coale could quite easily find someone else to take over, possibly someone much more competent that she to do the work. Probably a scholar who understood Greek and Latin and would not need to bother him. Zelah put her hands to her cheeks. If he should turn her off now, before she had secured another position, she would be penniless again, living on her family's charity. It had felt so rewarding to give her advance wages to Reginald, telling him it was for her keep and to pay Nicky's school fees. She needed the second instalment to put aside in case she fell upon hard times in the future.

She must finish her task here, whatever the cost. It shocked her to realise how much she wanted to complete it, to make this a library fit for a gentleman. No, to make it fit for Dominic Coale. She also wanted to see how the seasons played out on this terrace, once the gardeners had tamed the overgrown plants and removed the grass and weeds that invaded the cracked paving.

She clenched her fists.

'I'll show you, Major Coale. I am no poor, bullied soldier to be frightened by your bluster and ill humour.'

With renewed determination she applied herself to her work and returned to West Barton that evening tired, dusty but content.

She tried to be pleased when she heard the next day that Major Coale had gone off on business, but she missed his visits to the library, even when he was being odiously difficult. Now that most of the books were on the shelves, she was working her way through each section, recording, cross-referencing, enjoying the experience of being surrounded by so much knowledge. Her father, she knew, would relish such a wide-ranging collection and in her regular letters to her parents she always included details of her progress at Rooks Tower. It helped her to reinforce her growing sense of pride in her achievement.

* * *

'I thought I might accompany Reginald to Lesserton today, for the hearing. I would be very glad of your company.'

Maria was pouring coffee at the breakfast table as she made this request. Zelah glanced at her brother-in-law.

'I have told her it is not necessary, but she insists,' he replied jovially, but Zelah noted the slight shaking of his hand as he took the proffered cup. His was an easy-going nature and she knew he did not relish any sort of confrontation.

'Of course Maria will want to support you,' said Zelah stoutly. 'I shall come with you. Major Coale can spare me for one day, I am sure.'

They travelled to Lesserton in the carriage, Reginald in his best coat of olive superfine and the ladies suitably veiled. The hearing was to take place in the long room at the White Hart, the same room that had been used for the assembly, but now it looked very different, stripped of its garlands and the space filled with desks and benches. The room was already full to overflowing and Maria observed that the whole of Lesserton was represented.

'Which is not surprising,' agreed Reginald, 'since they have all been accustomed to grazing their animals on the land Sir Oswald is claiming.' He looked around the crowded room. 'My dear, I think after all I would prefer you to wait downstairs for me. The proceedings could become boisterous. Come, I will bespeak a private room for you.'

Maria protested, but Zelah could see her objections were half-hearted. They made their way downstairs to a private parlour overlooking the street, where Reginald left them and went to talk to the farmers gathered in a little knot around a tall, saturnine gentleman in a black frock coat and bagwig.

'That is Mr Summerson, the lawyer from London,' whispered Maria, drawing Zelah to the window. 'Reginald was closeted with him for hours yesterday. He has obtained copies of the charters filed with the Crown—' She broke off as another carriage pulled up at the door. She gave a little snort. 'And here is Sir Oswald himself. The rat-faced little man with him is his lawyer. Look how he follows, bowing and scraping. Ugh, quite repulsive.'

Soon everyone had gone upstairs and the ladies settled down to wait. The landlord sent in coffee and they sat in silence, listening to the tread of feet above them and the occasional rumble as the crowd muttered or protested over something that had been said.

* * *

An hour had gone by, two, and still the hearing had continued. There was a cheer at one point, and Maria had looked up hopefully, but it was another full hour before the thunder of movement above them told them that the hearing was over. They waited impatiently, listening to the clatter of feet on the stairs and watching the villagers pour out onto the street.

'They do not look particularly elated,' Zelah observed, not knowing how to interpret the expressions of the crowd.

She turned expectantly towards the door as her brother-in-law came in. Maria ran to him.

'Well?'

He took her outstretched hands and forced a smile. 'All is not lost.'

He guided the ladies back to the table as a servant came in with more coffee and a jug of ale and they sat down, waiting in silence until they were alone once more.

'It was going very well. Mr Summerson brought a charter that describes the common land and mentions the stream that forms the westernmost boundary. The description fits the Lightwater, which runs down from Rooks Ford and to the west of Prickett Wood. I thought we had it then, until Evanshaw's man pointed out that it could just as easily refer to the ditch that runs along the edge of the bluebell wood.' Reginald shook his head. 'Evanshaw then produced a map, which clearly shows the ditch as the boundary.'

Maria snorted.

'A forgery!'

'Very likely, my dear, but with that and the charter, Sir Arthur is minded to agree that Prickett Wood and the hill grazing does belong to Sir Oswald.' He sighed. 'Some of the older villagers claim their parents told them of a boundary stone, but it hasn't been seen in living memory, and Sir Oswald's man claims it will have been removed when the lane at the edge of bluebell wood was widened.'

'Oh dear,' said Zelah. 'Then the villagers have lost their fight. No wonder they were looking so downcast.'

'Well, not quite. Sir Arthur is not wholly convinced, and he has given us until the end of June to find more evidence to prove our case.'

'And must Sir Oswald allow the villagers access until then?'

'I'm afraid not. Evanshaw's lawyer argued most successfully against it. However, Sir Arthur has ordered that he remove the mantraps, but he has conceded that Evanshaw has the right to shoot any deer that wander into the wood, since they damage his valuable woodland.'

'It would seem Sir Arthur is well nigh convinced the land belongs to Lydcombe Park,' sighed Zelah.

'If that is the case, can we afford to fight it?' asked Maria. 'I know how hard it was for everyone to find the money to pay for the lawyer to come down for just this one visit.'

'You can perhaps find someone local,' suggested Zelah.

Maria looked doubtful. 'Perhaps, but it will still be costly.'

Reginald took his wife's hands. 'Perhaps I should have discussed this with you first, my love, but I have pledged that I will bear the costs for the next hearing. If we win then the farmers and villagers will pay me back, if we lose... I know that would leave us sadly short,' he said quickly, seeing the dismay in her face, 'but we shall come about, with a little economy. We have to try.'

'What is the alternative?' asked Zelah. 'What will happen if the villagers lose the hill grazing and the right to forage in Prickett Wood?'

Reginald shrugged. 'Many of them will not be able to survive. Some of them are our tenants and if they cannot pay their rents then that will affect us, too.'

'Then of course we must do what we can to avoid that,' said Maria. She glanced at the little bracket clock on the shelf. 'Pray order more refreshments, Reginald. If we wait another hour, we can collect Nicky from Mr Netherby's on our way home.'

When Dominic walked into the taproom of the White Hart that evening he found the mood distinctly sombre. He was on his way back from Exeter and had made good time, but the warm weather had left him parched and he decided to slake his thirst in Lesserton before the final stage of his journey.

He entered the inn, his coat collar turned up and his hat pulled down to shade the left side of his face, as was his habit, but several of the locals recognised him and nodded. Giles Grundy was sitting at one end of the bench beside the long central table and he shifted up to make room. Dominic hesitated, but he knew it would be churlish to ignore this small sign of friendship so he went over to join him, saying as he sat down, 'How went the hearing today?'

Giles grunted and after taking a long draught from his tankard he gave Dominic a brief account.

'Ah, 'tis all over,' grunted Abraham Judd, puffing morosely on his pipe at the other end of the table. 'Even Mr Buckland bringing down a fine Lunnon lawyer didn't make no difference. Evanshaw claims the ditch is the boundary stream and Sir Arthur do believe 'un.' He turned to spit into the fireplace at his back. 'Stream! There's more water in my pisspot than that there ditch, and allus has been!'

He stopped and glared at the doorway. Dominic felt the tension around him and looked up to see Miller, Sir Oswald's bailiff, had entered. His glance at the long table was met with sullen stares. With a scowl he turned away, then thought better of it and came over to the long table.

'Drownin' yer sorrows?' His lip curled. 'I heard how it went today, so here's a warnin' to you all to keep off Sir Oswald's land.'

'But 'tedn't his land yet, Miller,' growled Giles Grundy. 'Not fer another month.'

Miller shrugged.

'As near as damn it, an' I'll be out with me gun every night, as will my men. Should any of 'ee want to argue the point, we'd be only too pleased to shoot ye.'

'I really don't think Sir Arthur would approve of that,' remarked Dominic. He raised his head as he spoke and saw the bailiff's eyes widen slightly as he recognised the face beneath the wide-brimmed hat.

'Beggin' yer pardon, Major. I'm merely passin''

on a message from my master. Besides, we're permitted to shoot the deer, and how are we to know what's man and what's beast in the dark?'

'Aye, well now you've passed on yer message, get yerself back to the Three Tuns with the rest of yer cronies,' muttered Abraham Judd. 'You bain't welcome here.'

Miller scowled, and with a reluctant tug at his forelock towards Dominic he slouched off to the corner, nursing his mug of ale. The men around the table looked at each other.

'Well, 'tedn't too bad at the moment,' remarked one, shaking his head, 'but come summer we needs the high pasture for grazing. And in the autumn we'll need to be collectin' firewood. You've been very good, Major, lettin' us forage in your own grounds, but that won't be enough to keep us all going.'

'Then we must hope you find the evidence you need to win your case.' Dominic finished his ale and rose. 'Now I'll bid you goodnight.'

He strode out of the door, buttoning his coat, ready to continue his journey. Since the assembly he had been making a conscious effort not to drag his right leg and his stride was becoming easier. Perhaps the doctors were right, after all. There was nothing wrong with his leg. He grinned to himself. He had not been prepared to make the effort for the sawbones, but to please an impertinent slip of a girl…

'Ooomph!'

As he stepped out of the inn a shambling, unsteady figure cannoned into him and collapsed on to the ground, cursing roundly. Dominic grinned as he recognised the ragged heap.

'Old Robin.' He held out his hand. 'Up you come, man, and look where you are going next time.'

As he pulled the old man to his feet he turned his head away, grimacing at the stench of beer and onions on his breath.

'Major Coale,' he hiccupped and swayed alarmingly. 'Just goin' to wet me whistle…'

'You should be going home, man.'

Robin gave a grunt. 'A fine night like this, I'll be sleepin' in the woods.'

Dominic laid a hand on his shoulder. 'Then take care where you lay your head. Evanshaw has armed men patrolling Prickett Wood.'

'That's very kind o' you, Major, but I've been followin' the deer into Prickett Wood since I was a boy an' I don't plan to stop now. It'll take more'n Sir Oswald's men to keep me out!'

With a nod he shuffled off into the inn, singing roisterously as he bounced from wall to wall.

Shaking his head, Dominic went off to collect his horse.

Summer was nearly here. Zelah could smell it in the air as she walked across the lawn towards Rooks Tower. Even in the few weeks she had been coming to the house she could see the changes Major Coale had wrought. The new road was only one of the improvements he had made—clinging ivy had been stripped away from the windows, which had been cleaned and painted and gleamed in the morning sunshine. The gates from the new road had been repaired and oiled and now opened easily on to the freshly gravelled drive. The house stood proudly amid its scythed lawns and seemed to welcome her. The weather was so glorious that Zelah was reluctant to go indoors and once she had reached the library she lost no time in throwing up the windows.

There was no sign of the major. Zelah assumed he had not yet returned from Exeter. A pity, she thought, since the oppressive, sultry air hinted that the good weather would soon break and she would have liked him to see his house on such a beautiful day.

Even with the windows open it was very warm

in the library and she decided against emptying the last two crates that stood in one corner. She had peeked in them upon their arrival and knew they held large, ancient manuscripts that would require some exertion to move. Instead she settled down at her desk to continue cataloguing the books she had already sorted.

When the pretty ormolu clock on the man-telshelf chimed noon she looked up, surprised at how quickly the morning had gone. She got up and stretched. The still air was heavy and oppressive. She went to the double doors and threw them open, but the dark stillness of the shuttered salon did nothing to dispel the humid atmosphere. She stood for a moment, listening. The house was hushed, expectant, as if it was waiting for her to act. Zelah crossed to the first window and after a short struggle with the catch she folded back the shutters and threw up the sash. She went to the next window, and the next. As the fresh air and sunlight flooded in the room seemed to sigh and relax, like a woman released from her confining stays. Zelah chuckled at the image. The room was decorated in yellow and white with the ornate plasterwork of the ceiling and the magnificent chimneypiece picked out in gold and reflected in the straw-coloured sofas and chairs. She took up a cushion and hugged it, revelling in the glowing opulence of the salon.

'What in damnation do you think you are doing?'

Zelah dropped the cushion and spun around. Major Coale was standing in the doorway, his scarred face pale with anger.

'Well?' he demanded. 'What are you doing in here?'

'N-nothing. That is…I thought this room could use a little air.'

'I gave express instructions that this room is to remain shuttered. I hate this salon. It is not a room for levity.'

'Oh, but it is,' cried Zelah, throwing her arms wide and spinning around. 'Just look at the colours and the space. Can you not feel it? The happiness? It is a room for children, and laughter and lo—'

She stopped.

'Love? Marriage? A happy family?' His face twisted into a bitter grimace, making the livid scar even more noticeable. 'You are far too romantic, Miss Pentewan. In future you will confine your work to the library.'

He turned and stalked out. Zelah frowned, but even as she strove to understand his anger she saw what she had not noticed before, that between each of the windows was a pier glass, paired with its equal on the opposite wall. Wherever she went, whichever way she turned, she could not escape her reflection.

'Oh goodness. Major!' Picking up her skirts she flew after him. 'Major Coale, wait, please.'

He was crossing the hall and she caught up with him just as he opened the study door. She put out her hands to stop him closing it in her face.

'Please,' she begged him. 'Please let me apologise.'

He glared at her, eyes blazing, his chest rising and falling as he fought to contain his rage. She held her ground and after a moment he turned and walked away. Silently she followed him into the room and shut the door.

'I did not understand, until I saw the mirrors.' He was standing with his back to her, staring down into the empty fireplace. She said quietly, 'Forgive me, Major. I did not mean to make you angry.'

'So now you will go back and close the room up again.'

'Must I?'

'Yes! I do not wish to be reminded of the monster I have become.'

'You are *not* a monster!' Angrily she caught his arm and turned him towards her. 'You are a man, a soldier with a scarred face. Is that so very bad? You went to the assembly—'

'That was an aberration, a moment of madness.'

'Perhaps it was so, for you, but you were not shunned. One or two were shocked, of course, people who had not seen you before, but the majority—those who know and respect you—they accept you for what you are.'

'What I am is a *freak*.'

'Now you are just being foolish! There are many men with worse disfigurements than this, many whose wits are addled.'

'And there are many who lost their lives!' he flashed. 'Do you think I am not aware of that? Do you think I do not *know*? Every time I see this scarred face it is a reminder of all those men that died, good men, with more right to live than I will ever have—' He broke off and swung away towards the window. 'From the moment we crossed into Spain I was writing letters of condolence. To wives, fathers, mothers, as more and more comrades perished. And still they died, those poor souls, never to see their homeland again. You have no idea of what it's like to wake up at night asking, *why me?* Why should I live when all around me perished—Graddon was a fool to bring me back. And the others who helped him. They should have left me to die like the rest at Cacabelos—'

'No!' Zelah grabbed his arm and pulled him round again. 'How dare you say such a thing. Any life lost is a tragedy, yes, but a life *saved*—it shows the love and respect in which you were held that so many put themselves out to bring you home! So your scars remind you of your fallen comrades. Is that so very bad? You are not the only one to have bitter regrets about the past. Perhaps instead of wallowing in your self-pity every time you look in a mirror you should feel proud to have fought beside those men.' She stepped closer and put up her hand to touch his face. 'These marks are not so very bad—'

He grabbed her wrist and whipped her hand behind her back. They were so close that her breast brushed his waistcoat. Immediately her body tensed. She could see every detail of the long black lashes that fringed his eyes, the fine lines etched into his skin. She dropped her eyes to his mouth, the curve of his lips, the slight droop on the left where the scar ran close. In her mind she put her arms about his neck and gently touched her lips to the livid scar, kissing his brow, his cheek, his mouth, making him forget his injuries and remember that he was a man, like any other.

'You go too far, madam.' His voice was rough, not quite steady.

Not far enough. The words were on the tip of her tongue. She felt her body softening, yielding to the magnetic power of the man. She felt naked under his scorching glance. It had been so long since any man had held her thus, but the desire for that first youthful love had not been as strong as this, as unconfined. She had never wanted a man as she wanted Dominic. His eyes wandered to her mouth and nervously she ran her tongue over her lips. Surely he would kiss her now, or she would die.

He released her so suddenly that Zelah swayed.

Dominic turned away from her, rubbing his eyes. This would not do. Only by an extraordinary effort of will had he resisted the temptation to kiss her. She was willing enough, he knew that look; the darkening lustre of the eyes, the soft flushing of the lips. He could have taken her, made love to her there and then in this very room, but what then? To have her working in his library was giving rise to scandalous rumour, but while it remained only that, she could still become a governess and maintain her independence. If he took her as his mistress it would outrage the neighbourhood and ruin her reputation for ever. When they grew tired of each other what would there be for her, save another man, another protector, until her looks had quite gone.

'I b-beg your pardon,' she said quietly. 'I…perhaps I should leave. You could find another archivist.'

He swung round. She was very pale, but outwardly composed.

'Is that what you want?' She shook her head and Dominic realised he had been holding his breath for her reply. He nodded. 'Very well. We shall say no more of this. Go back to work, now, Miss Pentewan.'

She clasped her hands in front of her, twisting her fingers together and running the tip of her tongue over her lips. Dear God, if she continued to do that it would be his ruin! He said roughly, 'Well, madam?'

'The salon. May I…will you allow the shutters to remain open?'

A smile tugged at the corner of his mouth.

'You are nothing if not persistent, madam. If it is your wish.'

'Thank you. You might of course remove the pier glasses.'

'No, let them stay. The room is designed for them.'

He was surprised by his response and took a moment to consider how he felt. Exhausted, drained, but somehow calmer than he had felt for years. Somehow his outburst had been a catharsis. He had spoken to no one of his guilt and it had built inside him, reaching such proportions that it had distorted everything, even, he suspected, his view of his own disfigurement. When he looked up Zelah was still standing before him, uncertainty in her hazel eyes.

'Will—will it prevent you coming to the library?'

He thought about it. 'I do not know. Shall we put it to the test?'

He walked to the door and stood there, looking at her. After a brief hesitation she accompanied him back across the hall. The doors to the salon still stood wide. Beyond, the room glowed with the afternoon sunlight. It glinted off the gilded plasterwork, twinkled from the mirrors. His step slowed at the threshold and he held out his arm.

'Will you do me the honour?'

She placed her fingers on his sleeve and they processed slowly through the salon.

'I had no idea you had returned from Exeter, Major.'

'Evidently, or you would not have turned my house upside down.' She shook her head, refusing to respond to his teasing. He continued. 'I have ordered a carpet for the library. It will mirror the pattern on the ceiling, I hope you will approve.'

She looked up quickly, surprise and pleasure in her eyes.

'I am sure it will add the finishing touch.'

They had gone more than halfway across the long room before Dominic realised that he had held out his left arm to her, so that when he looked to the left his eyes were drawn to her reflection rather than his own. And there was something else. The man in the mirror was walking with a sure, steady gait. He was no longer dragging his right leg.

Dominic stretched and rubbed his eyes. He had slept well again, untroubled by dreams or nightmares. That was three nights in a row. He put his hands behind his head, thinking about the change in him. It was due to Zelah. She had accused him of wallowing in self-pity. He could not deny it. She had coaxed and bullied and nagged him until finally he had erupted, his pain, anger and guilt spilling out and the relief, to finally confess it all to someone, had been overwhelming. That was three days ago and now he felt purged, ready to rebuild his life, to face the world.

And it was all due to his little librarian.

Graddon brought his shaving water and Dominic considered how best he could reward her. Money? The razor rasped over his cheek. No. He knew her well enough now to know her proud independent spirit would never accept such a gift, or any gift. Damnation, then how was he to thank her? One thing was certain, he would not let her become a governess. She deserved to be her own mistress, with her own servants to command. But how was he to engineer such a change in her life? It must not look as if he had any hand in the affair. He could set up an annuity and have his lawyer tell her it was from some long-lost relative, but that would mean taking her family into his confidence, and if her father was the upright clergyman she had described then he might not be happy to collude in such a lie. Besides, there was not much time. The work in the library was almost complete. Every day he dreaded that Zelah might come to him and say she had accepted another post. And once she had left her sister's house—

'Marriage!'

Of course. He dropped his razor and dried his face quickly. Maria Buckland had already thought of an excellent plan. It was up to him now to carry it out.

When Zelah set off for another day at Rooks Tower, the sky was a blanket of unbroken grey and a freshening wind promised rain later. Spring was refusing to give way to summer. However, the lowering weather did not affect her spirits. When she thought of what she had achieved in the library she was pleased, but when she reached the house and walked through the salon, its window shutters now folded away to allow the light to fill the elegant space, her heart swelled with pride. She was pleased to think she was playing some part in Major Coale's rehabilitation, encouraging him to see that he need not lock himself away and live a solitary existence.

She must face up to the fact that she had grown fond of the major. Too fond. He could be overbearing and irascible, but she knew much of his ill temper sprang from the horrific injuries he had suffered, not just to his face, but to his mind. She had seen a softer side to his character and now her day was not complete unless she saw him—Zelah shook her head. Heavens, what was she thinking? She must not allow herself to become attached to Dominic Coale. It would be foolish to dwell upon his many kindnesses to her. They meant nothing, and if she should betray her feelings—she knew only too well how easily a man could succumb to temptation. It had almost destroyed her once, it must not happen again.

It was therefore a very cool and formal greeting

that she gave the major when he marched into the library the following morning, before returning her attention to her work. He appeared not to notice.

'You will leave off your interminable cataloguing, Miss Pentewan. I have another job for you.' He strode about the room as he spoke, his hands clasped behind his back. 'I want you to compile a list of all the families in the county. Those with the rank of gentlemen and above, naturally.'

She paused, her pen caught in mid-air.

'A list, sir? Very well, if that is what you want…'

'It is, and I want it complete by tomorrow. You may need to consult your sister on this.'

'Yes, I think I shall have to do that.'

She stared at his broad back, wondering if she dare ask him why he wanted these names. He swung round, catching her glance.

'I am going to hold a ball.'

Zelah dropped her pen.

'A—a *ball*?' She hurriedly blotted the ink that had splashed on to the ledger.

'Yes. Now we have opened up the salon it seems a pity not to use it.' He began to pace up and down the room. 'My sister will be coming down to play hostess. I have already written to her. You and I will compile a list and then you will write to everyone, inviting them to attend.'

'And…and when is this ball to be?'

'At midsummer. Three weeks from now.'

'Three weeks! So little time.'

'I know, but it cannot be helped. I have asked Mrs Graddon to let me know what is required to make all the bedrooms habitable and I will be sending someone to buy what is necessary—give me a list of your requirements, pens, paper, seals and so on and they shall be fetched for you.'

'Th-thank you,' said Zelah, her head reeling. She listened as he explained the steps he had already taken to prepare for the event and drew a sheet of paper towards her to write down a few notes.

'I think that is all,' he said at last, rubbing his chin. 'I must be off to find Phillips and ask him if Old Robin has been back yet to finish removing the moles from the south lawn.' He strode towards the door and stopped. 'Oh, and remember to put your own name on the list. You and your sister and brother-in-law will be my guests at dinner beforehand.'

'Me? Oh, I do not think I could—'

He turned to glower at her. 'You will do as you are bid, Miss Pentewan. If I am going to all this trouble, then I expect you to make a little effort, too!'

Chapter Nine

Zelah was still dazed when she returned to West Barton that evening and it was a relief to unburden herself to her sister.

'Do you not think it odd,' she mused, 'that a man who so very recently lived as a recluse should suddenly take it into his head to hold a ball?'

Maria was inclined to be complacent. 'That is the life he has been used to.'

'But up until a few days ago he could not bear to look at himself in the mirror. He kept the salon in darkness.'

'Yes, until you showed him how nonsensical it was. You are a beneficial influence, Zelah. Think how much he has changed since he has met you.'

'He would have come about, even without me, but a ball! That is most unexpected.'

'He appeared to be enjoying himself at the assembly,' returned Maria, her eyes twinkling. 'Perhaps someone gave him the hint.'

'Yes, but the worst thing is, he insists that I should be there. I suppose that he feels he cannot leave me out, since you and Reginald are invited. We are all to dine there, too, beforehand. And I am to tell you, sister, that he will have a suite prepared for you and the children, because he knows you will not stay away long from Baby.'

'Well, I consider that to be exceedingly kind, and beyond anything I was expecting.' She cast a shrewd look at Zelah. 'Major Coale must think very highly of you, my dear.'

'I think he values the work I am doing.'

'Are you sure that is all?'

'Of course. What else should a viscount's son think of a parson's daughter?' Zelah forced herself to speak lightly and she was glad to see the speculation fade from Maria's eyes.

'Oh well, at least this will give you the opportunity to mix in society.'

Zelah shook her head. 'But I don't *want* to mix.'

'Well, you should. Who knows? There will be many gentlemen there, and dancing has been known to lead to greater things, like an offer of marriage.'

'Maria, you know that is impossible.'

'Not so,' said Maria stoutly. 'You have many qualities that an honest man would look for in a wife—'

'Not if he knows of my past. Would you have me deceive an honest man?' Zelah bit her lip and fixed her eyes upon her sister's dismayed countenance. She said gently, 'I should not be attending this ball at all. I am a fallen woman, Maria. If anyone should discover that—'

'They won't. No one outside Cardinham knows what happened to you—why, even Reginald and I don't know the whole!'

No, thought Zelah, sadly, she had never told anyone about the man who had stolen her heart and her virtue. She thought back to that halcyon summer. She had been in love and thought herself loved in return. She stifled a sigh.

'Well,' she said brightly, 'at least it will give me the opportunity to find out if anyone requires a governess.'

Two weeks before the ball, the major's sister arrived. A handsome travelling carriage bowled up the drive and Zelah, watching from the tower room, saw a lady alight. She was elegantly attired in a travelling dress of olive green, her dark hair caught up under a stylish cap from which a number of curling ostrich feathers nodded in the breeze. Even as she shook out her skirts Dominic came striding out of the house and caught her up in his arms, swinging her around. Zelah turned back to her books. She had no right to feel jealous of the major's lovely sister.

Down on the drive, Dominic hugged his sister. 'It is good to see you, Sal. How was your journey?'

'Tiresome. If only all the roads on Exmoor were as good as this last mile!' She pushed herself free of his arms and stood looking him over. 'Hmm, a vast improvement, Dom, I would not have recognised you. The last time I saw you was at Markham and I thought then you bore a strong resemblance to a bear. And you are no longer limping.'

He grinned. 'The Exmoor air agrees with me. Come inside. We will drink a glass of wine while they take your baggage to your room.' He kept his arm around her as he swept her inside.

'So this is your new home.' She gazed up at the impressive roof of the hall as they passed through. 'A touch Gothic for you, Dom.'

'This side of the house is the original, but do not despair, the bedrooms have every comfort, including new windows that do not rattle in the night. Later I will show you the salon and the library, more recent additions to the building.'

'Ah, yes, the library. You wrote to tell me you had a home at last for all your books!'

'Yes.' He looked down to brush a speck of dust from his sleeve before continuing in a casual tone, 'I have found a librarian to put them in order for me.'

'Ah, good.'

'A woman.'

The choking sound from his sister made him smile inwardly, but his look was all innocent concern. Sally was not deceived.

'The devil you have,' she said rudely. 'She is a beauty, I suppose.'

'Not particularly. She is kin to the Bucklands and I took her on because she lives at West Barton, so I did not need to have her living here.' His lips curved upward. 'Actually, she has done an excellent job of creating order from the chaos that was the library. But that is not important—we have a ball to organise.'

He pulled out the list of names Zelah had written out and handed it to Sally, who perused it carefully.

'Well, you can add Jasper to the list. He will come, if he can. He is currently in town and waiting to see what changes Prinny will make now he is Regent.'

Dominic nodded. It would be good to see his twin again. 'What about Ben?'

'My darling husband is in the Peninsula and the last I heard he was with the army at Albuerra.'

Dom gave a mirthless laugh. 'Ah, yes, our so-called victory. The losses were terrible, I hear.'

'I know. It is very sad. I think Ben is safer as an intelligence officer.'

He nodded, then said abruptly, 'Do you worry about him?'

'Of course.' Sally's smile softened and her eyes took on a dreamy, faraway look. 'I cannot wait until he comes back again.'

Something twisted deep in his gut and Dominic found himself wondering if any woman would ever have such a look for him.

'You have finished your wine, Sal. Would you like more, or can I take you to meet my librarian? I fear if we wait until you have changed your gown she will have left.'

'Take me to her,' said Sally immediately. 'I am agog to see the woman you will trust with your precious books.'

Sally's tone was light, but her interest in the unknown employee was very real. She followed him across the hall, not knowing what she would find. Some harpy, perhaps bent on securing a wealthy husband. Or an eccentric bluestocking. What she did not expect was a slender girl with sun-streaked brown hair and golden skin. She would be looked upon askance at Almack's, where pale skin was so fashionable and even the odd freckle was frowned upon. Not a harpy, then. Her high-necked grey gown was plain to the point of severity and with her hair strained back into a knot at the nape of her neck, Sally thought the girl was doing her best *not* to attract any man's attention.

Observing Dominic's constraint as he made the introduction, and Miss Pentewan's faint blush, Sally was even more intrigued. She gave Zelah her most friendly smile.

'Dominic tells me you are making excellent progress with his wretched books. Why he had to collect so many I really cannot think! I do hope you will be able to spare some time to help me organise this ball.'

'Yes, ma'am, if you wish it.'

Her voice was soft, musical even and the smile lurking in her hazel eyes hinted at a mischievous sense of humour. A pleasant enough child, but nothing to attract her brother. When he had been on the town, his flirts had always been diamonds of the first water and even his mistresses—of whom she was supposed to know nothing—had been ripe beauties. What he saw in this unremarkable young woman she did not know.

'You are free to give Mrs Hensley as much assistance as she needs,' barked Dominic, as if impatient to be gone. 'The library can wait until after the ball.'

Sally inclined her head. 'That is very kind of you, Dominic.'

'Not at all. There is still a deal of work to be done out of doors and I shall not be able to give you as much attention as I would like.'

'Ah, I see now. You are shuffling off your responsibilities, brother. Very well, Miss Pentewan, we shall begin tomorrow by looking at the lists you have drawn up and seeing how many have replied. But that will have to be in the afternoon. Tomorrow morning I want to be shown around the estate.' She turned to Zelah. 'Do you ride, Miss Pentewan?'

'I was used to, but not any more. There are no mounts suitable for a lady at West Barton.'

'Oh, if that is all then I will provide you with a mount. I brought two of my own hacks, because Dom warned me how bad the roads can be. Do you have a riding habit?'

'Yes, but—'

'Then that is settled. We will go riding tomorrow, if the weather holds.'

She paused, raising her brows at Zelah, who clasped her hands together, saying, 'I am very grateful for the offer, but I am afraid I cannot ride out with you. I am a librarian—'

'Hell and damnation,' growled Dominic, 'you will be whatever I pay you to be!'

Zelah's head went up.

'I am no bondservant! If that is what you think, then I am sorry to disappoint you and we will part now.'

Sally put up her hands. 'Of course he does not think that, Miss Pentewan. Shame on you, Dominic, did you leave your manners behind when you moved here?'

After a tense interlude he shook his head. 'I beg your pardon, Miss Pentewan,' he ground out. 'I would be *much obliged* if you would accompany my sister when she rides out tomorrow. Since I cannot go with her myself, I would feel happier knowing she did not go with only a groom for company.'

There was a proud tilt to Zelah's chin and the stormy look was still in her eyes as she met Dominic's fiery glare. So the drab little librarian had steel in her soul.

Good for her, thought Sally appreciatively, *but is she a match for Dominic?*

She waited silently and saw the anger fade from

her brother's eyes. His tone was quite cordial as he posed his next question.

'Do you *dislike* riding, Miss Pentewan?'

'On the contrary, but there is no place for it in my life now.'

'Not even if it will assist me?'

'Dominic, do not press her,' Sally began, but he waved his hand and continued in a coaxing tone,

'Come, are you so eager to finish working in my library that you cannot leave it for another day?'

A soft blush suffused Zelah's cheeks. 'It—it is not that,' she stammered. 'I really do not think it is my place...'

'My dear Miss Pentewan, I really would be most grateful for your company,' said Sally. 'I shall keep you away from your work for no more than two hours—three at the most. Do say you will come.'

'I would enjoy it very much, ma'am, but I do not think it possible. I could not sit down in here in all my dirt, and to go home and change would severely curtail my day...'

'Then take the whole day off, madam. I am not such an ogre that I will prevent you having any pleasure.'

'There you are,' said Sally triumphantly, 'You are to take a day's holiday, Miss Pentewan!'

* * *

'My dear, you will wear out the carpet!'

Maria's laughing protest halted Zelah as she paced up and down the morning room and she dropped into a chair, albeit one with a view of the drive.

They were in the morning room at West Barton. Breakfast was finished, Zelah had donned her riding habit and was waiting for Sally Hensley to arrive. She could not deny she was looking forward to riding out. She had enjoyed riding her father's hack at Cardinham and she had brought her riding habit with her to West Barton. However, Maria had explained to Zelah that she had sold her horse, for there would not be any opportunity for her to ride until little Reginald was older. What Zelah knew, although it remained unspoken, was that there was no money to spare for such a luxury. Zelah had resigned herself to the fact that she would never ride again, but now Major Coale's delightful sister had not only invited her to ride, but was willing to provide a mount, too.

Zelah had spent some little time wondering if she should have held fast and refused to go. But it had been far too tempting an offer and when Sally eventually arrived, and Zelah was at last mounted upon the spirited bay mare, she could not regret her decision. The mare tossed her head and snorted, playfully sidestepping across the drive while Zelah kept control with the lightest hold on the reins.

'She is very lively, but you have her measure.' Sally nodded approvingly as Zelah brought her mount alongside Sally's glossy black horse.

'She is delightful.' Zelah laughed. 'What is her name?'

'Portia. After Shakespeare.' Sally chuckled. 'Dom and Jasper had taken me to see *The Merchant of Venice* as half of my birthday treat. Portia was the other half. She is a delightful ride and can cover miles without flagging, but then my husband bought Ebony for me.' She leaned forwards and stroked her horse's gleaming neck. 'Poor Portia was ousted.'

'I do not know how you can choose between them,' commented Zelah as they rode out into the lane.

'Ebony was a present from my darling Ben. When you have a much-loved husband you too will value any gift he gives you.'

'I do not intend to marry. I am going to be a governess.'

'Goodness. Wouldn't you rather have a husband?'

'No.' Realising this bald answer might be a little rude, she added, 'I would rather be independent than marry the wrong man.'

'Very true, but if you could marry *any man* you wanted…?'

Zelah was silent. There was no possibility of her being able to marry the man of her choice, so she would rather not think about it. She said carefully, 'It is all too easy to be deceived by a charming man.' They followed Sawley into a field and she took the opportunity to change the subject. 'The land is well drained here, shall we gallop the fidgets out of these horses?'

After racing across the open ground they settled down to follow the groom as he pointed out to them the extent of the land belonging to Rooks Tower. It was impossible for Zelah to keep up her reserve when Sally was so naturally friendly. She could not, of course, agree that they should do away with formality completely and while she was happy for Sally to use her first name she was resolved never to call her companion anything other than Mrs Hensley.

They had finished their tour with another gallop across the moors and were about to turn back when a lone rider appeared in the distance. Zelah's heart skipped a beat. She instantly recognised the upright rider on the huge grey horse.

'Here is my brother now,' declared Sally. She waved. 'Just in time to escort us home.'

The major spotted them and raised his hand. The grey mare broke into a canter and very soon he had caught up with them. He did not smile in response to Sally's greeting and the downward turn of the left side of his mouth was more pronounced than ever. Zelah regarded him anxiously.

'Is anything the matter, Major?'

'It's Old Robin. They found his body in the Lightwater today.' His voice, his whole manner, was terse.

'Oh, good heavens!'

'Who is this Robin?' demanded Sally, her frowning glance moving between them.

'An old man from the village who spent most of his time living wild in the woods. He earned a little money doing odd jobs for me or the other landowners. There was nothing he didn't know about this land. A useful fellow.'

'He will be sorely missed,' added Zelah, thinking of Nicky. 'Who found him?'

'Buckland was out with Giles Grundy early this morning, trying to prove that the Lightwater is the river referred to in the charter. They came upon him just where the Lightwater enters Prickett Wood.'

She shuddered. 'Poor man. How long…?'

He shook his head. 'No one knows. I saw him outside the White Hart on the night of the hearing. He was drunk, then. No one seems to have seen him since that night.'

'Perhaps that was it, then,' suggested Sally. 'He lost his footing and slipped into the stream and drowned. How sad. Has he any family?'

'A sister. Buckland has gone to see her.'

'Is there anything to be done?'

'No. Buckland and Sir Arthur, the local magistrate, have everything in hand. Let me escort you home.'

The little party was subdued as it cantered back across the fields to Rooks Tower. When they reached the fork in the path which led to West Barton, Zelah drew rein.

'This is where I must leave you. My brother-in-law will send someone over with the mare tomorrow, if you wish, or Sawley can come with me now.'

'I would not hear of you going home alone,' said Sally. 'Dominic shall accompany you.'

'No, please,' cried Zelah, alarmed. 'There is no need for that!'

'It is the least he can do when you have given up your time for me this morning. And we must do it again—I have enjoyed it so much. I know! We will keep your riding habit at Rooks Tower, then when we want to go riding you only have to change into it, and can go back to your work in the library afterwards. What do you think, Dom?'

'I think you are imposing upon Miss Pentewan's good nature, Sal.'

'Nonsense. You enjoyed riding out with me, did you not, Zelah?'

'Very much, but—'

'Then it is settled. Dom shall send the carriage over for you in the morning, so that you can bring everything with you. Is that agreed?'

Overwhelmed, Zelah could only nod and earned a beaming smile from Sally.

'Good. That is settled. Now, see her home safely, Dominic. I should come too, but I fear the journey yesterday tired me more than I first thought.'

'Very well,' said Dominic. 'Take Sawley with you, Sal. I will see Miss Pentewan home.'

Once they had watched Sally and the groom cantering off towards Rooks Tower, Zelah turned her horse towards West Barton, the major bringing the big grey into line beside her. He said quietly,

'You will have to explain to Nicky about Robin.'

'I was thinking of that. Nicky has seen much less of Robin since he has been attending classes with Mr Netherby, but he will still be upset, I think.'

'Would you like me to come with you?'

She looked up, surprised. 'Th-that is very kind of you, Major, but I think I can manage.' She gave a little smile. 'After all, I need to learn to handle things like this, if I am to make a good governess.'

He gave an impatient huff. 'You still hold by your absurd plan?'

'Of course.' Zelah blinked. 'Why not?'

'You are attending the ball. It is not impossible that you will meet some gentleman—'

'Not you, too!' she exclaimed bitterly. 'I do not *want* to meet some gentleman. I can never marry.'

'*Can* never marry?' He jumped on the word. 'Is there some impediment then?'

Her hands jerked on the reins and Portia sidled nervously.

'N-no, of course not,' she stammered, aware that her cheeks were hot and most likely very red. 'I am merely determined to maintain my independence. In fact…' she put up her chin, suddenly remembering a letter that had been delivered yesterday '…I have received an enquiry for a very good situation as a governess. In Bath. I have to send references.'

'Do not look to me for that.' His tone made her frown and he gave an exasperated sigh. 'However good your work has been, you must be all about in your head if you think any respectable family will consider you upon *my* recommendation.'

'Then I shall find others to recommend me,' she said stiffly. 'I cannot afford to miss this opportunity.'

'But you will still come to the ball.'

'If you wish it, sir.'

'Damnation, it has nothing to do with my wishes!' he exclaimed wrathfully. 'I want you to come and dance. I want you to enjoy yourself. As you did at the assembly.'

She turned an indignant glance upon Dominic. 'You cannot order me to enjoy myself!'

'I can, and do.'

The glinting smile in his eyes set her heart bounding in her chest as if desperate to break out. Her mouth was dry. Somehow she tore her eyes away. Somehow she found the strength to speak. 'Absurd, Major. What an arrogant thing to say.'

When they reached West Barton he jumped down and ordered Cloud to stand. He reached up and plucked Zelah from the saddle. For one dizzy moment she was suspended in mid-air, then she slid down into his arms. Her eyes were level with his mouth and she found herself wondering what it would be like to be kissed by him, to have those firm lips gliding over her skin. Her body went hot at the thought. She pushed away from him and thrust the reins into his hand.

'I must go. Thank you for allowing me this holiday, Major Coale. I shall work extra hard tomorrow, to make up for it. There is one final crate of books from Lydcombe that I must unpack, ancient books that might be of interest.'

She knew she was gabbling but she dare not stop, fearing a silence between them. Looking anywhere but in his face, she gave a little nod, picked up her skirts and ran into the house.

Since Reginald was still in Lesserton, Maria had not heard of Robin's death and Zelah passed on the few details she knew. Nicky had been invited to spend the day with one of his school friends and when he returned the news had already reached him. He had been sad, of course, but, as Zelah had predicted, school and his new-found friends occupied so much of his time that he had not seemed overly disturbed and when she peeped into his bedroom before retiring for the night she was relieved to see that he was sleeping peacefully.

Zelah envied Nicky's slumber when she eventually lay down in her own bed, for sleep eluded her. She had enjoyed her day, but riding out with Sally Hensley only served to highlight what she was giving up. But what choice was there? She could not marry any man unless he knew of her past, and what honest man would want her then?

Tossing restlessly in her bed, she glanced towards the window. There was no moonlight to disturb her sleep, but a star twinkled brightly and she remembered just how she had felt all those years ago, dishonoured, betrayed, her life in ruins. She had been fooled by one man—who was to say it couldn't happen twice? Gazing out at the distant star, Zelah renewed her vow never to put herself in any man's power.

Chapter Ten

Life at Rooks Tower was very different with Sally Hensley in residence. She carried Zelah off for long walks or to go riding with her and set the household by the ears with her arrangements for the forthcoming ball.

'We really must use the orangery, now it has been painted and reglazed,' mused Sally, as she toured the gardens with Zelah. 'I will leave that to you, my dear.'

'We will need lamps, then. Perhaps a few coloured ones would look pretty—I could paint some of the glass lanterns.'

'You could? How clever you are, Zelah! We will move some of the statues in there from the house, too, and you can arrange them. And that reminds me,' Sally continued. 'We will need to use the tower room as a bedchamber.'

'No!' Zelah stopped, appalled. 'Surely that is not

necessary? It—it is far removed from the rest of the accommodation.'

'Well, I have thought and thought about it, but we have invited so many cousins and uncles that even if we send the servants into Lesserton we will be overflowing, and I need to keep a room spare for Jasper.'

'But I moved all the clutter from the library up there when you said we would need to open up the library,' objected Zelah. 'I can work up there while all the guests are in residence without being in any-one's way.'

Sally took her arm and urged her to walk on. 'There is one solution…' she said thoughtfully.

'Yes?' Zelah looked at her eagerly.

'We could use it as your bedroom. That would free up another bedchamber.'

'If that is all, we could make up a truckle bed for me in Maria and Reginald's suite.'

'No, that will not do. I have already crammed in a bed for the children's nurse. It will have to be the tower room.' She laughed suddenly. 'Do not look so downcast, Zelah. It will only be for the one night and you will not object to being surrounded by your books and ledgers, I am sure.'

'All this effort for one night,' exclaimed Zelah. 'I wish to goodness I did not have to attend.'

'Nonsense.' Sally patted her arm. 'It will be quite delightful. Now let us go indoors and we will decide which of the marble statues we should move to the orangery.'

With three days to go to the Rooks Tower ball it seemed that the event was all anyone could talk about. Nicky was thrilled when he was told they would all be staying at the house overnight and Maria spent hours deciding which gown she would wear. Only Zelah refused to show any enthusiasm. She declined a new gown, declaring that she would not waste her money on something she would never wear again.

It was almost impossible to think of working when everywhere was in such upheaval, but Zelah did her best. When she arrived at Rooks Tower the following day she was informed that Mrs Hensley had gone into Lesserton and would not be returning until dinnertime, so she hurried off to the tower room, determined to catch up on some of her work. The room was far more cluttered than when she had left it. The small writing desk and the remaining crate of books still stood by the window, but the rest of the furniture had been moved up to make room for an oak tester bed, one of several old beds Sally had discovered dismantled and stored in the nether regions of the house. There were no fluted footposts, no light-as-air draperies. The headboard and canopy were elaborately carved and the two supporting posts were as thick as young trees. She was thankful that the bed-hangings had long ago disappeared and when she peeped beneath the scarlet-and-gold bedcover and cotton sheets, the mattress looked to be quite new. Sally had thoughtfully provided a stepping stool and Zelah climbed up on to the bed. She gazed out through the leaded windows and felt a little *frisson* of excitement at the thought of waking up there and seeing the moors in the early morning light.

Another memory to be locked away.

Zelah slipped off the bed. She must not worry about the future. Her work here was as yet unfinished.

Having windows on three sides made the tower room very light, it also made it very warm with the June sun beating down. Zelah opened all the windows before setting to work, listing another set of books in the ledger. She was writing in details of the last volume when she heard a hasty step on the wooden stairs. She smiled. It was Major Coale. There was no longer any hesitation or unevenness in his step, but no one else moved about the house so quickly, or entered any room with such a burst of energy. He came in now, wearing boots and buckskins and the old jacket she had seen on him the first time they had met, his restless presence filling every corner of the room.

'So this is where you are hiding yourself.'

'Not hiding, sir. The library has been prepared in readiness for your guests' arrival tomorrow. I can as easily work up here.'

'The devil you can.'

She laughed.

'It is true. I bring a few books up here, enter the details, then return them to their place on the shelves. It takes a little longer, but it means I am not in the way.'

'Hmmph.'

He looked around the room, his eyes coming to rest upon the bed.

'Good God, where did that monstrosity come from?'

'Mrs Hensley said it was in storage. Presumably left here by the last owners.'

'More likely abandoned by the builders! It is a relic of the last century at least. It should have been thrown out.'

'Fie, Major, if that had happened then I should have had nothing to sleep on.'

'You are sleeping here?'

'Why, yes, sir. For the night of the ball. Did your sister not tell you?'

'No, she did not,' he replied grimly. 'It is out of the question. It is too remote. There is no accommodation for a maid—'

'I do not have a maid, sir.'

'That is not the point. What was Sal thinking of to put you here?'

'Mrs Hensley needed one last room and if anyone had to have this room I would much rather it was me.' She waved her hand in the direction of the desk. 'For anyone else all this would have to be removed. Believe me, sir, I shall be quite comfortable.'

'As you wish.' He shrugged, as if tired of the conversation.

'Did you want to talk to me, sir?'

'Mmm? No, I just wanted to know where you were. I am going out. There is a dead beech tree in the woods that needs felling and my sister has seen fit to set all my best men to prettifying the grounds ready for this damned ball.'

She said, hoping to mollify him, '*My* sister says it will be the most magnificent event in the county this year.'

'Is that supposed to please me?'

'Yes, it is. Why else are you holding the ball?'

She waited for his answer, her head tilted on one side. His eyes narrowed.

'Another momentary aberration, Miss Pentewan. They are becoming quite common since I met you!'

He swept out again and Zelah returned to her work.

Mrs Graddon brought her a glass of wine and a little bread and ham at noon and while she enjoyed her solitary meal, Zelah considered the final crate of books. She would empty it now and have Graddon take the box away. That would be a little less clutter in the room.

She lifted out the books, three large volumes each in panelled calf. Carefully she opened the first one and read the inscription. It was the first volume of *Vitruvius Britannicus*. She had never seen Lydcombe Park, but she had heard that it was a delightful Palladian mansion. Its owner was quite likely to have taken the design from one of these volumes. Sir Oswald would be quite sorry not to have them, if that was the case. She picked up her duster and carefully ran it over the book before putting it to one side and wiping down the next volume. The cloth snagged on something between the pages. Fearful that she had damaged a loose page she carefully opened the book.

* * *

'Have you seen Major Coale? Is he back?'

Zelah asked the question of a startled footman as she hurried across the great hall. The man stuttered out that he thought he had seen the master crossing the lawn from the woods towards the stables some ten minutes ago. The stables were situated in a block beyond the north-west corner of the house, as far from the library as it was possible to be. With scarcely a pause Zelah set off through the twisting passages to the back of the house, hoping that her quarry did not enter by some other door unknown to her, or walk around to the front entrance and miss her altogether.

Outside the sun was blazing down, and the heat was intense after the shady corridors of the house, disastrous for a lady's complexion, but Zelah did not waste time going back for her bonnet. She set off towards the stables, nearly running in her haste to find Dominic. As she rushed through the arch into the yard she heard voices mixed with the creak of the pump handle and the splash and gurgle of water. The sight that met her eyes made her stop in her tracks, open-mouthed.

Dominic was bowed down with his head under the pump while one of the stable lads worked the handle, drenching his head and shoulders with clear, cold water. He straightened and shook himself like a dog, sending diamond droplets of water flying in every direction. Zelah was unable to look away. He was naked to the waist and she could plainly see the white line of the sabre slash running from his left shoulder and across the dark shadow of hair on his chest. But it was not the jagged scar that held her spellbound, after all she had seen that before. It was the sight of his powerful torso, tanned from working out of doors, the muscles flexing as he grabbed a cloth and began to dry himself. She stared, taking in the broad shoulders, the flat stomach with its tapering line of hair that disappeared into his breeches. A powerful ache tore at her insides. Even the man who had taken her virginity had not roused such a powerful physical longing.

Dominic stilled when he saw her, slowly lowering the cloth. He resisted the temptation to hold the towel against his chest, covering the scar. She continued to stare at him in silence. What the devil was she doing in the yard? He threw the drying cloth at the grinning stable hand and barked out a command which sent the lad scurrying away. The movement woke Zelah from her trance and she blinked, a hot flush flooding her cheeks.

'I—um—I came to find you.'

He spread his hands. 'Well, here I am.' Her confusion angered him and he said roughly, 'I am sorry if the sight of me disturbs you.'

He picked up his shirt and threw it over his head. His shoulders were still damp and the soft linen stuck to his skin, but at least he was covered.

'No, no...' She trailed off, then her flush deepened as the meaning of his words hit her. 'Oh heavens, please do not think I was upset by the scar! I hardly noticed. That is, I was looking...' Her eyes were still fixed on his chest, but the look in them was not horror, or revulsion. It was something he had not seen in a woman's eyes for a long time. Desire. His heart swelled and he stood a little taller. Drawing a deep breath, she started again. 'I have found something—a paper—in the tower room. I think you should see it.'

He picked up his discarded waistcoat and jacket and came towards her.

'Propriety would suggest I should dress first, but there seems to be some urgency in your coming to find me.'

'I *do* want you to see this as soon as possible.'

His lips quirked. 'Are you sure you can cope with my, er, informal attire?'

She saw the glinting smile in his eyes and her chin went up. 'I am sure it is no concern to me!'

He laughed. 'Perhaps not, but I will change, all the same. Give me five minutes and I will follow you.'

She stood for a moment, uncertain how to respond to his teasing. Then she picked up her skirts and swept ahead of him back to the house.

Zelah went back to the tower room, wishing she could lock the door against the major. She had been shocked by her reaction to seeing his naked body. She had allowed herself to be carried away once before, but then she had thought herself in love, and if she was honest she had been more anxious to please her lover than herself. Their love-making had consisted of one fumbling, disappointing night and the consequences for Zelah had been disastrous. She had had no difficulty after that in eschewing all men and could honestly say that she was content to lead a celibate life—until now.

She pressed her hands to her stomach. Her body felt strangely light and out of balance. She looked around in a panic, her eyes alighting on the huge bed. She could not see him here, in this room!

Zelah ran to the desk and was about to pick up the manuscript and carry it to the library when she heard him coming up the stairs. It was too late to remove, she must concentrate on her news. He was hardly through the door before she began to speak.

'I emptied the final crate from Lydcombe Park this morning. It contained all three volumes of Campbell's *Vitruvius Britannicus*.'

'Are you suggesting I should remodel Rooks Tower into a Palladian mansion?'

She threw him a scornful glance but was grateful for his tone—she could deal with his light banter.

'It is what is inside the second volume that is important.'

Carefully she opened the book to display a single sheet of parchment, covered with closely packed rows of bold, black handwriting.

'It is a contract for the sale of Lydcombe Park.' Zelah could hardly keep the excitement out of her voice.

'But not a recent one. It is dated 1779.'

'I know, but it describes in detail the eastern boundary of the park and look here—it says that the easternmost point of the boundary is marked with a large stone in Prickett Wood. The charter that was produced at the hearing mentioned a boundary stone and everyone thought it was the marker that used to be on the lane running past the bluebell wood.'

'And that was removed over fifty years ago,' said

Dominic slowly. 'At least twenty years before this document was written.'

'So there must be another marker stone, in the wood itself. Could we go and look? If we could find it—'

'No. We must proceed cautiously. Evanshaw may well know about the marker. That may be why he has his men patrolling the wood, but they are more likely to shoot you than ask what you are doing there. We should take this document to Buckland. He will be able to verify it and then he can ask Sir Arthur to authorise a search.' He carefully rolled up the manuscript and tied it with a ribbon. 'Sally has taken my curricle, but I expect her back any time now. Once she is returned I will take you and this document to West Barton.'

Zelah frowned. 'Could I not take it now? I could walk…'

'Are you so keen to get this to your brother-in-law?'

'Well, most likely he will not even be at home, but I will not rest until he has seen it.'

Dominic hesitated, then shook his head. 'No. It is too hot for such exertion. I will take you in the curricle.'

His autocratic tone made her long to retort, but

she closed her lips firmly together. Dominic saw her response and his mouth quirked upwards.

'You must have patience, madam. Your family would berate me soundly if I allowed you to walk home in this heat.'

He was right, she knew it. She looked at the manuscript.

'I suppose it would be foolish to set off yet. But after finding this I do not think I can sit down and work.'

She risked looking at him and immediately realised her mistake. Once he had captured her glance she could not look away. She was trapped. The smile in his eyes deepened. He lifted one hand and gently rubbed the backs of his fingers over her cheek.

'There is one way to pass the time.'

His eyes dropped to her mouth and she responded by running her tongue over her lips. She should step back, but her wayward limbs refused to move. She was drawn like a magnet to the man in front of her. He had changed into a clean shirt, waistcoat and buckskins, but without a jacket the white sleeves billowed out, making the breadth of his shoulders even more impressive. He dominated the space before her and she could not look away.

Very slowly he lowered his head and kissed her. It was the gentlest of touches, his lips gliding across her mouth. She closed her eyes, almost swooning as desire swamped her. His kiss deepened as he sensed her reaction, his mouth working on her lips until they parted and his tongue flickered, seeking her own. She wound her free hand around his neck, pulling him closer while he plundered her mouth, his tongue dipping, diving, driving her senses wild. She responded by pushing against him, returning kiss for kiss. When he released her mouth and raised his head she gave a whimper, turning her face up, standing on tiptoe as she reached up for him.

He put his hands on her shoulders, holding her away from him, his eyes hard and bright.

'You are not…repelled by my disfigurement?'

'Repelled? No.' She reached out one hand and gently placed her fingers on his ragged cheek, then she brought up the other hand to pull his head down until she could kiss his scarred brow, his cheek, his jaw.

Dominic put up his hand to cover hers and dragged it to his mouth, pressing a kiss into the palm before pulling her into his arms again. She lifted her face, inviting his kiss and eagerly returning it as he pushed aside the muslin scarf that covered her neck and shoulders, his thumbs gently rubbing along her collarbones. She threw back her head as his mouth grazed her throat and moved on to kiss the soft swell of her breasts. Zelah trembled, the desire that had been smouldering inside her bursting into a flame that threatened to consume her, but even as she felt her body slipping out of control she began to fight. She pushed against Dominic and immediately he let her go.

With a sob she turned away. 'Oh, what have I done?'

'Zelah.'

'Oh, do not call me that! I am—must be—Miss Pentewan to you.'

'Of course.' His voice was harsh. 'I should have known. You were merely taking pity—'

'No!' She spun round, saying indignantly, 'What I feel for you is *not* pity.'

'Then why push me away?'

She put her hands to her burning cheeks, forcing herself to tell him the truth.

'I was afraid that if I did not stop you now I would not be able to do so. You—you arouse such feelings in me as I have never known.'

As she spoke she fumbled to straighten her neckerchief. Dominic pushed her hands aside and carefully rearranged the folds of muslin decorously across her shoulders.

He said quietly, 'Such feelings are natural between a man and a woman.'

'Not to me! I cannot afford such a luxury.'

'It is not a luxury, it is a blessing.' He slid his hands down her arms and grasped her fingers. 'Believe me, I would not have kissed you if I didn't think you wanted it, too. I saw the way you looked at me in the yard.'

She pulled away, confused and embarrassed. 'Fine words, sir. It is very easy for you to return to your rakish ways!'

'Hell and confound it, madam, do you think I am toying with you?'

'Of course you are. But it is partly my fault, for coming here to work, putting myself in your power.'

'My power!' He laughed savagely. 'You make me sound like the villain of a melodrama.'

'And that is just what you are,' she flashed. 'With your black scowls and tortured looks—' She stopped, her hands flying to her mouth. 'Oh, I should not have said that, I am so sorry—'

'Nay, why should you hold back? I cannot deny that I have the physiognomy for a rogue!'

'That is not what I meant.'

'Isn't it? Do I not feature as the villain in your fantasy, a grotesque being who has ensnared you, drawing you in against your will? Do I not exert an evil fascination?'

'No, no,' she said unhappily. 'You wilfully misunderstand me. I will not stay here—I shall walk home now and never return.'

At that moment a sudden crack of thunder ripped the air. Zelah gave a little cry of fright and shrank towards Dominic. Instinctively his arms closed around her.

'So,' he muttered, 'the thunder frightens you more than I do.'

Zelah extricated herself from his embrace and said with as much dignity as she could muster, 'I never said you frightened me. I merely wish to quit this house—and you!—as soon as possible.'

The quiet patter of raindrops intensified to a roar. Dominic went over to close the window.

'Well, you can hardly walk to West Barton now.' He glanced back and saw that she was looking out at the rain sheeting down, her bottom lip caught between her teeth. He said coldly, 'Do not fret, madam. I will not inflict my presence on you a moment longer than necessary. Once my sister returns, Sawley shall drive you to West Barton.'

He turned on his heel and stormed out. Damn the woman! Did she think he was made of stone? He was no saint, but she would turn him into a veritable Lothario. He had not meant to kiss her, but she had looked so damned alluring with the flush on her cheeks and those sparkling eyes.

And she had wanted him to kiss her, he would stake his life on that. She had been right to stop him, another few moments and he would have made good use of that ancient bed. But why had she ripped up at him? Why was she so afraid to admit the attraction?

He had reached the yellow salon by this time and saw the answer in the mirrors. A dozen reflections of his scarred face. Gritting his teeth, he strode through the room. She had touched that scar, kissed it, but in the end the thought of his disfigured body was too much for her. Well, the sooner she was removed from Rooks Tower the better!

It was another hour before Sally returned in the curricle. Dominic took an umbrella out as the carriage pulled up on the drive, but when he informed his groom that he was to take Miss Pentewan to West Barton, Sawley shook his head.

'Not with this team, sir. I've nursed 'em this far, but I don't want to take 'em any farther.'

'We had a slight mishap as we were leaving Lesserton.' Sally took Dominic's proffered hand and alighted. 'The doctor's hack broke loose from the smithy and charged into us. The off-side horse took a blow to his thigh.'

'Aye, and t'other's started limping,' added Sawley. 'I think he might've taken a kick on his fetlock.'

Dominic handed the umbrella to Sally and went to inspect the horse, running his hands gently over the suspect leg.

'You are right. It's beginning to swell.'

'Pray don't blame Sawley,' Sally implored him, observing his black frown. 'He did well to avoid overturning us. You can imagine that everything was confusion, until the blacksmith's apprentice managed to quieten the poor runaway creature.'

Dominic straightened, exhaling. Just his luck for this to happen today. He waved Sawley away.

'Take the team round to the stables and look after them, Jem, and have my match greys harnessed to the curricle. I shall drive to West Barton myself.'

Thus when Zelah presented herself at the front door it was to find Major Coale holding the reins. Briefly he explained the situation, adding when he observed her hesitation, 'I am afraid Sawley must stay here to look after the horses and I will allow no one else to drive my greys.'

For a moment Zelah thought it might be a ploy, but Dominic looked as dissatisfied with the arrangement as she was, so she allowed herself to be handed up into the carriage.

'You have the manuscript?'

'Yes.' She held up the rolled parchment, safely wrapped in oilskin.

They set off, Dominic holding the greys to a sedate trot along the drive. The rain had eased, but the grey clouds were still threatening and Zelah hoped they would not have to stop to put up the hood. It was bad enough to have to sit next to a man whose whole demeanour was one of barely controlled anger, she had no wish to be trapped in a confined space with him. She stared ahead, trying to maintain a dignified silence, but her conscience was making her uncomfortable. The tension between them was palpable and they had not gone far before she could no longer bear the strained atmosphere.

'Major Coale!' She clasped and unclasped her hands, forcing herself to speak. 'What happened earlier, it was as much my fault as yours. For me to say such terrible things to you—I am ashamed. It was unjust and...and I beg your pardon.'

His countenance did not change. Not by the flicker of an eye did he acknowledge that she had spoken. Zelah's spirits sank. He could not forgive her.

She ought not to be surprised. She had intended

to wound him and had done so magnificently. She was mortified now even to think of it and to be barred from Rooks Tower—and its owner—for ever would be a fitting punishment. A silent tear slid down her cheek.

'My own conduct was reprehensible.' Dominic spoke without taking his eyes from the road. She sucked in a ragged breath.

'Oh, if you only knew how much I wish my words unspoken!'

'That is impossible, but if we both regret what happened this afternoon, if we admit that we were both at fault, could we not put it behind us?'

She looked down. 'I had determined never to come back to Rooks Tower.'

'That would be sad indeed. Is that what you really want?'

She blinked back the tears. 'Not at all.'

He took one hand from the reins and reached out to cover hers. 'Then let us cry friends, Zelah.'

'Do…do you think we can?'

He turned his head to smile at her. 'I have a damnable temper, my dear, but if my black scowls don't frighten you…'

'They do not. They never have.'

'Then, yes, I think we can be friends.'

Her fingers twisted under his and she clasped his

hand. She said shyly, 'Then I would like that very much, Major.'

'Dominic.'

'Dominic.' The name rolled off her tongue. She relished each syllable.

The sun breaking through the clouds lifted her spirits, so much so that when Dominic mentioned the forthcoming ball she was able to reply with perfect candour.

'I am glad I am not to be excluded, I am looking forward to it, very much.'

'And will you save one dance for me?'

'As many as you wish,' she replied recklessly. 'I am unlikely to have many partners, I know so few people.'

'You underrate yourself, my dear—' He broke off to guide the curricle through the gates of West Barton. A closed carriage was already standing at the door.

'Well, that is very good timing,' declared Zelah. 'Here is Reginald just arrived home. Now you will be able to give him the charter yourself.'

Dominic brought his team to a stop and a groom ran out to hold the greys. Zelah climbed down and shook out her skirts, glancing towards the carriage where her brother-in-law had alighted and was waiting while another gentleman clambered out.

'Reginald has brought a guest home,' she murmured, as Dominic came round to join her. She handed him the manuscript. 'It makes no odds, you can still give this to him, it is too important to wait and I am sure he will be...'

Her words trailed away. The fashionably dressed gentleman beside Reginald smiled, lifting his hat from his carefully arranged blond curls.

'Zelah, my dear. How good to see you again.'

Chapter Eleven

Zelah could not speak. She did not resist when the gentleman picked up her hand and pressed a kiss upon her fingers, holding them for far longer than was polite. He looked up and smiled into her eyes and the years fell away. She was eighteen again, gauche and tongue-tied. Dominic shifted impatiently at her side and she pulled her hand free, giving only the slightest nod of recognition.

Reginald was beaming.

'What a stroke of luck, my dear. I met Lerryn at the White Hart. Major Coale, let me present Mr Timothy Lerryn to you. His father is the squire in my wife's home town of Cardinham.'

Timothy's eyes flickered over Dominic's scarred face, but his smile never wavered.

'I am travelling to Bristol and I thought, since it is on my way, that I would call upon Mrs Buckland at West Barton. When Buckland told me that

Miss Zelah Pentewan was staying here too, I could hardly believe my good fortune.'

His smile had turned to a caress, but it only made her shiver. Reginald laughed and patted him on the shoulder.

'What could I do but invite him to join us for dinner. And you too, Major, if you are free.'

'Thank you, I regret that I cannot stay. I came only to give you this.' He handed Reginald the manuscript. 'It relates to the dispute with Sir Oswald. Miss Pentewan will explain it all.'

Reginald's eyes lit up.

'Another charter, is it? This could be important. Come along to my study now and tell me everything. My man will look after your horses. Lerryn, you will not object if I leave you with Zelah?'

'On the contrary.' Timothy Lerryn held out his arm to her. 'We are such old friends I am delighted to have her to myself.'

Zelah wanted to say that *she* objected, but Reginald bore Dominic away, leaving her with Timothy Lerryn. His blue eyes roved over her.

'You have not changed one jot.'

She had thought the same of him, but now that he was closer she could see that he was different. He was still a handsome man, in a florid way, but the last four years had added inches to his waist and tiny lines at the sides of his mouth and around his eyes. Lines of dissipation, she thought.

'What do you want here?'

He looked pained. 'I came to find you. I heard you were visiting your sister.'

Once such words would have delighted her. She would have given anything to hear them. Now her lip curled.

'You can have nothing to say to me.'

'How can you speak so?' He followed her into the empty hall. 'Remember what we were to each other.'

She stopped. 'No one here knows of that!' she hissed at him. 'I do not want them to know.'

'And nor shall they. I did not come here to make trouble for you, Zelah. I wanted merely to see you.' He lowered his voice. 'I have missed you.'

'You are a married man.'

'That was a mistake. I see that now.'

'Ha!' She turned from him. 'I will take you to my sister. You shall have dinner here, but then you must go, do you understand?'

Head high, she led the way into the drawing room. Maria was reading to Nicky, but she stopped when they came in, regarding Mr Lerryn with a polite, questioning air. She listened to his explanation, flattered if a little bemused that he should break his journey to see them.

Zelah made her excuses and went off to change her gown. Her nerves were jangling, not only from the events at Rooks Tower but also from the unexpected appearance of Timothy Lerryn. He said he had come to find her and that could only mean trouble.

She tarried as long as she dared, but when she returned to the drawing room she was surprised to find Major Coale taking wine there. The sight of Dominic and Timothy Lerryn talking together did nothing to calm her nerves. She could not help comparing the two men—Dominic no longer turned the injured side of his face away from the room, but the sight of his terrible scars only added to his dark, powerful presence. By comparison she thought Timothy's tightly waisted coat and fashionable blond locks looked positively effete.

She had to steel herself not to run away as Timothy crossed the room to her.

'My dear Zelah—Miss Pentewan,' he corrected himself smoothly, seeing the flash of anger in her eyes. 'Your brother-in-law was explaining to me about the current land dispute going on in Lesserton. I understand you were instrumental in finding a new document that will help the villagers' case.'

'Yes. I certainly hope that will be so.'

She went to leave, but he put his hand under her elbow. 'Will you allow me to escort you to a chair?

She quickly pulled her arm free. A swift glance assured her that Maria and Reginald were engaged in conversation with Dominic so she walked to the bay window where they would not be overheard. Timothy followed her, as she knew he would.

'Let me make one thing plain,' she began. 'I am not your dear anything and I do not wish to renew our acquaintance. After tonight I never want to see you again.'

'I am very sorry to hear that.'

'Are you? I should have thought you would be pleased to know that I am making a new life for myself, that does not involve you.'

'Ah, yes, your sister told me you are working for Major Coale, as his librarian. Are you sure that is wise?'

She eyed him coldly. 'I do not know what you mean.'

'With your, er, history.'

She fought down the blaze of anger at his words and the knowing look that went with them. 'No one knows about my *history* here and my employment at Rooks Tower is perfectly respectable.'

'People might not think so, if they were to know the truth about you…'

'Which they never will,' she flashed, 'unless you tell them!'

He put his hand on his heart. 'My dear Zelah, it is not my intention to say a word.' He reached for her hand, but she snatched it away. His eyes hardened. 'Of course, if you are unfriendly I might inadvertently let something slip.'

His hand remained outstretched, the challenge in his eyes unmistakable. Reluctantly she gave him her fingers. He lifted them to his lips.

'There, that is not so bad, is it? Now, as long as you are sweet to me, your secret is safe.'

She put up her chin. 'It is *our* secret, Mr Lerryn, and if it was to become public then you would not appear in any very honourable light.'

His grip tightened. 'True, but a man's reputation will survive the odd scandal—a woman's good name is a very different matter.'

Zelah clamped her lips closed upon the angry retort that rose within her and with a slight nod she moved off, inwardly seething.

Disinclined to join the others, she moved to the piano on the pretext of tidying the pile of music, but Dominic soon followed, carrying two glasses of wine. He held one out to her.

'You look troubled. I am sorry if you did not wish me to stay. I merely came to pay my respects to your sister and see how Nicky goes on.'

The roughness of his tone rubbed at her raw nerves.

'Your presence does not trouble me.' She forced herself to smile. 'I have a headache. The weather…'

Her gaze shifted to Tim Lerryn, who had come up. She kept the smile fixed on her lips as she hid her dismay at his interruption.

'Poor Zelah never could endure thunder. The storm this afternoon was particularly bad, was it not? However, the sky is clearing now and I am in hopes that the weather will improve for the remainder of my visit.'

'How long are you staying in Lesserton?' Dominic enquired.

'Oh, a few days more, at least. Having caught up with my friends again we have a great deal to talk about, do we not, my dear?'

Zelah felt her cheeks burn with anger and embarrassment at his familiar tone. She dare not risk her voice, so she turned her attention to straightening the sleeve of her gown.

'I shall not see much of them tomorrow, I fear,' Timothy continued. 'Mrs Buckland tells me the family are joining you at Rooks Tower for your summer ball, Major Coale. I hope the weather holds for you.'

'You are welcome to join us for the dancing, if you wish, Mr Lerryn. My sister has already sent out all the invitations, but I will see to it you are not turned away if you present yourself at the door.'

Zelah froze.

'Why, that is exceedingly kind of you, sir, most obliging, is it not, Zelah?' Timothy beamed with pleasure. 'It means I shall have the opportunity to dance with you again, my dear. By heaven, that will bring back some memories, eh?'

She murmured something incoherent. After listening to Timothy repeat his gratitude, Dominic gave a little nod and walked away. He exchanged a few words with Maria and took his leave. Beside her, Timothy expelled a hissing breath.

'Dashed ugly brute, ain't he? Didn't know where to look when we was first introduced, my eyes kept going back to that damned scar.'

'One hardly notices it after a while.'

'*You* might not, but others will, take my word for it. I heard about this Major Coale of yours in Lesserton. Allowing villagers grazing rights, letting them forage in his woods—trying to buy his way into their favours, I don't doubt.'

'You know nothing about him,' snapped Zelah.

His brows rose. 'Oho, and you do? I hope you are not growing too attached to the Major, my dear. He won't be interested in the likes of you, at least not in any honourable way.' He leaned closer. 'Better to let me look after you…'

She hunched a shoulder and turned away, just as Reginald came up to escort her to dinner. Zelah placed her fingers on his arm, steeling herself for an interminable evening.

'Ah. I did not expect to see you here today, Miss Pentewan.'

Zelah looked up as Dominic strode into the library. His formal address did not escape her notice. After Timothy's remarks yesterday perhaps it was for the best. She could be formal, too.

'Good morning, Major Coale. I wanted to finish listing the books on mathematics today. I understood you and your guests were going riding, so the library would be empty.'

He spread his hands, looking down at the buckskins. She wished he had not drawn her attention to them, for they clung to his powerful thighs in a way that made her feel quite weak. 'I am dressed for riding, as you see. I was on my way to the stables when I heard a noise in here and came to investigate. Your devotion to your work is admirable, but it is the summer ball this evening.'

'I am aware of it. My sister is bringing my ball gown. I shall go upstairs and change when she arrives.' She was quick to note his frowning look and added, 'Mrs Hensley has no objection to my working here today.'

'Hmm.' The major walked over to the window while Zelah continued to pull the books off the shelf. She was about to take them upstairs to the tower room when he spoke again. 'I thought you would spend the day with your friend Mr Lerryn.'

She stopped. 'Mr Lerryn is not my friend.'

'Oh?' He turned to face her. 'I thought he was damned friendly towards you yesterday.'

'Mr Lerryn is an old acquaintance, nothing more. He is a married man.'

'Married! His behaviour towards you did not give me that impression.'

Zelah had no answer to that. Silently she started towards the door. In two strides he had crossed the room and blocked her way.

'And you were not exactly spurning his advances.'

The accusation hurt her, but she could not deny it. She merely gave him a scorching look and went to walk past him. He caught her arm.

'Let me warn you to be careful, madam. I'll not have an employee of mine embroiled in a scandal.'

Her face flamed. Anger, indignation and dismay warred within her breast. Silently she shook off his arm and stalked off. Only when she reached the seclusion of the tower room did she allow her self-possession to crumble. She dropped the books on to the desk and sank down on the chair, shaking.

Scandal.

How could it be avoided? If she allowed Timothy Lerryn to dance with her, to flirt with her this evening, she risked Dominic's wrath, possibly even dismissal. If she followed her inclination and refused to have anything to do with him, she knew Timothy would not hesitate to make her past known to everyone.

She tried to get on with her work, doggedly listing details of each book in her ledger, but Dominic's uncompromising words kept coming back to her. He would not tolerate a scandal. Perhaps she should not go to the ball, but then Dominic would know she was avoiding Timothy Lerryn and draw his own conclusions. Even worse, Timothy might decide he had nothing to lose by exposing her. At length she admitted defeat, put down her pen and dropped her head in her hands. Whatever happened she was ruined.

Eventually the heat roused her from her reverie and she went to open the window, looking down at the gardens shimmering in the summer heat, while beyond the park she could see the ragged outline of the moor, bare but majestic above the trees. She stared about her, trying to memorise every detail. It might be the last time she ever enjoyed this view. She had been a fool to think the past could be so easily left behind.

A party of riders crossed the park, cantering towards the house. Dominic was easily recognisable on his grey mare and she spotted Sally Hensley beside him, tall and elegant in the saddle. The rest of the party were the relatives and friends invited to stay for the summer ball and she knew none of them. Zelah had begged Sally to wait until this evening's dinner to introduce her, not wanting the other guests to see her in her role as librarian. Now her caution seemed laughable. If she did not dance to Tim Lerryn's tune, then they would soon know her as something far worse and how embarrassing that would be for Dominic, when he discovered she had deceived him.

Yesterday Dominic had asked her to cry friends with him. What sort of friend was it that kept secrets? She squared her shoulders. What was it her father had always said? Tell the truth and shame the devil. If Dominic was to learn the truth about her, then she would tell him herself.

She ran down the stairs and made her way to the great hall, where the riding party was milling around, chattering and laughing. As she hoped, no one spared a second glance for the dowdy little figure in her grey gown and linen apron hovering in the doorway of the yellow salon, but she managed to catch Dominic's eye. With a word here, a smile there, he left his guests and made his way across the hall. It occurred to her that he looked very much at home amongst his friends. He was no longer the surly recluse she had first met. Surely she could take some credit for that? The thought gave her courage as he approached, even though his eyes were as hard and cold as the stone on the moor.

'If I might beg a word with you, Major?'

He did not disappoint her. With a slight nod he led her to his study.

'Well?' He closed the door, shutting out the laughing, chattering crowd. 'I perceive it must be important for you to come down from your eyrie to seek me out.'

'It is.' She dared not stop to think of the consequences now.

'Then will you not sit down?'

He gestured to the armchair beside the empty fireplace and once she was seated he pulled up a chair to face her. She would have preferred him to keep his distance, to stand over her, looking down in judgement like some omnipotent deity.

'You said this morning that you would not countenance a scandal.' She looked down at her hands clasped in her lap. 'Before I sit at your table for dinner tonight there is something you should know about me.' She stopped. How would he react? Would he have her escorted from the house immediately? 'I wanted to tell you about myself, before you heard it from anyone else.'

He sat back in his chair. 'Then tell me.' His expression was cold, his tone indifferent. Her courage faltered. He said brusquely, 'Go on.'

Zelah's hands were clasped so tightly her knuckles went white. There was no going back now.

'There was a man, in Cardinham. He called himself a gentleman. He was handsome and so very, very charming. I suppose I was flattered by his attentions.' She screwed up her courage to continue. 'When he said he would marry me I believed him. I allowed him to…to bed me. It happened only once, but that was enough to get me with child.'

'And then I suppose he disowned you.'

His dispassionate tone made it easier for her to continue.

'Yes. My parents were deeply hurt, but they refused to abandon me, even though I would not tell them who the father was. I thought it best that everyone should think it was a stranger, a traveller from the annual fair that passed through our town each summer. I wanted no repercussions. It was my mistake and I would suffer the consequences. I was sent away to live with an aunt until my confinement.'

She stopped. She felt physically sick, but there would be no relief until she had finished her story.

'The baby was stillborn—a just punishment for my wickedness, I suppose. After a period of recuperation I returned to Cardinham. Everyone was told I had gone away for my health, but you know what villages are, I doubt if anyone really believed that. There were sly glances, whispers. No possibility of finding work with any local family.' She risked a quick glance at him. He had not moved, his face remained inscrutable. 'Reginald met Maria while she was on a visit to Bath two years ago and married her immediately. He knows my…unfortunate history, but he is very good and agreed to my coming to live with them for a short while. I hoped I would be able to make a new life for myself. I thought I could be respectable.' She lifted her chin. 'I *am* respectable. That is why, when you kissed me yesterday, I could not let it go on.'

The silence that followed was unnerving. She dared not look up again, but threaded her handkerchief through her fingers, over and over.

'And why are you telling me this now? Ah, but you said, did you not, someone else is likely to tell me?'

'Yes.'

'Mr Lerryn.'

'Yes.'

'He was your lover.'

She flinched. 'How did you know?'

'From what you told me this morning, and what I observed yesterday. He has threatened to expose you, I suppose?'

She flushed. He made it sound so sordid. 'Yes.'

He rose and paced the room once, twice. Zelah remained in her seat, her head bowed. He said abruptly, 'Do you still love him?'

'No. I doubt if I ever did. It was a foolish infatuation. I was very young and he was very…experienced.'

'What does he want for his silence?'

'My…co-operation.'

His angry snort told her he knew just what that would involve.

'Damnation, if I had known I would not have invited him to come here this evening.'

She raised her head. 'Why *did* you invite him?'

He scowled. 'Your sister wants you to marry, and I, too, consider it would be the best thing for you,' he said bluntly. 'I thought…Lerryn seemed to be keen to fix his interest with you. I did not know yesterday that he was married!'

Zelah stared at him. 'So you thought to promote his suit?'

'And why not? He is a squire's son.'

A cold hand wrapped itself around her heart. She jumped to her feet. 'Oh, why is everyone so keen to marry me off?'

'Because it would be a better future for you than a governess. Good God, there is no knowing what might befall you. Believe me, I know this world. There are many men, outwardly respectable, who would not hesitate to seduce a servant. If you marry a man of means you will have the protection of his name, servants, a carriage. A family.'

'No.' She shook her head, tears starting to her eyes.

He caught her arms. 'So you have been hurt once and lost a baby, but that need not be the end. There are other men than Lerryn. Good men.' His grip tightened.

She closed her eyes, but the tears squeezed out and made hot tracks down her cheeks. She heard him sigh. He put one arm about her shoulders, holding her to him while he pulled a clean white handkerchief from his pocket.

'You should not be anyone's drudge, Zelah.' He wiped her cheeks gently. 'You should be respected, loved.'

He put his fingers under her chin and forced her to look up at him. His grey eyes were no longer hard rock, but something hotter, darker. Her head was thrown back against his arm, he had only to lower his head and their lips would meet. Her heart was beating such a heavy tattoo she thought he must hear it. Her breasts had tightened and ached for his touch. She placed her hand on his chest and felt the powerful thud of his own heart against her palm. With sudden, startling clarity she knew she wanted him to kiss her, more than anything in the world.

'No.' The heat faded from his eyes. Gently he released her.

Unable to speak, she watched him walk away from her, his shoulders straight, his back rigidly upright as he continued. 'You need not fear Lerryn.

I will not turn him away tonight, that would give rise to the type of gossip we are trying to avoid, but I will make sure he does not trouble you. Now, I have detained you long enough. It wants but a few hours to dinner, so I suggest you finish your work. I have given orders that the library is to be opened to my guests tonight, so perhaps you will make sure it is looking its best before you go off to change your gown.'

He turned back, smiling, urbane, his face shuttered. She was dismissed.

Chapter Twelve

Zelah made her way back to the library. She kept her head up as she passed through the salon where an army of servants were fitting fresh candles to the chandeliers and polishing the mirrors. The carpet had already been rolled away and the floor cleared for dancing. The double doors to the library would be thrown open once the ball commenced, but now she closed them, preferring to be alone with her thoughts. Not that they were very coherent. Dominic would protect her from Timothy Lerryn's threats, she was sure, but he had made it plain that he had no interest in her. She had known that all along, of course. He liked her, he respected her work and he was anxious for her happiness, which he thought would be best achieved by marriage. To someone else. In all likelihood he was right, but this foolish heart of hers had decided otherwise, and Zelah knew that if she could not have Dominic Coale she would have no one.

'Well, you had your plans, you were determined to earn your own living.' She spoke aloud as she walked around the empty library. 'You should be happy. Nothing has changed.'

But in her heart Zelah knew that nothing could ever be the same again.

A burst of laughter from the salon reminded her of the servants next door. She hurried off to the tower room, where she made a few last entries into the ledger and began gathering together the books to be returned to the library. She was soon joined by a harassed-looking Hannah bearing a tray.

'Mrs Graddon thought you might like some lemonade, miss, seeing as how she has made plenty for this evening.' She wiped her hand across her brow. 'My, 'tis hot, miss. I've opened the windows in the library, to let in some air.'

'Thank you, this is very welcome.' Zelah took the lemonade and sipped it. 'This must be a great upheaval for you, after living so quietly.'

'Aye, it's all at sixes and sevens. We have hired more girls from the village, though, the master insisting that Mrs Graddon should have all the help she needs, as well as the grand French chef who is come down from Lunnon to take over the kitchen.

But 'tis good to see the master taking his rightful place,' Hannah continued. 'And I hear that Master Nicky is coming to stay and his little brother, too, so I hopes I might be allowed to wait on them, dear little mites.'

She bustled away, leaving Zelah feeling slightly more cheerful. There was a definite buzz of excitement around Rooks Tower. The old house had come alive with so many people in residence.

Zelah took her empty glass back to the kitchens and begged a piece of lemon to clean the ink from her fingers. Once she had done that she checked the clock. There was a good hour yet before she needed to disappear and transform herself from employee to house guest and there were still a dozen or more books in the tower room that needed to be returned to the library. She ran to fetch them. She found it was still possible to lose herself in her work, matching up books, wondering if Ehret's botanical prints should be placed beside the works of philosophy and science rather than with the book entitled *Modern Voyages and Travels.* As she straightened the volumes of *Vitruvius Britannicus* she remembered the paper she had found and wondered if it would prove useful to the villagers in fighting Sir Oswald Evanshaw's claims.

Sir Oswald would be at the ball that evening.

Zelah had been present when Sally and Dominic had discussed it. Zelah remembered how flattered she had been when Dominic asked her what she thought. She had agreed with Sally that it would be impolitic to exclude him.

Now, standing alone in the library, a little flush of pleasure nudged through her depression. Dominic valued her opinion. Despite everything, he clearly wanted her to be present at the ball, so perhaps he would dance with her as he had at the assembly. The thought cheered her immensely and, determined to remain cheerful, she began to sing as she placed the last few books on the shelves.

'Well now. Minerva, in her element.'

The deep, warm voice held a laugh and she swung around, smiling when she saw Dominic. He was sitting astride the open window, his back against the jamb with one booted foot upon the sill. Her smile wavered. It *was* Dominic, and yet…he looked slightly more modish than usual. The top-boots seemed to fit more snugly, the buckskins were a shade lighter. His riding jacket was just as tightly fitting, but the buttons were larger and his neckcloth was a froth of white folds. His dark hair glowed like a raven's wing in the sunlight, but it had obviously been cut by a master. The eyes were a shade lighter, more blue than grey, and his face, that beautiful face with its smooth planes and lean jawline, was just too perfect. On both sides. Her hands flew to her mouth.

'You must be Lord Markham.'

With a laugh he swung himself into the room and came towards her, tossing his hat, gloves and crop on to a chair. 'How do you do—no, no, none of that.' He reached out and caught her hand, pulling her up as she sank into a curtsy. 'I should be saluting *you*, fair Minerva!'

He bowed over her hand and she chuckled, even as he placed a kiss upon her fingers.

'I am merely the librarian, my lord.'

'You are not merely anything. You are important enough to be invited to the ball.' His eyes were laughing at her, joyous, carefree, with none of the sadness she detected in his brother. He continued. 'You are Miss Pentewan, are you not? My sister told me all about you when she wrote.'

Her cheeks grew hot. 'There is nothing to tell.'

'No?'

It was impossible not to warm to the viscount. His likeness to Dominic would have endeared him to her in any event, but she found his charm irresistible and she responded, quite at her ease, 'No. I am merely going about my business here.'

'That in itself is unusual. A female in the library.'

'I am very grateful to Major Coale for the opportunity.'

'Sal speaks very highly of you.'

'She is most kind.'

She could think of nothing more to say, and with a little smile of apology she went back to tidying away the books.

'I hear my brother is improved a great deal.'

'You have not seen him yet?'

'No. I have only just arrived and was taking a look around the house when I heard you singing.'

'Then I beg your pardon for distracting you.'

'I was not distracted, I was enchanted.'

The compliment came easily to his lips and she giggled. 'I think you are trying to charm me, my lord.'

'Would you object to that?'

She considered the question. 'That depends upon your reason for doing so. If it is purely to put me at my ease, then, no, but if your intention is more mischievous then I do object, most strongly.'

His brows lifted. 'Straight talking, madam.'

'But necessary, sir. I may be an employee, but I am not to be imposed upon. I would not want to fall out with you.'

He laughed. 'Nor I with you, Miss Pentewan. I shall treat you with the utmost respect.'

Her lips twitched. 'Very well, my lord, then I beg you will leave me to finish tidying this library.'

'Oho, am I to be dismissed summarily?'

Zelah could not suppress a smile. She was beginning to enjoy herself. 'You are indeed, sir. You said yourself you have only this minute arrived. You should make your presence known to Major Coale. You will find your way lies through those doors, which lead to the salon and then to the great hall.'

He was laughing down at her, not at all offended by her dismissal. She was struck again by the similarity between the brothers, both tall, broad-shouldered and dark-haired, and although there was more laughter in the viscount's eyes she was reminded of Dominic every time she looked at him. Perhaps that was why she felt so little restraint with the viscount. He gave a little bow.

'Very well, Miss Pentewan, I shall leave you to your books.'

He sauntered off, whistling, and Zelah went back to work, her spirits lifted even further.

When the party from West Barton arrived Zelah made her way to the suite of rooms set aside for her sister and brother-in-law, where she received a warm welcome. A footman was despatched to the tower with the small trunk containing Zelah's evening clothes, but she did not immediately follow and instead asked Reginald about the charter.

'I think it proves the case for the villagers, but I don't plan to tell anyone about it until we get to the hearing next week. Sir Oswald's lawyer is as cunning as a fox.' He frowned. 'I understand Evanshaw is expected here tonight. I don't deny it goes against the grain to meet the fellow on friendly terms.'

'Well, I don't know how I shall look at the man,' exclaimed Maria, 'when I think how roughly he has treated anyone wandering into Prickett Wood, even catching Nicky—'

'That was his bailiff, Mama, and I came to no harm.' Nicky came running in at that moment and threw his arms around Zelah, who hugged him back.

'No, because your aunt and the major were on hand to rescue you,' retorted Maria, who could not bear the thought of any danger to her child.

'Now, now, my love, if Evanshaw thinks people are trespassing he is perfectly entitled to put a stop to it,' said Reginald mildly. 'I admit I cannot like the man, but I do agree with Coale, it does not do to fall out with a neighbour if it can be avoided.'

Zelah could not listen to more because Nicky demanded that she come and look at the room that had been allocated to him and his baby brother.

'Major Coale says I can watch the dancing from the landing,' he told her. 'And he is going to send up supper for me.'

'The major has been very kind,' declared Maria. 'Having this apartment means I will be able to slip away and feed the baby and then return for the dancing.'

'Will there be ices, do you think?' asked Nicky, his eyes wide.

'Alas, no,' laughed Zelah. 'However, there will be little pastries and definitely lemonade, because I have already had some.'

'So you will have a little party all of your own,' said Maria, scooping up Nicky and kissing him soundly. 'Now we must not keep Zelah, she has to change. I have already sent Bess to your room, my love. She will help you get ready.'

Zelah protested, but only half-heartedly. She wanted to look her best tonight and she knew that Bess would be able to dress her hair far better than she would be able to manage alone.

By the time she arrived back at the tower room the maid had emptied the trunk and laid out everything upon the bed.

'Oh.' Zelah stopped. 'That is not my dress.'

Bess curtsied. 'The mistress bought it for you,

miss. She said this ball is the biggest event of the summer and she wanted you to have something new. It's Indian muslin,' she added, helping Zelah out of her grey gown. 'And madam thought the green bodice would suit your colouring. I hope you aren't displeased?'

'How could I be?' She fingered the filmy skirts, then, looking up, her eyes fell upon a little cup full of rosebuds on the desk. 'Oh!'

'The mistress picked them from the garden today,' explained Bess. 'She sent them over specially for me to put in amongst your curls.'

Zelah wondered if she should protest at such frivolity. After all, if she was going to be a governess should she not put herself above such worldly considerations? But her doubts were quickly suppressed. Her work at Rooks Tower was coming to an end and this might be her last opportunity to dance. And besides, she wanted to see if she would win a look of warm admiration from a pair of sombre grey eyes.

She looked at her maid and allowed a smile to burst forth. 'Well, Bess, will you help me to get ready?'

The chiming of a distant clock reminded Zelah that it was time for the dinner guests to meet in the drawing room. She left her temporary bedchamber and made her way downstairs. Her route lay through the empty salon and she could not avoid seeing her reflection in the mirrors as she crossed the room. She stopped and moved closer to one of the mirrors. There was no hint of the bookish librarian in the elegant stranger she saw there, with her hair piled up and white rosebuds nestling amongst the curls. Her neck and shoulders rose gracefully from a short green velvet bodice that was ornamented at the neck and wrist with twisted white-and-gold braid. The low neckline fell to a point at the centre of the bosom and the braid continued down the front of the muslin skirts. It gave the illusion of height and she smiled to herself. She looked almost as willowy as the elegant models on the fashionplates. She flicked open her new spangled fan and held it before her, experimenting with different poses. When she held it across the lower part of her face her eyes appeared to sparkle invitingly.

The sound of the door opening made her jump and a guilty flush heated her cheeks.

'I beg your pardon, I did not mean to startle you.' Dominic stood in the doorway.

'I—there is no mirror in the tower room....' Her words trailed off. She knew she must sound very conceited.

'You look very well.' He cleared his throat. 'Everyone else is in the drawing room. I was merely coming to check that the salon and the library were in order. The orchestra will be setting up in here while we are at dinner.'

He seemed ill at ease, whereas Zelah's fine new clothes gave her an added confidence.

'I have just come through the library, Major, and I can assure you there is not a book out of place.'

'No, of course.' He seemed to battle with himself for a moment before meeting her eyes. 'Very well, then, shall we join the others?'

He held out his arm to her. Zelah placed her fingers on his sleeve. She could feel the ribbing of the wool-and-silk fabric through her glove. Expensive. Everything about his coat—the sheen of the material, the fit, the exquisite cut—it all shouted quality. Tonight he was every inch a viscount's son.

And she was a parson's daughter, an encumbrance that he was trying to marry off by inviting her to his ball. Had he not said as much?

The silence was uncomfortable and she searched for something to say as they crossed the hall.

'I met your brother earlier. He came into the library.'

'I know. He said you had given him his marching orders.'

'I hope he did not think me uncivil. I tried very hard not to be.'

'No, but you surprised him.' A glancing smile touched his lips. 'He is not accustomed to being turned away.'

As the footman jumped to open the door, Dominic released her arm and allowed her to precede him into the drawing room. It was filled with a chattering, glittering crowd and Zelah knew a moment's panic, but it subsided when Sally Hensley came forward to meet her.

'My dear, how charming you look. I have just been talking to your sister. She is over there by the window, but you can find her later. First I want to introduce you to everyone....'

It was not to be a large dinner, a mere ten couples were sitting down, but that was more than a dozen new people for Zelah to meet and remember their names. She realised Sally had chosen the company with care, they were all close friends of Dominic or family. No one to stare or comment upon his scarred face.

At dinner she found herself beside one of Dominic's army colleagues. Colonel Deakin was a jovial, bewhiskered gentleman who lost no time in telling her that he had served with Dominic in the Peninsula. He patted his empty sleeve.

'Wasn't long in following him home, too! I'll not complain, though, my wife and I have settled into a nice little house in Taunton and she says she's glad to have me under her feet all day, even if I only have the one good arm.' He raised his glass at the plump little woman sitting opposite, who twinkled back at him and addressed herself to Zelah.

'I'm lucky to have him and I thank the Lord for it, every day.'

Colonel Deakin chuckled. He leaned a little closer to Zelah, lowering his voice. 'And I'm pleased to see Coale looking so well. He was a good officer. Thought we might lose him, y'know.'

'Was he very badly injured?'

'Barely recognisable,' replied the colonel, cheerfully helping himself to a large slice of raised pie. 'Fortunately we had a good sawbones who patched him up pretty well, but even then when we sent him off to England I never really expected to see him again. Pity about his face, of course. He was a dashed handsome fellow.'

Zelah glanced to the head of the table, where Dominic was engaged in conversation with his brother. With the two of them together she had no need to try to imagine how Dominic had looked before he went to war, but the scars mattered very little to her now.

* * *

By the time the guests left the dining room the first carriages were pulling up on the drive. Zelah and Maria went off to tidy themselves before the ball and Zelah took the opportunity of thanking Maria for her gown.

'With the fan, and new shoes and gloves—it is all too much. How I wish you had not spent your money on me, Maria.'

'Oh, tush! If you will not think of yourself, then please think of what my feelings must be on the occasion. Reginald is highly respected here and I would not have it thought that we could not afford to dress you.'

Zelah hugged her sister, tears starting to her eyes. 'Then I will accept it all very gratefully, my love. Thank you, dearest sister!'

Maria had to stay to feed the baby, so Zelah made her way back downstairs alone. The great hall and the salon were already full and she saw Dominic greeting his guests. She thought she had never seen him look better. His black frock coat, tight-fitting breeches and stockings only accentuated his powerful physique. Now he was no longer limping his movements were graceful and assured, those of a man at the peak of his physical power. Dragging her eyes away, she spotted Reginald talking to Sir

Arthur Andrews and on the far side of the room stood Sir Oswald Evanshaw, resplendent in a lime-green coat. She descended the final few steps and was caught up in the crowd. Almost immediately Dominic was at her side.

'I was looking out for you.'

'You were?'

Her spirits soared, only to plummet at his next words.

'Yes. Lerryn has not arrived yet. I have given instructions that if he turns up he is not to come in until I have had a word with him.' He touched her arm. 'Do not worry. He will do nothing to harm you.'

She murmured her thanks and watched him walk away. The harm was already done. Dominic knew what she was. Sally came up and took her hand.

'You are looking very pensive, Zelah. I hope everyone is being kind to you?'

'Oh, yes, in all the noise and confusion no one has time or inclination to question too deeply why Major Coale should invite his librarian to the summer ball. Indeed, most have no idea of my identity, and I think the guests who were at dinner merely look upon me as a poor little dab of a girl who is on the receiving end of the major's charity.'

Sally laughed. 'Oh, no, my dear, you are much

more important than that! All Dom's friends know he was becoming a positive recluse. When he moved to Rooks Tower we thought we had lost him but now, barely six months later, he is holding the most important local gathering of the summer.'

'But I had nothing to do with this—' Zelah protested.

'You taught him that he is still a person worthy of note,' Sally cut in. 'He told me as much. We all owe you a great deal.'

Zelah saw her chance. 'Then perhaps I could ask a favour of you,' she said. 'Would you be kind enough to supply me with a reference? I am sure a good word from yourself would mean a great deal to any future employer.'

'Oh, my dear, you are looking so lovely tonight that I am sure you will have no need of a *reference*—'

'But I *will*.' A note of desperation crept into Zelah's voice. 'My work here is almost done and I have had a very favourable enquiry from a widow in Bath. She has three children in need of a governess and has asked me to provide references. My father has offered one, and Reginald, but they are family and therefore not as valuable… I would be most obliged if you would provide one for me.'

Sally squeezed her hands. 'I will, of course, Zelah, if that is what you wish. But on one condition.'

'Anything!' was Zelah's grateful response.

'That you forget all about being a governess for tonight and enjoy yourself!' Bestowing an airy kiss upon Zelah's cheek, she dashed off to greet more guests.

When the music began Zelah moved to one side of the room. She knew so few people that she had little expectation of dancing, although, with Sally's words still ringing in her head she did hope that Dominic might claim her hand later in the evening. That could not be for some time, of course, because there were many ladies with whom he must stand up first. She watched him from the side of the room. He strode proudly through the crowds, seemingly unaware of his scarred face and because he took no note of it, most of his guests did the same. She was aware of one or two sly looks, the odd hesitation when someone was introduced to him, but she saw no signs of the repulsion Dominic had feared would mar his return to society. She was glad, for his sake.

'Zelah.' Timothy Lerryn was beside her. 'You need not look daggers at me,' he muttered savagely. 'I have already been warned not to importune you.'

'Then there is no reason why we should not be civil to one another.'

'Will you dance with me?'

'Thank you, I would rather not.'

His face darkened. They were surrounded by people and she did not wish to quarrel openly with him. She said pointedly, 'My sister tells me your wife is expecting a happy event soon. That must be cause for celebration.'

'Yes. Thank you. It will be our third child.' His smile remained, but there was a spiteful note in his voice as he added, 'My wife breeds like a sow. We expect no still births in *our* family.'

Zelah's hands went immediately to her stomach, as if to protect herself from the cruel blow. Feeling sick and disgusted, she turned away, grateful to hear her brother-in-law's cheerful voice close at hand.

'There you are, my dear. Maria is not yet downstairs so I shall carry you off to dance in her stead.'

'I'll dance with you, Reginald, with pleasure!' Zelah accepted with alacrity and went off, determined to forget Timothy Lerryn.

Despite his duties as host, Dominic found his eyes drawn constantly to Zelah. He watched her dance with her brother-in-law, then Colonel Deakin led her out, and finally Jasper.

Dominic watched his brother taking Zelah down the dance. How had he ever thought her an insignificant little thing? She was the most elegant woman in the room. Her only ornament was the string of fine pearls around her neck, but she outshone the other ladies with their flashing jewels. He was standing beside Lady Andrews, who saw his concentrated gaze and gave a little chuckle.

'Lord Markham appears quite taken with young Miss Pentewan. I am not well acquainted with her, but she seems a pleasant, well-mannered gel.' There was a pause. 'She is employed here, I understand, as your archivist?'

'That is correct, ma'am.'

'How unusual. And, may I say, very daring.'

'Oh?' He frowned. 'How is that? Why do you call it daring?'

Lady Andrews fluttered her fan nervously. 'Oh well, perhaps I am old-fashioned,' she tittered. 'Sir Arthur says he sees no objection, but to have an unmarried lady employed in a bachelor's establishment...'

'I have several housemaids working here. They are unmarried—do you consider them at risk, too?' he countered bluntly.

'Oh, no, no, Major, of course not—' She broke off, flustered, then gathered herself and came back to say brightly, 'And you have your sister staying here, so there can be no objection, can there?'

Dominic forced himself to smile before he moved away. He had known from the outset there would be gossip, but he had ignored the voice of caution and hired the girl, wanting only to help her. He had thought only the meanest of tabbies would consider there was anything improper in the situation. After all, she did not live at Rooks Tower and he had a house full of female servants, so there should be no question of impropriety. Yet if he was honest with himself, Dominic knew that he had failed to keep a proper distance between himself and his employee. By God, if anyone found out he had kissed her! He knew his world, it fed upon sordid intrigue and gossip—that was the reason he had refused to give her a reference: the more glowing his recommendation, the greater the belief that she was his mistress.

Dominic nodded to one acquaintance, threw a brief word to another, but continued to move through the crowd, his thoughts distracted. Hell and damnation, he had no wish to ruin the chit. The work in the library was all but complete now. He would end her employment before Sally left Rooks Tower.

Chapter Thirteen

Dancing with Lord Markham set the seal on Zelah's success at the ball. After that there was no shortage of young gentlemen begging for the pleasure of leading her out. She whirled from one partner to the next in a heady round of gaiety, but her enjoyment was cut short when she left the floor at the end of one dance to find her way blocked by Timothy Lerryn. He bowed elegantly and held out his hand.

'Dance with me once,' he coaxed her. 'For old time's sake.'

There was no escape. The matrons on the nearby benches were all smiling and nodding encouragement, pleased to see the young people so enjoying themselves.

She could declare that she would dance no more that evening, but Dominic had not yet asked her to dance, and she desperately hoped he would do so before the end of the ball. Putting up her chin, she gave Timothy a challenging look. 'One dance,' she told him. 'No more.'

Triumph gleamed in his eyes as he led her back to the floor. While they waited for the other couples to take their place in the set he leaned towards her.

'Have I told you how well you are looking tonight, my dear? Quite beautiful.'

She ignored his compliment and returned only short answers to his remarks as they went down the dance, impatient for the ordeal to end. But even when she made him a final curtsy he took her hand and placed it on his arm.

'You sister and her husband are over there, I shall escort you to them.'

Zelah merely inclined her head, keeping as much distance as she could between them. A moment later he spoke again.

'By heaven.' He raised his quizzing glass. 'Who is that fellow in the lime-green coat, talking to Buckland?'

Zelah shifted her gaze. Reginald was standing beside Maria's chair, looking very much like a terrier guarding a bone.

'That is Sir Oswald Evanshaw.'

Even as they watched, Maria rose from her chair and Reginald swept her off towards the door.

'Well, well, they have cut him dead!' He stopped. 'No point in taking you over there now, your sister and brother have gone off to the supper room, I suppose. So what do you say to one more dance?'

'No.' She tried to pull her hand free. 'Release me, if you please.'

'If you will not dance, then I shall escort you in to supper.'

She could smell the brandy on his breath as he leaned closer. She tugged again at her hand. 'Let me go,' she hissed. 'You have been warned.'

He leered at her, a reckless look in his eyes. 'Coale can do nothing to me if you come with me willingly.'

'But the lady does not want your company.' With relief she heard Dominic's voice behind her. 'I suggest you leave now, Mr Lerryn.'

Dominic spoke very softly, but there was no mistaking the menace in his tone.

Lerryn glared at him for a moment, his jaw working, then he flung himself away, shouldering his way through the crowd.

Zelah closed her eyes and released a long, grateful sigh. 'Thank you.' She put out her hand and he took it in a warm, reassuring grip.

'I did not expect him to stay so long. His attachment to you must be stronger than you thought.'

She shuddered. 'His attachment is nothing more than pique, the desire to have the unobtainable.'

'We are all guilty of that,' muttered Dominic. He pulled her hand on to his sleeve. 'Come. Let us go to supper. My sister is waiting for you there.'

Timothy Lerryn lounged out of the salon. Damn the chit, who was she to set herself up against him? He would show her! He had half a mind to tell her story now, to anyone who would listen. But his brain was not so befuddled that he had forgotten Major Coale's quiet threats when he had arrived. They had been issued in a cold, matter-of-fact tone that was much more effective than any blustering arguments and he did not doubt that if word of Zelah's past got out the major would indeed hunt him down and ruin him. Well, the slut was not worth the risk. Seething with frustration he set off across the great hall.

He had almost reached the door when a flash of bright green caught his eye and another idea came into his sly brain. He stopped, stepping back and across to put himself in the way of his quarry.

'Sir Oswald.' He bowed. 'Timothy Lerryn, at your service. I wonder if I might have a word with you. There is something I think you should know...'

* * *

In the supper room Zelah found her sister sitting with Sally Hensley while Reginald paced up and down behind them.

'He is still fretting over his words with Sir Oswald,' Maria explained when Zelah came up with Dominic.

'Aye, blast his eyes, the man came bang up to me to say that his men had found Giles Grundy on his land and sent him home with a broken arm. Then he had the effrontery to suggest the hearing next week was as good as settled!' Reginald scowled blackly. 'He thinks he has Sir Arthur in his pocket, but when I show them that new document—!'

'Yes, dear, now sit down, do and calm yourself.' Maria shook her head at him. 'The man is indeed a scoundrel, but we will not stoop to his level. I will visit the Grundys tomorrow and offer what help I can and you will use the law against Sir Oswald.'

'I'll ride over, too,' said Dominic, holding a chair for Zelah. 'I can spare some of my men from the woodcutting if Grundy needs help on his farm. Now if you will excuse me—'

'Are you not going to eat with us?' asked Sally.

Dominic shook his head. 'I promised a certain young man he would have some supper. So I am going to take it to him!'

* * *

The last dance had ended and the salon was rapidly clearing. Dominic looked for Zelah, but she was nowhere to be seen. Perhaps she had gone off with Jasper to the drawing room. He and his twin had made a habit of that in their younger days, seeking out the prettiest girls and carrying them off at the end of the evening to engage in a desperate flirtation.

Dominic tugged at his neckcloth. It was all he could do not to go storming off to find them. Instead he forced himself to remain outwardly calm as the last of his guests took their leave. He escorted them out to the drive and watched the final carriages rattle away until the silence of the summer night was restored. For once there was no wind to freshen the balmy air, the moon rode high in the cloudless sky, dimming the stars and bathing everything in a silver blue light. After the clamour of the evening, the peaceful calm was soothing and he did not want to return to the house immediately. He set off across the grass rather than have the scrunching of the gravel under his feet disturb the night.

Even before the ball was over, Maria was congratulating Zelah on her success. She began to talk of having a small gathering at West Barton.

'Nothing as grand as this of course, but we could perhaps invite one or two of the gentlemen who danced with you...'

Zelah stopped her. 'I know what is in your mind, Maria, you think to persuade one of those eligible gentlemen to offer for me.' Timothy Lerryn's scowling image rose up before her. 'I do not *want* a husband.'

She read the determination in her sister's face and made her excuses to walk away. The orchestra was playing the last dance of the evening and she could see Dominic partnering his sister. There was no chance now that he would dance with her and Zelah slipped quietly away to her room.

There were no curtains or shutters on the windows and the moonlight flooded in on all sides, making candles unnecessary, but it was oppressively hot. She wanted to be out of doors, but that was impossible. It was the middle of the night and not safe for anyone to be wandering around alone, especially a young lady. She remembered the flat roof above her. That surely would be safe enough. Quickly she slipped out of the room and up the stairs.

Zelah stepped out on to the roof. She gazed about her, entranced. It was a magical world, all grey and blue moonshadows. She paced around, her slippered feet making no sound on the stone slabs. It was easier to think up here, for the rest of the world seemed very far away and somehow less important. There had been no lack of partners this evening, she had enjoyed the dancing and for a short time she had felt like a carefree girl again. That was what she had hoped for, wasn't it? A few hours of enjoyment before she settled down to the sober existence of a governess.

She gazed out at the distant moors, silver under the moonlight. She would not deceive herself, she had hoped for more. She had wanted Dominic to dance with her. It was too much to hope that he would flirt with her, as his brother had done, bringing a flush to her cheeks with his cheerful nonsense, but she had thought perhaps he might compliment her upon her appearance.

She wrapped her arms across her chest as a huge wave of anger and futility welled up. She wished there had been no summer ball, that the world had remained shut out of Dominic's life.

That she could have kept him to herself.

It was a despicable thought and she quickly dismissed it. She did not want Dominic to be a sad, lonely recluse. He needed to take his place in society, even if that meant he had little time for her.

And what did that matter? She would not be here

much longer. The books were all in order now and in another few weeks the cataloguing would be finished. She really must remind Sally to write her a reference and make efforts to secure another position, although she knew that nothing could compare to being at Rooks Tower.

'What the devil are you doing here?'

She jumped as Dominic's angry words cut through the night. 'I—I beg your pardon. I did not think there could be any harm...'

'Harm? Foolish girl, you know the stonework is unsound. Come away from that wall.'

His anger sliced into her like a knife. Not for her the soft, civil tone he used for his guests. Just because she had been allowed to attend his summer ball she must not think herself anything other than a servant. The unhappiness within her tightened into a hard knot.

'I had not forgotten. I am sorry. I shall not come here again—'

She ran for the stairs, but as she passed him his hand shot out, gripping her arm. He was not wearing gloves and she could feel the heat of his fingers through the thin sleeve.

'Wait. There are tears on your cheek.'

She turned her head away from him. 'Please, let me go.'

Instead he pulled her closer, putting one hand under her chin and forcing her to look up at him. The moonlight glinted in his eyes, twin devils sent to mock her. Gently he wiped her tears away with his thumb.

'Has someone been unkind to you tonight?'

'N-no.' It was a struggle to speak with more tears ready to fall.

He said roughly, 'Perhaps you are regretting sending Lerryn away.'

'You know that is not so!'

'Then why are you crying?'

'I—um—I am just…very tired.'

How could she tell him the truth? His eyes bored into her and she prayed he would not read her thoughts. At last he looked up at the moon, letting his breath go in a long sigh.

'Yes, it has been a long day.' He pulled her close and enfolded her in his arms. She did not resist, it was the most natural thing in the world to allow herself to lean against him. 'It has been quite exhausting, having so many people in the house.'

'Did you not enjoy it?' she murmured the words into his coat.

'I did, after a fashion. It is good to know I am not a pariah, a social outcast.' His arms tightened.

'And it is you I have to thank for that, Zelah. You made me see that all was not lost.'

'Then…then you are not angry with me?'

'Angry? No. I was worried lest you lean on the parapet and the stonework should give way.'

'Oh.'

It was a spark of comfort. The tiny flame warmed her heart. She let herself relax against him, her cheek against his shoulder. His breath ruffled her curls, softer than the night breeze.

'I am pleased I could help,' she murmured.

'And now I shall do something for you. Sally told me you had asked her to recommend you. With her support I have no doubt that we can find you a suitable post. I was talking to her earlier—are you set upon becoming a governess? Because we thought perhaps you might find the role of companion more to your taste. Sally has many contacts.'

The little flame flickered and died.

'You are very kind, Major.' Steeling herself, she pushed away from him. 'I should go in now.'

Dominic caught her fingers. His body was alive, aroused and he wanted to succumb to the attraction he felt for her, to seduce her here on this moonlit terrace far above the everyday world. He could do it, too. She had responded to him before, and here, with the darkness to hide his face, why should it not happen again? But she was pulling away from him and he could still see the trace of tears on her cheeks. He buried his own desires and squeezed her hands.

'Of course. It is very late.'

For a brief moment her fingers clung to his. Perhaps she wanted comfort, but he was not the one to give it. He would do nothing that she might regret in the morning. He said formally, 'Goodnight, Miss Pentewan.'

Without a word she walked away, her figure a pale blur on the stairs before she disappeared from his sight. There. It was done. He had saved her. From himself, possibly from her own weakness.

Why, then, did he feel no pleasure in his chivalrous deed?

Zelah did not sleep well and was relieved when the morning came and she could leave the tower room and go in search of her sister and brother-in-law. She found them at breakfast, being entertained by Sally and Lord Markham.

'Dominic has already gone out,' explained the viscount, rising to escort her to her chair. 'Taking his duties far too seriously, if you ask me. He should be here looking after his guests.'

'But he knows he can rely upon us for that.' Sally beamed at Zelah across the table. 'So you are to leave us this morning and go back to West Barton. What shall I do without my little companion?'

'Any number of things, I should imagine.' Zelah had lost all her shyness with Sally and treated her in the same friendly manner as her own sister. 'But perhaps before I leave this morning you will write a reference for me, as we agreed?'

'By all means, if that is what you wish.'

Zelah nodded, saying firmly. 'It is, madam.'

'I have a great deal to do before the hearing next Friday,' said Reginald. 'How soon can you be ready to travel, Zelah?'

'Hannah has already packed for me.' She pushed her plate away. 'I can leave as soon as Mrs Hensley has furnished me with my reference.'

'Then I shall go off and write it now,' said Sally, smiling.

'Well, I need to feed Baby before we can set off,' put in Maria. 'It will be at least another hour.'

A sudden burst of sunlight filled the room, making everything jewel bright and sending glittering rays bouncing off the breakfast silver.

'Ah, the sun is making an appearance.' The viscount put down his napkin and looked at Zelah.

'Perhaps Miss Pentewan would care to take a stroll around the grounds with me until the carriage is called?'

Zelah assented readily. The viscount was an entertaining companion and, knowing her heart was in no danger, Zelah could relax and enjoy his company. She encouraged him to talk about his brother, hoarding each little nugget of information. Jasper's revelations only confirmed her impression of Dominic. Honest, loyal and honourable, a man determined to do his duty.

'And now he is throwing his energies into Rooks Tower,' said Jasper as they reached the orangery. He opened the double doors and stood back for her to enter. 'I thought at first he wanted it merely as a retreat, to hide away from the world, but his holding a ball has made me think again. Perhaps he is intending this as a family home. What do you think, Miss Pentewan, is my brother on the lookout for a wife?'

The thought was a body blow to Zelah, robbing her of breath. She hoped it did not show in her face and she pretended to give her attention to looking about the summer house, admiring the arrangements of plants and marble while she considered her response. At last she said carefully, 'There were several very eligible young ladies here last night.'

'I know, I danced with them all,' he replied promptly. 'Dominic, on the other hand, danced with none. But perhaps he was just being cautious. He is not the sort to raise false hopes.'

'No. He is far too chivalrous for that.'

Jasper did not notice the bleak note in her voice. He merely nodded, gazing around him in admiration.

'Now, madam, you are to be congratulated. You have created here the perfect trysting place. Do you not find it most romantic?'

Zelah summoned up a smile. 'Not in the daylight, sir, I see only the empty glasses that the servants failed to clear away because they were hidden behind the plants.'

He looked pained. 'You are far too practical, my dear.'

'My besetting sin,' she told him cheerfully.

'You puzzle me, Miss Pentewan. Why do you resist all my attempts to flirt with you?'

His worried tone amused her and she gave him a mischievous look.

'Since you attempt to flirt with every young lady, my lord, it will do you no harm to be rebuffed occasionally.' She moved towards the door. 'Shall we go back to the house?'

Jasper was in no way discomposed by her response and they strolled back across the lawn in perfect accord. The entrance door was standing open and as they approached Dominic came out.

'Good morning, brother,' Jasper hailed him cheerfully. 'You were up and out before I had even shaved this morning!'

'I went to see Giles Grundy,' he replied shortly.

'Ah, yes, how is he?' asked Zelah.

'A little bruised, but he will mend. Doctor Pannell has set his arm—he says it is a clean break and should heal well.'

'And while you have been busy with your tenant, you have left me with the very agreeable business of entertaining your guests,' Jasper responded, putting his free hand over Zelah's where it rested on his sleeve.

Dominic shifted his stony gaze to Zelah. 'I have just ordered the carriage for your sister.'

She knew him well enough now to know he was angry about something, but she said calmly, 'Then I shall fetch my wrap.'

She moved past him into the great hall, wondering if he had received bad tidings. Poachers, perhaps, or news that Sir Oswald had destroyed more deer. She had not quite reached the top of the stairs when his gruff, furious words echoed off the walls.

'By heaven, Jasper, it is bad enough that you flirt with every woman you see. Must you also attempt to charm my librarian?'

Chapter Fourteen

Librarian. Yes, that is all she was to him, thought Zelah as she sat in the tower room the next day, working at her ledgers. She tried to ignore the huge bed that still dominated the room, a constant reminder of her attendance at the summer ball. The weather had broken and the rain had fallen steadily all day. She saw no one save Mrs Graddon, who brought her a tray at noon, along with an invitation from Mrs Hensley to join the other guests in the drawing room later to play charades.

Zelah sent back her apologies. She had lost too much time already. She wanted to finish her work at Rooks Tower and be ready to take up the post in Bath, should her application be successful. Dominic had told her that Sally could find her a position with someone of her acquaintance, but Zelah wanted to sever all ties with Major Coale's family and had already sent off the required references to Bath.

She was relieved when at last she could return to West Barton, but even there the talk was still of the ball. Learning that Maria was in the nursery, she ran upstairs to find Nicky telling Nurse how exciting it had been.

'Major Coale brought me supper, and by sitting on the edge of the landing I could hear what people said when they came into that little spot beneath the stairs.'

Maria threw up her hands. 'Lud, my son is an eavesdropper! He now knows all the secrets of the village.'

'Devil a bit, Mama,' grinned Nicky. 'It was only Lord Markham telling one of the ladies that her eyes reminded him of the stars, and then Sir Oswald came over with—'

'Enough!' Maria put up her hand. 'It was very naughty of you to be listening, Nicholas, and you must say no more about it. Eavesdroppers will never hear any good of themselves.' She turned her attention to her sister. 'Good evening, Zelah. Did you get very wet walking home? I had hoped Major Coale or his sister would have the goodness to send you home in the carriage.'

'I slipped away without telling them.' Zelah recalled the shouts and laughter coming from the drawing room when she had crossed the empty hall. She raised her chin a little. 'It was never part of the agreement that the major should provide a carriage for me.'

'It was never part of the agreement that you should catch a chill,' retorted Maria. 'But never mind, it is done now and you are here safe. Mr Lerryn has sent word that he is resuming his journey to Bristol so we shall be able to enjoy a quiet family dinner together.'

Zelah uttered up a silent prayer. Dominic had assured her that she was safe from Timothy Lerryn, but it was still a relief to know he had quit Lesserton. It was one less problem to worry her.

When Zelah arrived at Rooks Tower the next morning her spirits were as leaden as the overcast sky. Two more weeks, three at the most, and she would be finished here. The library was just as she had left it, no sign that the major had been there to check her progress. She had the lowering suspicion that he was avoiding her.

She had not been working long before Sally Hensley burst into the room, saying impetuously, 'Oh good, you are here! I have come to say goodbye!'

'G-goodbye?' Zelah rose from her seat and was immediately enveloped in a scented embrace.

'Yes! I had planned to stay another two weeks at least, but I have today had a letter from my darling husband! Ben is well, and in England, and on his way to our house at Fellbridge. He may already be there, because his letter went to Markham and they have sent it on to me. I must go home immediately. I only hope this rain does not slow my journey. Oh, I cannot *wait* to see him again.'

'Yes, yes, of course. I am very happy for you.' Zelah barely had time to murmur her words before she was caught up again in another fierce hug.

'Thank you. I count you very much my friend now and I am very sorry to be leaving, but I shall write to you at West Barton—'

'I—I doubt I shall be there for much longer. My work here is almost finished. I hope to hear soon about the post in Bath.'

Sally regarded her for a moment, as if she would protest, but in the end she merely nodded. 'Very well, but if you take it you must let me know where you are. I do not want to lose touch with you now.'

Then, like a whirlwind, Sally was gone, leaving only silence and the faintest hint of perfume behind her.

Zelah resumed her seat and picked up her pen.

It was unlikely they would ever meet again. Sally would be preoccupied with her husband for the next few weeks and by the time she was able to think about her new friend, Zelah hoped to be far away from Exmoor.

The rain persisted well into the afternoon, but about five o'clock there was a break in the weather. The sky was still a thick grey blanket, but Zelah decided she should set off for West Barton before there was another shower. She was just crossing the hall when she heard her name. Dominic was standing in the doorway of his study.

'Perhaps you will grant me a few minutes of your time before you go?'

'Yes, of course.'

He stood aside and allowed her to enter. The hearth was empty although the smell of wood smoke lingered in the air. There was a large desk by the window and two glass-fronted cupboards that housed the estate's papers. Everything was orderly, businesslike, as was the major's tone when he spoke.

'You have done an excellent job, organising my library. You are to be congratulated.'

'Thank you, sir. The catalogue of titles is almost

complete, I shall begin the final section to-morrow—'

'That will not be necessary.'

She frowned. 'I do not understand you.'

He turned on his heel and walked across to the window. 'You have done enough, thank you. I will arrange for your final payment to be made. It will be brought to West Barton tomorrow.'

She blinked. 'You do not wish me to return to Rooks Tower?'

'That is correct.'

'But I have not finished!'

'You have done enough.'

She clutched her hands together. 'Are you—are you dissatisfied with me, with my work?'

'I have already said that is not the case.'

'But that does not make sense. It will take only a few more weeks—'

'No!' He swung back. 'Don't you understand? I am trying to protect your reputation. While my sister was here, there was a modicum of propriety, but now—'

'You never worried about that before.'

'That was an error. I should never have allowed you to work here.'

'You *invited* me to come here,' she retorted, anger beginning to mount.

'I know. It was wrong of me. I admit it.'

Beneath Zelah's annoyance was another emotion. Panic. He was sending her away. She would never see him again.

'Please,' she said quietly. 'Let me finish what I have started. If you are anxious for my reputation, I could have a maid in the library at all times—let Hannah attend me!'

'No. My mind is made up. This will be the last time you come to Rooks Tower.'

Her eyes searched his face, but his eyes were shuttered, withdrawn. He would not be moved.

The rumble of voices filtered through the door, but she barely noticed.

'Then will you not shake hands with me?' He looked as if her outstretched hand was a poisoned chalice and a strangled cry was wrenched from her. 'I thought we were friends!'

The stony look fled. 'Friends. We could never be that.' He reached for her. 'Zelah—' He broke off as the door opened and Reginald burst in.

'Coale—and Zelah. Thank God. Have you seen Nicky?'

Chapter Fifteen

Dominic's hands fell. He stared uncomprehending at Reginald Buckland, who had stormed into his study without so much as a knock. Then he saw the look of strain in the other man's face and he said sharply, 'What is it?'

'My son. He has gone missing. Because of the rain I sent my man to collect him from Netherby's house today, but the boy had already gone. The other boys said he had set off for home, but my man did not pass him on the road. I thought he might have come here.'

'I have not seen him, but he could have gone straight to the kitchens.' Dominic strode out of the room and barked an order, sending a footman scurrying away. A few minutes later he returned and Dominic went back to the study, frowning.

'No one has seen him. Could he have stopped off with friends?'

Reginald shook his head. 'I have checked that. I beg your pardon, if he is not here then I must get back…'

'Yes, let us get home with all speed,' said Zelah quickly.

'Wait.' Dominic caught Reginald's sleeve. 'You are on horseback?'

'Yes.'

'Then we will follow in my curricle.' He glanced at Zelah's pale face. 'I know it is a greater distance, but it will be almost as quick as walking and will leave you in a better state to support Mrs Buckland.'

His heart lurched. She looked utterly bewildered, and little wonder. A few moments' earlier he had been telling her he wanted nothing more to do with her.

He sent Reginald on his way and ordered his curricle to be brought round. When he returned to the study Zelah was still standing in the middle of the floor, clasping and unclasping her hands. He pushed her gently into a chair.

'Try not to worry, Nicky might well be home by now.'

'Yes, yes, of course.'

The curricle was soon at the door and Dominic drove his horses hard, praying that they would not meet anything in the narrow lanes. He stopped only once, to drop his groom off in Lesserton, with instructions to make enquiries at the local inns. Then it was off again at a breakneck pace. A swift glance showed him that Zelah was hanging on to the side of the carriage with one hand, the other clamped firmly over her bonnet. 'My apologies for the bumpy ride, ma'am.'

'Do not slow down on my account,' she told him. 'I, too, want to get to West Barton as soon as possible.'

When they reached West Barton a servant ran out to grab the horses' heads. Zelah jumped down before Dominic could run round to help. He followed her into the house, where the butler's careworn expression told them that the boy had not come home.

They were shown into the drawing room. Reginald was pacing up and down and Maria sat on a sofa with her head in her hands. When the door opened she flew out of her seat and threw herself into Zelah's arms, sobbing wildly.

Dominic looked at Reginald, who shook his head.

'No one has seen him. I have sent my people into the village to ask questions, but the answer is always the same. He was seen leaving the vicarage and walking out of the village in this direction, but then he disappeared.'

'I left orders for my woods to be searched,' said Dominic. 'Everyone at Rooks Tower is fond of the boy, they will make every effort to find him.'

'Oh, my poor child,' cried Maria. 'Where can he be?'

They sat in silence, until Maria pushed herself out of Zelah's arms.

'I am forgetting my duty,' she sniffed, taking out her handkerchief and wiping her eyes. 'You would like some refreshment, Major Coale. Tea, perhaps?'

'I think brandy might be preferable,' suggested Reginald.

When Dominic assented he rang the bell.

'I would like tea,' said Zelah, hoping her sister would find some comfort in the well-rehearsed ritual.

Conversation had been stilted as they waited for news. Every knock on the door heralded the return of another search party, but each time they had to report failure. The dinner hour had come and a place was laid for Dominic, but no one had much appetite. The hours passed. Maria dragged herself up, saying she must feed the baby and Dominic announced he would go.

'No, please, Major, stay,' Maria beseeched him. 'Stay at least until I return.'

He could not refuse, but the inaction irked him. By the time Maria came back to the drawing room it was growing dark. He rose.

'I must get back, my groom is waiting for me in Lesserton. I will come over again in the morning, and if there is still no news we will work out a plan...'

There was a scratching at the door and the butler entered. He crossed the room, holding out a folded piece of paper to his master.

'Someone slipped this under the door, sir. I looked outside, but I could see no one.'

'Then go out and search the grounds,' barked Reginald, taking the note.

'Too late,' muttered Dominic, peering out of the window. 'They'll have gone away immediately.' He returned to the hearth and waited. Reginald's usually cheerful countenance became increasingly grim. 'Well?'

'What is it?' demanded Maria, her hands clasped to her breast. 'Tell us!'

Silently Reginald handed Dominic the note. 'Read it out, Coale, if you please.'

If the Parents of a certain Young Man want to see him Alive again, then they will not be presenting any new evidence at the White Hart on Friday next. Neither will they make any effort to find him. If they comply with these instructions, the Young Man in question will be delivered to them, unharmed, on Sunday next.'

'Oh!' Maria's hands flew to her mouth.

'Evanshaw,' ground out Reginald. 'It has to be.' He drove his fist into his palm. 'But how did he know? He came up to me at the ball and mentioned the hearing. He was bragging that he could not lose, crowing so hard that I cannot believe he knew about the new document.'

'You told no one about it?' asked Dominic, pacing the room.

'No, of course not. I told you I wanted to keep it from that rascally lawyer Evanshaw has engaged.'

'And I mentioned it to no one at Rooks Tower,' muttered Dominic. 'No one outside this room knew of it.'

'Mr Lerryn.' Zelah put her hands to her white cheeks. 'Timothy Lerryn was here when we brought over the manuscript.'

'By heaven, you are right,' declared Reginald, horror dawning in his eyes. 'He asked me about the case, while we took brandy together after dinner.'

'And I pointed out Sir Oswald to him at the ball,' whispered Zelah. 'He must have warned him.' She turned her eyes, dark with horror, towards Dominic. 'It is all my fault. This is his revenge upon me...'

Dominic saw the bewildered looks bent on Zelah and he said abruptly, 'Lerryn tried to impose upon Zelah. I sent him packing. If it is anyone's fault, it is mine for allowing him into my house in the first place!'

Reginald shook his head. 'Never mind that now, what are we going to do?'

Maria jumped up and gripped his arm. 'You must go to Sir Arthur now, Reginald. He is the magistrate, he can get a party together and go to Lydcombe Park—'

'That will not work,' put in Dominic. 'Sir Oswald will deny everything.'

'But it *must* be his doing,' protested Zelah. 'We could search Lydcombe—'

Dominic shook his head. 'You may be sure the boy will not be hidden anywhere on Evanshaw's land.'

Maria looked at each of them in turn, her eyes wide with apprehension. 'Will he keep his word, do you think? Will he return Nicky to us if we do as he says?'

Reginald rubbed a hand across his brow. 'Why should he not? Once the hearing is concluded it will be too late to change anything.'

'But we cannot just sit here,' declared Zelah.

Reginald snatched the note from Dominic's hand and waved it at her, his eyes bleak with despair. 'It says if we try to find him—' He broke off, swallowing. 'I dare not do anything.'

The sound of voices in the hall caught their attention. Maria leapt up as the door opened, only to slump back again when she saw Jasper. He was dressed for riding, his spurs jingling cheerfully as he walked in.

'Lord Markham!' Reginald sounded more hopeful.

Jasper nodded to the assembled company as he began to strip off his gloves.

'I was out looking for your boy when I came across Sawley.' He glanced round as the groom followed him into the room, having stopped to wipe his boots thoroughly before entering the house. Jasper fixed his eyes on Dominic. 'He was rushing here on foot, so I thought it might be important and took him up behind me.'

Jem dragged his hat off and twisted it between his hands.

'I thought to see you on the road, sir, seein' as you hadn't got to the White Hart an' I wanted to tell you as soon as maybe.' No one spoke, no one even moved while he paused to wipe his face with a red handkerchief. 'I did what you said, sir, and took myself off to the Three Tuns for some home-brewed.' He grimaced. 'Rough place, it is, but I pulled me cap down over me face and settled in a corner of the taproom. Anyway, one or two of Sir Oswald's people was in there, drinking, when a man comes in looking for Miller, the bailiff. Said he had some gaming cocks for him. "He's gone off to see 'is brother," says one, only to have 'is foot stamped on by his mate, which shut him up. "Well, that's odd," says the man. "When I saw 'im the night afore last he said he'd be 'ere to take these birds off me hands." Well, there was some mutterings and shifty looks, and it struck me as a pretty rum do.' Jem rubbed his nose, his brow wrinkled in concentration. 'They all left soon after, so I took meself off to the High Street to see old Mother Tawton, the washerwoman. Regular gossip, she is, and knows everything about everyone around Lesserton. It being a warm evening I found her sitting in her doorway, smoking her pipe. She told me that Miller's brother runs a tavern down at Beston Quay. And according to Mother Tawton, that's who supplies Sir Oswald with his brandy and tea.'

'Smugglers,' declared Reginald.

'Most likely they wouldn't be above aiding a kidnap, too,' muttered Dominic.

Reginald rubbed his chin. 'But that is what, thirty…forty miles away. Would they take the boy that far?'

'If Evanshaw is involved, he wouldn't risk hiding the boy locally,' said Jasper. 'We should take a look.'

'Yes, yes!' cried Maria. 'You must go there this minute, Reginald.'

'Yes, we—' Reginald stopped, his animated look replaced by one of wretchedness. 'But it won't work. You saw the note, Coale. He threatens the boy if we try to find him. Our hands are tied.'

Dominic handed the paper to Jasper.

'*Yours* may be,' he said slowly, 'but mine are not. No one will be any the wiser if I am gone from Rooks Tower for a day or two, and you can make sure you are seen in Lesserton, to allay suspicion.'

Jasper immediately spoke up. 'I shall come with you, Brother.'

Reginald shook his head. 'No, no, I cannot let you do it. If Evanshaw finds out—'

Zelah put her hand on his arm. 'What is the alternative?'

His shoulders drooped. 'We let Evanshaw redraw the boundary. The villagers lose their land. And I will have spent a great deal of money I could not afford bringing the lawyer down from London for nothing.'

'But we will have our son back.' Maria's voice broke and she dropped her face in her hands again.

'But if he is at Beston,' said Dominic, 'and we can bring him back safe before the hearing?'

'I think it is worth an attempt.' Jasper nodded.

'But it is not your son's life at stake,' retorted Reginald, strain beginning to take its toll of his nerves.

'True,' said Dominic, 'but what guarantee do you have that Evanshaw will keep his word and return the boy?' The awful reality of his words hung in the silence. He continued urgently, 'Let us try this, Buckland. If Nicky is not there, we have lost nothing. If he is…'

'Oh, yes,' sobbed Maria. 'Yes, Major, please try. I only wish I could go with you. My poor little boy will be so frightened.'

'I will go, if you will provide me with a horse.' Zelah's words were quietly spoken and Dominic thought he had misheard until Jasper protested.

'No, Miss Pentewan, there is no call for that.'

'Nicky may need me,' she said simply. 'He is a little boy, snatched away from his home and everything he knows. He will be very frightened.'

Dominic shook his head. 'Out of the question,' he said curtly. 'It is far too dangerous.'

He found Zelah's agonised gaze fixed upon him.

'Please,' she whispered, 'let me do this. Nicky is like my own son. To lose him…'

He read the anguish in her eyes and suddenly he understood: she was racked with guilt. About Lerryn, Nicky's disappearance—about her own stillborn child. His judgement said she should not go, but he could not deny her.

'We will be riding hard,' he warned.

She returned his look, her own hazel eyes now steady and unafraid. 'I am used to that, and thanks to your sister I have had some practice these past weeks.'

She looked pale but resolute and Dominic's heart swelled. Her spirit was indomitable.

'Sal has left Portia at Rooks Tower,' put in Jasper. 'I will have her saddled up for you. And we will need to leave at dawn.'

Zelah nodded.

'My habit is still at Rooks Tower, I will come back with you now.' She went to her sister. 'You and Reginald must convince Sir Oswald that you are complying with his demands, Maria. Do not worry, if Nicky is at Beston Quay we will find him.'

Maria hugged her tightly. 'Bring him back safely, Zelah.'

Dominic felt better now that they had a plan. He

turned to Reginald. 'Can you trust your servants, Buckland?'

'Aye, they've all been with me for years.'

'Very well, then, impress upon them that no one must know what we are doing. And put it about that Miss Pentewan is confined to her room.'

She met his eyes in a fleeting glance that held the hint of a smile.

'I am of course exhausted after the ball.'

'Can you do it?' asked Reginald. 'It is Thursday tomorrow. Can you get to Beston and back before the hearing?'

'We will do our level best.' Dominic held out his hand to him. 'Keep that paper ready to produce at the hearing, Buckland. With luck we will beat Evanshaw at this!'

By the time they arrived back at Rooks Tower Zelah could not see anything in front of the horses and she wondered just how Dominic kept the curricle on the road. Jasper had stabled his horse and was waiting to hand her down.

'All our guests have retired, so we do not need to offer any explanations yet,' he said, escorting her into the hall. 'I took the liberty of asking Mrs Graddon to make up a bed for you, Miss Pentewan. She tells me the tower room is ready. And I have ordered refreshments to be served in the morning room. I hope you don't mind, Dom?'

'Of course not.'

His tone was curt, but she was used to that. She did not think he was angry with her, merely that he did not want to take her to Beston Quay. When Jasper excused himself and went off to change out of his muddy clothes, Zelah followed Dominic into the morning room.

'I promise I shall not hold you up,' she said, 'if that is worrying you.'

He walked over to the window and closed the shutters. 'I know that. I have seen you ride, Miss Pentewan.'

She winced at his formality. 'You had begun to call me Zelah,' she reminded him gently.

With a smothered oath he swung round. 'I am doing my best to protect you, madam, and at every turn you thwart me!'

She raised her brows. 'Do you think I am doing this to thwart you?'

He looked up at the ceiling, exhaling. 'No, of course not. But this could leave you open to gossip, when it becomes known.'

She lifted her shoulders. 'It does not matter. I will soon be gone from here.' He did not contradict her. Another blow, but she shut her mind to it and said fiercely, 'Besides, rescuing Nicky is far more important than any reputation.'

They set off at sunrise, riding away from the moor, through wooded valleys towards the Devon border. Zelah rode between Dominic and his brother, Jem Sawley following behind on a large dappled roan. Jasper had laughed when the groom had brought it into the yard.

'Good God, Dom, do you have only ugly horses in your stable?'

'Aye.' Dominic grinned. 'They are a good match for their master!'

Jasper winked at Zelah before scrambling up on to his handsome bay gelding. The exchange had lightened the mood a little—until then Dominic had behaved with numbing politeness and she was relieved that he had now returned to his usual habit of barking orders at everyone.

On they rode, mile after mile, down ancient tracks and across open land, following the route Dominic and Jasper had memorised the previous night. They skirted towns and villages for the first part of their journey, only coming on to the main routes to cross the rivers. The last major crossing was at Torrington, and as they trotted across the bridge Dominic gave Zelah an encouraging smile.

'Not long now.'

She nodded, easing her aching thighs on the saddle. At any other time she would have relished the challenge, but for now her mind was fixed on rescuing Nicky.

They followed a narrow lane and soon found themselves travelling across a desolate plateau of bare fields and scrubland. Ahead of them was the sea, a deep grey line between the edge of the land and the heavy grey cloud bank on the horizon. Zelah could taste the salt in the fresh breeze as they rode on, skirting the village itself and heading directly towards the quay, which was a mile or so to the west. Then, suddenly, their goal was in sight and they reined in their horses as the ground fell away sharply before them. On each side the black, ragged cliffs dropped into the choppy grey waters, while directly below them a haphazard collection of buildings straggled across a promontory. The inn was easily identified, a low stone building with its blue sign and a row of barrels standing against the wall.

'I think it best if I go down alone first,' said Jasper. 'It is possible that some of Evanshaw's people might be there and they could recognise one of you.'

Zelah gazed down at the little hamlet.

'It looks a very poor, isolated sort of place. What will you say?'

Jasper grinned. 'No need to worry, I am quite adept at playing the eccentric traveller.' He pointed to a small stand of trees. 'Wait for me over there, where you will not be seen.'

While Jasper set off down the winding track, the others moved back into the trees, where only the sighing wind and the distant cry of the gulls broke the silence. It was impossible to ride into the small wood because the overhanging branches were too low, so they dismounted and Sawley led their horses along a narrow path. Zelah was thankful that the thick canopy of leaves sheltered them from the hot sun. Their path led to a small clearing. The groom took the horses to one side while Zelah and Dominic found a convenient tree stump and sat down.

'This reminds me of the first time I saw you,' said Zelah, removing her bonnet and wiping her hand across her hot brow. 'You had been working in the woods and you were carrying a fearsome axe.'

'With my wild appearance I must have been very frightening.'

She considered for a moment. 'No, I was never really frightened of you.'

'Not even when you attacked me with that tree branch?'

She laughed. 'A mere stick, which you disposed of quite summarily!'

He looked at her, the faint smile in his eyes causing her heart to beat a little faster. 'You were very brave, you know, to stand your ground against me. You did not know who I was, or what I might do.'

'But I could not leave Nicky.'

'No, you are very fond of him, are you not?'

'He is like my…' She stopped, shaking her head a little.

'Go on,' Dominic urged her gently.

Zelah drew in a long, steadying breath.

'He is like my son, the baby that n-never lived, that I never held in my arms. I shut it out, all the pain and loss, until I came to West Barton and met my sister's little stepson. He was so bright, so very much alive—I could do nothing else but love him.'

Dominic gave a short laugh. 'I know what you mean. He soon found his way past my defences!'

'And now he has been snatched away—' She gripped her hands together tightly in her lap. 'Do you think Jasper will find him?'

Dominic's heart lurched when she spoke his twin's name. Were they on such good terms already? He tried to dismiss the thought and concentrate upon her question.

'I doubt it will be quite so easy. If they have the

boy, you may be sure they will keep him out of sight. But he may glean some useful information. Then we will act.' She shivered, instinctively leaning closer. Dominic put his arm around her shoulders. 'Try not to worry. If the boy is here we will find him.'

She leaned against him and he lowered his head until her honey-brown curls brushed his chin. Desire stirred, but Dominic knew it was more than that. He wanted to protect her, to wipe away the anxious frown that creased her brow. It was a jolt to realise that her happiness was the most important thing in the world to him. With a sigh she reached for his hand, twining her fingers with his.

'Thank you. It is such a comfort to have you here. You really are a true friend to me.'

The knot in Dominic's stomach hardened. There was that word again. Friend. She kept insisting it was what they should be, but it was a million miles away from what he wanted from her.

They sat thus for a long time, each lost in their own thoughts. Behind them was the quiet snuffle and chomping as their horses nibbled at the tender young shoots pushing up through the ground.

Chapter Sixteen

'Listen!'

Dominic's soft hiss brought Zelah's head up. She sat very still, straining to hear. Someone was approaching, whistling a jaunty tune that mingled with the sighing of the gentle breeze through the leaves. Minutes later Jasper appeared, leading his horse through the trees. Dominic jumped up to meet him.

'What did you discover?'

'There's the usual customs house, some warehouses and a few cottages down by the quay, and the inn of course. The Anchor. It's a rundown tavern used mainly by the fishermen, so it's pretty quiet at the moment because all the boats are out.' He stripped off his gloves, grinning. 'Landlord's name is Miller—'

'The bailiff's brother!' declared Zelah.

Jasper nodded. 'Very likely. He and his wife run

the place, but they were not very welcoming, told me they had no rooms to spare and suggested I should try the Ship in Beston village.'

'You saw no sign of Nicky?' Zelah questioned him anxiously.

'No, but I thought I heard a child's voice coming from one of the upper rooms.'

'Then we must go back immediately,' she said quickly. 'If Nicky is there we must rescue him—'

'I intend to,' replied Dominic, 'but we won't go rushing in.' He nodded towards the coast. 'We are less likely to be seen once the rain sets in.'

A bank of cloud was rolling in from the west. The minutes dragged by but at last it had enveloped the fields and as it crept ever closer to the trees, the gentlemen unstrapped their greatcoats from the saddles and prepared themselves for bad weather. Jasper and Dominic pushed their cuffs out of sight and each wrapped a muffler around his neck to conceal the white linen. Zelah, shrouded in her enveloping cloak and with the capacious hood hiding her face, thought they would look like grey wraiths riding out into the swirling mist that had swept in from the sea.

Zelah picked up Portia's reins. 'Will one of you help me to mount?'

'It would be best for you to wait here with Jem,' stated Dominic.

'I am coming with you.'

'You are not!'

'But—'

He flung up his arm. 'I do not have time to argue, Zelah. We need to concentrate on finding Nicky and getting him away safely, not protecting you from danger.'

She opened her mouth to protest, but Jasper put his hand on her arm.

'Dominic is right,' he said quietly. 'You would distract us. We would both be far too anxious for your safety if you come with us. Let Dom and me rescue the boy. Besides, if anything should go wrong, you and Sawley will be free to raise the alarm.'

She closed her lips against further protest—it would only add to their belief that she was a distraction, she thought bitterly. With a nod Jasper began to lead the big bay out of the clearing. Dominic stepped in front of her, hesitated, then briefly placed his hands on her shoulders.

'Don't worry, if the boy is there we will find him and bring him back to you.'

Silently she nodded. *I am a distraction*, she thought, and fought down the desire to throw her arms about his neck and kiss him, to wish him good luck and urge him to be careful. Instead she tried to keep her worries hidden as she watched them walk away. They were soon swallowed up by the mist and she was left with only Jem Sawley for company.

Dominic followed Jasper down the narrow track. The drizzle and mist enveloped them and within minutes their outer clothes were dusted with tiny water droplets. When they reached the small promontory Jasper led the way to a derelict barn. The door had disappeared, but the roof was almost intact.

'We'll leave the horses here,' said Jasper. 'The inn lies at the other side of the quay, but it's not far.'

'Good.' Dominic drew his pistol from its saddle holster. 'You go to the inn and call for service, I'll slip in the back way and search the rooms.'

'I shall go to the front door and make a lordly fuss.' Jasper looked at Dominic, his eyes unusually sombre. 'Be careful, Brother.'

He slipped away and was soon lost to sight between the straggling buildings. Dominic waited a few minutes, then set off after him. The whole area was deserted, no fishing boats were tied up at the quay, the houses and outbuildings were empty and an air of quiet desolation hung over everything. He kept close to the buildings, the rain splashing from the roof tiles onto his hat and shoulders as he hurried along the muddy lane and into the narrow alley that led to the rear of the inn. The long, low building formed an L-shape around a cobbled yard. On one side the roof was extended to form a covered way, which looked as if it had once been a skittle alley, but was now filled with empty beer barrels stacked untidily against the back wall.

He could hear Jasper's voice, loud and bombastic as he shouted for the landlord. Dominic moved cautiously towards the open doorway. He found himself in a narrow passage. An open door immediately on his right led to the kitchen and a set of narrow stairs ran up to his left. He slipped up the stairs, which mercifully did not creak. A series of doors led off the landing. Boldly he put his hand on the latch of the first one and walked in, prepared to apologise and retreat if it was occupied, as if he was a genuine guest.

The room was empty, shabby but clean with the bed made up and ready for use. The second and third attempts revealed similar empty rooms.

'Hmm,' he muttered to himself, 'that gives the lie to their being full.'

The next door was locked and a heavy bolt had been fastened to the outside, the freshly splintered wood evidence that it had been fitted very recently. He knocked softly and heard a sobbing whimper.

Dominic took out a pocket knife and set to work on the old lock, which soon gave way.

Cautiously he opened the door. The room was as sparsely furnished as the others, but Nicky was there, alone, sitting disconsolately on the edge of the narrow bed. As soon as he saw Dominic he threw himself at him.

'Thank God,' muttered Dominic, laying a hand on the boy's shoulder. 'Come now, let us get out of here—'

'Not so fast, my fine friends.'

The rolling West Country vowels made Dominic's head snap around. The landlord was at the door, a shotgun held menacingly in his hands.

'Ah. I thought I heard a noise up 'ere.'

Dominic stepped in front of Nicky. 'Don't be a fool, man. Put the gun down. The game is up now, unless you mean to murder us.'

The landlord shrugged. 'Murder, abduction, it makes no odds. We'd hang anyway if we was found out—and keep yer hands where I can see 'em,' he ordered, as Dominic reached for the pistol in his pocket.

'Dan'l, what're you doin'…?' the landlady's shrill tones preceded her up the stairs. A slatternly looking woman with untidy hair and a greasy apron appeared beside her husband, who sniffed.

'We got a visitor, Martha. Come to get the boy. Do you check 'is pockets, and see if he's carryin' a weapon.'

The landlady wiped her hands nervously on her apron and approached Dominic, keeping well to the side so there was no possibility of blocking her husband's aim. She lifted the pistol from his pocket and the man called Daniel gave a satisfied nod.

'I thought as much.'

'So are you going to shoot 'im, Dan'l?'

'No!' cried Nicky, clinging to Dominic.

'It's all right, Nicky,' said Dom quickly. 'Don't worry, lad.'

'Aye, that's right, you tell 'im,' leered the landlord, waving the shotgun menacingly. 'If you are wise, you'll both behave yerselves.'

'And if *you* are wise, you will let them go.' Jasper's cool drawl came from the landing, a pistol in his hand.

'Is that right?' The landlord spat on the floor. 'Seems to me that pop gun o' yers might get me, but not afore I've pulled the trigger, and one blast from this would send the nipper *and* yer friend to kingdom come. And it's not to say that Martha here might not loose off yer friend's shooter, too.'

A cold chill ran down Dominic's spine. He wondered how quickly he could drop down and shield the boy. If he was quick enough, he could take the force of the blast and Nicky might survive.

'So what's it t'be?' the landlord demanded. 'I ain't gonna stand here all day. Either you comes in here with yer friend and the boy, or I'll shoot 'em both.'

'Don't 'ee be too hasty, Dan'l.' The woman placed her hand on the landlord's arm. 'If we has trouble here then we'll have the Revenue men crawling all over the place.'

'She's right,' agreed Jasper. 'You cannot fire that thing without an almighty disturbance that will bring every Revenue man for miles down upon you.'

The landlord shrugged. 'No matter. They ain't found nothing yet so I reckons I'll tek my chances, if I 'as to. And as to shooting anybody...' his lip curled, displaying a mouth full of yellow, rotted teeth '...a man's entitled to defend his property. No, my fine buck, I thinks you'd better give that pretty pop o' yours to my good lady, afore my finger gets itchy on this trigger and I shoots the boy.'

Through the open doorway Dominic met Jasper's eyes and read the message there. The risk was too great. Jasper lowered his pistol.

'Well, fellow, it seems you have me there.'

The landlord stood away from the door. 'You come on in here, then, where I can see thee. And, Martha, you go and fetch some cord to tie up these fine gennlemen!'

'I'm sorry, brother,' murmured Jasper as he came to stand beside Dominic. 'Perhaps we will have another chance.'

'Perhaps.' Dominic shrugged.

Faced with the shotgun pointing at them, they could do nothing but wait until the landlady returned with a length of thin rope, with which she proceeded to bind their hands behind their back.

'Tight, mind,' ordered Daniel. 'They's big divils and I don't want no messin with 'em.'

'Aye, but what now?' said Martha, when she had finished. 'Do you want to leave 'em all here?'

'No, the boy can stay—the lock's bust, but the bolt on the door will hold'n.' He looked up suddenly. 'Where's your horses?'

'Back at the village,' said Dominic. 'At the inn.'

'Aye,' added Jasper. 'We told them we were here to paint the landscape.'

The landlord's face twisted into a cruel grin. 'Well, then, they won't think nothing of it if you takes a tumble off the cliff into the sea. We'll put you in the cellar 'til nightfall, then tek you out to sea an'—'

'No!' shouted Nicky, 'You shan't hurt them, you shan't.'

The landlady pulled him against her greasy skirts. 'No, no, they won't be 'armed, my babby.' She glared at her husband. 'Do you want to have the nipper bawling and troublesome all night? Will said we was to keep 'im safe—no marks, 'e said.' She looked down at the little boy. 'Don't 'ee worry, me lad. We're jus gonna put yer friends into the cellar for a while, till William comes to take you all home, ain't that right, Dan'l?'

'Aye,' growled Daniel. 'So you two get yerselves downstairs, now, and don't try anything, I ain't afraid to deal with you.'

'No, of course not, now we have our hands tied behind our backs!' retorted Dominic. He turned and nodded at Nicky. 'We will see you later, Nicky.'

Daniel waved the shotgun again. 'That's enough, now get yerselves down them stairs.'

The landlord kept a safe distance behind them and the landlady, waving Jasper's pistol in her hand, informed them that she was quite prepared to use it.

A door under the stairs led to the cellar. The landlord waved them forwards, waited until they were both on the stairs, then kicked his foot into Jasper's back, sending them crashing down into the darkness.

* * *

Zelah paced up and down the clearing. The light within the trees had faded to a grey dusk. Surely Dominic and Jasper should have returned by now? It was still raining, but the mist had lifted a little and she could see where the lane dropped away to the quay. There was no one in sight. She felt quite sick with apprehension, imagining the most horrendous scenes. It was almost too dark to see now and with grim determination Zelah made her way back to where the groom was sitting with the horses.

'Help me to mount, Sawley. We will go and find out what has happened.'

'Nay, madam, the major said—'

'The major should have been back by now,' she retorted fiercely. 'Now it is up to you—either you come with me, or I shall go to the quay alone!'

Chapter Seventeen

The darkness was complete. Dominic and Jasper sat back to back on the cellar floor, each in turn trying to untie the other's wrists. Dominic ran his tongue over his lips, tasting blood. He guessed he had cut his face when the landlord had pushed them down the stairs, but that was a minor concern. He thought of Nicky locked in the room upstairs and his anger grew. He would give everything he had if he could save him, not only for his own sake, but because of what the boy meant to Zelah.

Jasper swore softly. 'It's no good, Dom. That damned fishwife has tied the ropes too well.'

'We'll rest for a moment, then I'll try again,' muttered Dominic. He leaned against his twin. 'How long do you think we have?'

'Heaven knows. I wouldn't think he would try to get rid of us while he has any customers, and by the sound of it the inn's pretty full tonight.'

'A couple of hours at most, then.'

'Our best chance would be when they take us to the ship,' said Jasper. 'We might be able to make a run for it then, perhaps get help at the customs house from the Revenue officer.'

Dominic said nothing. They both knew it was a slim chance, but neither was willing to admit defeat.

'We'll just have to conserve our energy and—'

'Hush!' Dominic whispered urgently. 'Someone's coming.'

They struggled to their feet and waited, tense and expectant. They heard the soft rasp of bolts being drawn back from the door at the top of the stairs. Dominic swallowed the bitter bile of frustration. If only his hands were free he would punish that damned landlord—

'Nicky!'

Jasper's exclamation mirrored his own surprise. The soft glow of candles appeared at the top of the steps and Nicky came racing down towards them, Jem Sawley following quickly, but it was the figure behind the groom that caused Dominic's heart to stand still.

'Zelah! By heaven, what are you doing here?'

She closed the door carefully behind her before descending, holding her candle high to give as much light as possible.

'We guessed something had gone wrong and came to find you. Here, Nicky, hold the candle for me.'

'Did you call at the customs house for help?' Dominic demanded, looking past her.

'No,' she said. 'Everything was in darkness and we did not want to waste time.'

With a furious oath Dominic turned to his groom. 'Hell and damnation, Jem, you should not have brought her here!'

Zelah did not wait for the hapless groom to muster his arguments.

'He could not very well leave me behind!' She pulled a long-bladed knife from the folds of her cloak. 'I found this in the kitchen and thought it might be useful. Turn about, if you please, and I will cut you free.'

It was the work of moments to cut through their bonds. Dominic stood for a moment, rubbing his sore wrists. His relief at being free was tempered by anger. He wanted to rail at Zelah for putting herself into such danger, but because he knew it was foolish and unjustified he kept silent. Jasper knew no such reticence. He put his arm about Zelah and kissed her soundly on the cheek.

'Well done, my dear!' He looked across at Dominic and grinned. 'I don't know about you, brother, but I have had enough of this inn's hospitality. Shall we go?'

'Yes, immediately,' returned Zelah. 'We left our horses with yours, at the old barn.'

The three men went first, cautiously opening the cellar door. The laughter and chatter from the tap-room filtered through the narrow passage, but there was no one in sight as they crept out.

They had almost reached the doorway when the landlord appeared from the courtyard. His eyes bulged when he found his way blocked by the men he thought safely trussed up in his cellar, but Jasper's fist caught him squarely on the chin and laid him low. Hurriedly Dominic and Jem dragged the landlord's unconscious body into the shadow of the building and signalled to Zelah and Nicky to come out into the wet twilight.

Once in the yard Zelah found her breathing easier: it was good to be outside again, even though the mist was thicker than ever. She held Nicky's hand as they followed Jasper out of the yard, Dominic and Jem hovering protectively behind them. Her spine tingled. She was fearful of hearing the alarm raised, or, even worse, a shot ringing out. Even when they reached the horses she could not relax. Jasper threw her up into the saddle while Dominic took Nicky up before him and they left the village at a canter, not slowing up until they were up on the plateau again, with only the mist and the rain for company. Zelah glanced nervously over her shoulder.

'Do you think they will follow us?'

'It's possible,' said Dominic. 'We should get as far away as we can while there is some light.'

Jasper nodded.

'I agree, although it pains me to lose two good pistols to the villains. But we may yet recover them. I do not intend to let that rascally landlord and his wife get away with this. But first we have to return Nicky to his parents, and before tomorrow's hearing, if that's possible. Let's press on, if you feel up to it, Miss Pentewan?'

Zelah nodded and Nicky, cocooned inside the front of Dominic's greatcoat, raised his head.

'Yes, please,' he said, his voice breaking. 'I w-want to go home.'

They had ridden hard until it was too dark to travel, then broken their journey at a coaching inn, where all Jasper's considerable address and his full purse had been required before the landlord was persuaded to admit them. They had set off again at dawn, but heavy rain hampered their progress and they had to divert several times to avoid the swollen streams that blocked their route. There was no

time to go to West Barton before the hearing started
at ten o'clock so they made directly for Lesserton,
where the church clock was already striking the
hour when they reached the White Hart.

'Your brother is here,' observed Dominic, nodding towards the carriage pulled up across the
street.

'Good, I hope Maria is with him too, I cannot
think she will be sitting at home on such an important day,' declared Zelah, as Jasper helped her
dismount.

He pulled her hand on to his arm. 'Come along,
then, we will all go in together.'

Their entrance caused immediate confusion.
Sir Oswald, facing the door, saw them first. His
eyes narrowed and a dull, angry colour mottled
his cheeks. Maria gave a little scream and Reginald, who was sitting beside Mr Summerson, his
lawyer, jumped up, gazing at his son and unable
to speak for some moments. Maria ran forwards to
take Nicky in her arms while the rest of the crowd
muttered in surprise, knowing nothing of what had
ensued.

Dominic stepped into the centre of the room and
addressed the magistrate.

'I beg your pardon for the intrusion,' he announced. 'We came to tell Mr Buckland his son is safe.'

'Aye,' declared Reginald, his eyes bright with anger. 'He was abducted, Sir Arthur, and this note was sent to me, warning me not to present my new evidence to this hearing!'

The surprised mutterings around the room swelled as Reginald handed the paper to the magistrate. Sir Arthur hammered on the desk again, then looked at the little boy, now held safely in his mother's arms.

'You were taken, young man, against your will?'

Nicky nodded solemnly. 'Yes, sir.'

'And do you know who it was who did this to you?'

'Yes, sir. He's there.' Nicky pointed towards Sir Oswald's bailiff. 'It was Mr Miller, the man who is trying to leave.'

The villagers raised their voices in a howl of outrage and those nearest Miller held him fast as he edged past them. The bailiff swore and tried to shake them off, but found himself trapped.

'It weren't my idea to take the boy!' he cried. 'Sir Oswald ordered me to do it.'

Sir Oswald jumped to his feet. 'Be quiet, you fool!'

Mr Summerson rose and directed a stern look at

the bailiff. 'If you know anything more you should tell us now, Mr Miller. The charge against you is a serious one.'

'He told me to do it!' Miller was gabbling now, fear loosening his tongue. 'Just like he told me to get rid of Old Robin, to stop'n talking.'

There was a moment of shocked silence, then fresh cries of fury filled the room. Giles Grundy rose to his feet, his broken arm strapped up securely across his chest.

'We found Old Robin drowned in the Lightwater,' he said slowly. 'But his head was bashed open fearsome bad.'

'Sir Oswald said I was to frighten 'im,' said Miller, still trying to free himself. 'Said I was to get him to leave the area, but the old man were stubborn. Drunk, he was, and we came to blows.'

'So you knocked him unconscious and threw him in the Lightwater,' pursued Sir Arthur.

Maria gasped and Zelah saw that her sister was holding Nicky tight to her and covering his ears.

'He'd have fallen in anyway, like as not,' muttered Miller sullenly.

Sir Arthur hammered on the desk to regain order. 'Take him away and lock him up,' he commanded. 'We will deal with this later.' He turned to Sir Oswald. 'I find it hard to believe, sir, that you would resort to abduction to prevent new evidence being put to the court.'

'Of course I would not,' declared Sir Oswald impatiently. 'I knew nothing about any new evidence.'

'Oh, yes, you did.'

Silence fell over the room as Nicky's young voice rang out. All eyes turned towards him and he flushed, shrinking closer to his stepmother. Sir Arthur turned to him.

'And how do you know anything about this, young man?'

Nicky swallowed hard. 'It was at the ball at Rooks Tower. I was on the landing. Major Coale said I might stay up and watch.' He turned his eyes towards Dominic, who nodded. Encouraged, Nicky continued. 'I heard Mr Lerryn tell Sir Oswald that Papa had a new document that would win the case for the villagers.'

'Utter nonsense,' blustered Sir Oswald. 'The child is dreaming.'

Sir Arthur put up his hand and directed his solemn stare at Nicky. 'I was at the ball, young man, and I know how crowded it was. How could you have possibly heard what was said?'

'It was supper time, and there weren't many people in the hall. Mr Lerryn brought Sir Oswald over to the corner of the hall, beside the stairs. Directly below where I was sitting.'

'And you are sure that is what was said?' Sir Arthur asked him.

'Yes, sir,' affirmed Nicky. 'When Sir Oswald asked him how he knew about it, Mr Lerryn said he was there when Papa received the paper and that he wanted to...to *put a spoke in Buckland's wheel*. He said he knew Papa meant to keep the paper a secret until the hearing.'

The murmur amongst the crowd swelled again. Sir Oswald jumped up, banging his fist upon the table.

'You will never take that child's word over mine, Andrews!'

'It explains why you thought it necessary to abduct my son!' roared Reginald.

Shouts and cries of 'shame' filled the air. Sir Arthur hammered on his bench.

'I will have order!' he bellowed. He fixed a stern gaze upon Sir Oswald. 'I will question you about the matter of abduction later, but first I am obliged to finish this hearing. I charge you, therefore, not to go out of my sight.'

'Don't 'ee worry, sir, we'll keep'n safe for 'ee,' shouted someone in the crowd, amid much cheering.

Reginald murmured something to his lawyer, who handed the magistrate a rolled parchment.

'My client informs me this paper was found amongst the books Major Coale recently purchased from the Lydcombe Park estate. You will see, Sir Arthur, that it is a contract of sale for Lydcombe Park, a transaction that took place some thirty years ago, and it describes the boundary between the village land and Lydcombe Park in great detail, placing it quite clearly on the Lightwater, which flows along the western edge of Prickett Wood, and marked by a white boundary stone.'

'And you were not going to declare this?' demanded Sir Arthur, frowning heavily.

'I think, in the circumstances, we can understand my client's reluctance,' stated Mr Summerson. 'But this contract is quite precise in the boundary's location.'

'Aye, but rivers can change their course over the years,' cried Sir Oswald, his face still alarmingly red. 'And I tell you there is no stone in Prickett Wood. If there was, then surely someone would know of it.' He glared at the packed courtroom. 'Well, have any of you ever seen it?'

'It would appear not,' mused Sir Arthur, shaking his head. 'In the absence of a boundary stone...'

'But there *is* one,' cried Nicky, his high young

voice piping clearly over the hubbub. 'There is a white stone in Prickett Wood. I've seen it!'

'The boy's deranged,' Sir Oswald sneered, but when Sir Arthur had again called for order Dominic stepped up and placed his hand on Nicky's shoulder.

'Let the boy tell us what he knows.'

'I've seen it,' Nicky said again, his eyes wide. 'Old Robin took me following the deer and we often tracked them into Prickett Wood, and the pricketts always use the white stone.'

'Pricketts are the young bucks,' Reginald explained to Mr Summerson. 'They like to rub their new antlers against favourite trees and rocks.'

Dominic's contemptuous gaze fell upon Sir Oswald. 'So that is why you were killing the deer.'

Sir Oswald glared at Nicky, fury etched into every line of his face. 'By God, you young devil, I should have told Miller to dispose of you rather than—' He broke off, realising what he had said.

'The boy has certainly got the better of you, Evanshaw,' said Dominic with grim satisfaction.

Sir Arthur turned again to Nicky. 'Can you show us where to find this stone, young man?'

'Yes, sir.'

'No, no, not today,' cried Maria. 'My son has suffered far too much. He needs to rest.'

'Devil a bit, Mama,' retorted Nicky, stoutly. His

courage faltered slightly and he cast a quick be-seeching look at Dominic. 'Will you come with me, sir, you and Papa?'

'Of course. And your mother and aunt. Lord Markham, too. We will all be there for you.'

'Well, that is most satisfactory,' declared Reginald as he walked back to the High Street with Maria on his arm. 'It was delightful to see everyone from the courtroom traipse off to Prickett Wood like that. No one can be in any doubt now of where the bound-ary stone is situated. The villagers have won their dispute and Evanshaw and Miller have been locked up to await trial. All in all a good day's work. But now, my love, I think you should take Nicky and Zelah home; they look exhausted.'

'Of course,' said Maria. 'I have to get back for Baby, too. You will come home as soon as you can?'

'I will follow on, once I have instructed Sum-merson to conclude the business of the boundary with Sir Arthur.'

He turned and hailed Dominic and Jasper as they passed. Zelah stepped back behind her sister. She felt as drawn and exhausted as Reginald had said and did not want to face anyone, especially Dominic.

'How can we ever thank you, gentlemen, for returning my boy safely to us?'

'I am pleased we could be of service,' returned Jasper with his cheerful grin. 'Sir Oswald should not bother you any more, I do not see how he can explain away the evidence against him.'

Maria put out her hand first to Dominic, then to his brother. 'I know you must be very tired,' she said, smiling mistily up at them, 'but you are very welcome to come to West Barton. Join us for dinner—it is the least we can do after all you have done for us.'

'And do not forget Miss Pentewan's efforts, too,' put in Dominic, his words and the trace of a smile that accompanied them making Zelah feel as if she might cry at any moment. 'But, no, thank you. We will stay until Sir Arthur has concluded the hearing, then we must go back to Rooks Tower. I still have guests there. I shall send Sawley ahead to tell them what has occurred, but I know they will be anxious to hear the story from us.'

'Of course.' Maria nodded. 'I quite understand, but pray believe me when I say that you are both welcome to take pot luck with us at any time.'

'Thank you, ma'am.'

Jasper bowed over her hand and Zelah's before ruffling Nicky's hair. 'Good day to you, Master

Nick. Do not frighten your mama too much with the tales of your adventures!'

Zelah stood by, smiling, supposedly listening to Nicky's reply, but all the time she was painfully aware of Dominic, standing beside Reginald. He would be taking his leave any moment. She would give him her hand for the last time. There would be no 'until tomorrow' because she no longer worked at Rooks Tower.

Dominic stood outside the little circle, watching. Jasper found it easy to converse, to do the pretty and bow over the ladies' hands, but Dominic held back. What was wrong with him? His manners could be every bit as polished as his brother's, but somehow today he could not push himself forwards. If Zelah had given him the slightest encouragement, a mere look, then he would have stepped up, taken her hand, but she had been avoiding him ever since they had arrived in Lesserton this morning. Now he watched the way she smiled up at Jasper when he took her hand and the demon jealousy tore at his gut so that he could manage no more than a curt nod of farewell before he turned away.

Zelah's heart sank. After all they had done together, all they had been through, he could not wait to get away. Bitterly disappointed, she climbed quickly into the carriage.

Dominic cursed himself for a fool. How could he leave her without a word? He owed her more than that. Quickly he turned back, but she was already in the carriage. The moment was lost.

'Well, we did it, Brother,' declared Jasper once they had collected their horses and were trotting out of the village. 'We brought the boy home safely, the principal villains have been locked up and a party is even now on its way to Beston Quay to apprehend the innkeeper and his wife. Everything has worked out very well.' Jasper laughed. 'By Gad, I never thought Exmoor would prove so interesting! You are the hero of the hour, Dom. And Miss Pentewan is the heroine.' When Dominic was silent he continued. 'By Gad, what a woman. Came into the inn, cool as you please, and cut us free. Heaven knows what would have happened if she hadn't come looking for us.'

'Utter recklessness,' retorted Dominic, chilled at the thought of what might have happened. 'To put herself in danger like that! If she'd had any sense she would have gone to Beston village for help.'

'And that might have come too late. Admit it, man, she's a damned fine woman. I thought so the first time I met her in your library. Not one to say yea and nay because she thinks you want to hear it.'

'Certainly not,' agreed Dominic with feeling. She had challenged him from the first moment they had met.

'Graddon says Rooks Tower has been transformed since she first entered it.'

'Aye,' growled Dominic, 'if you call setting the place on its head, opening up rooms and encouraging me to hold a ball—a ball, mark you!—a transformation then, yes, she has changed it out of all recognition.'

'And you too, Dom. When Sal wrote and told me how you had recovered I could scarcely believe it, but it is true.' His shrewd gaze slid to Dominic, who strained every muscle to keep his countenance impassive. 'How much of that is due to your little librarian?'

'I agree she was a civilising influence,' Dominic said carefully, 'but any woman would have been the same.'

'It takes more than just any woman to put up with your moods and your curst temper,' retorted his fond brother. 'You know you have been the very devil to live with since you came back from the Peninsula. And with good reason, I admit. The state you were in, we were surprised you survived at all. What you suffered would have tried the patience of a saint. But from what I've heard Miss Pentewan has been more than a match for you.'

Exhaling in frustration, Dominic kicked his horse into a canter, relieved that they had reached a stretch of open ground, but when they drew rein to make their way onto the road he found his brother had not finished with the subject of Zelah Pentewan.

'And the way she kept up with us all the way to Beston Quay and back. Never a murmur of complaint. Pluck to the backbone. Do you know, brother, I think I am in love.'

A short laugh escaped Dominic. 'Again! How many times has that been this year?

'No, this time I am serious.' Jasper brought his horse to a stand, a look of dawning wonder on his face. 'Zelah Pentewan is intelligent, courageous, generous—not a beauty, perhaps, but very lovely. There is something quite out of the ordinary about her.'

Dominic swung round in the saddle, scowling fiercely. 'Devil take you, Jasper, Zelah is not one of your sophisticated society ladies. She has no more guile about her than a kitten! I'll not have you break her heart with your flirting!'

'Flirting?' Jasper looked genuinely shocked. 'Dom, I have no intention of flirting with her. I want to *marry* her!'

Chapter Eighteen

If he had taken a blow to the solar plexus Dominic could not have been more winded. For a full minute he stared at his brother, and his stunned countenance brought a rueful flush to Jasper's handsome face.

'Oh, I know I have thought myself in love before, but this time I am convinced it is for real. It has been coming on ever since I danced with her at your summer ball. She was so graceful and with such a natural wit that she completely bowled me off my feet. Of course, I don't know if she'll have me, but I'd like to put it to the touch. What do you think, Dom, do you think I have a chance?'

Looking at Jasper with his perfect features, his clear brow and the smooth, unblemished planes of his face, Dominic knew he was looking at one of the most handsome men in the country. Add to that a generous nature, a noble title and enough charm to bring the birds out of the trees, and it was inconceivable that his offer should not be accepted.

'Damn you, I do not see how you can fail.'

Jasper's black brows snapped together and he subjected his brother to a searching scrutiny.

'Dominic? Do you have an interest there yourself? Because if that is so...'

Dominic wished he had bitten off his tongue rather than have Jasper guess his secret. In his mind's eye he compared himself with his twin. What woman would want a scarred wreck with a comfortable income when she could have the exceedingly rich and handsome Viscount Markham? Not only that, but Jasper's unfailingly cheerful disposition was a stark contrast to his own foul temper. It was time to be honest with himself. He had held the ball for Zelah's sake, had he not? So that she might find a prospective husband. Now it seemed he had succeeded only too well, for she had won the biggest prize on the matrimonial market. He forced himself to laugh.

'I?' He spoke with all the ease and nonchalance he could muster. 'Good God, man, what makes you think that? No, I merely want her to be happy. Go to it, Jasper, and I wish you every success. She is indeed a diamond.'

'Thank you, Brother!' Jasper reached across to

slap his shoulder. 'Do you know, I think I should put it to the touch today, before I lose my nerve. Mrs Buckland invited us to take pot luck at any time, did she not? Very well, then, I'll ride over there now. Pray make my excuses to everyone—if I am in luck then I will not be back for dinner.'

Dom found it more and more difficult to maintain his smile. He managed a nod. 'Aye, go on then. Take your lovesick sighs to West Barton and leave me in peace!'

Dominic took out his watch. Nine o'clock and no sign of Jasper. The faint, barely acknowledged hope that Zelah would refuse him had finally died. How he had managed to get through dinner without his guests realising that he was totally preoccupied was a mystery. He remembered nothing of the meal, prepared by the London chef Sally had sent down to relieve Mrs Graddon, but as soon as the ladies had withdrawn he excused himself from the table. It had not taken long for the events of the past two days to become known to his guests. They were being discussed at Rooks Tower even before Dominic returned, so his male friends and relatives were happy to send him off, declaring he must be exhausted after his heroic efforts.

Dominic *was* tired, but he did not go to his bedchamber. Instead he had come here, to the tower room, where the last flare of the setting sun beamed in through the windows and bathed everything in a rosy-golden light. Now even that was gone, replaced by grey twilight that robbed even the bed's garish cover of its colour. It was just as she had left it, the books and ledgers on the desk beside the inkwell and the freshly trimmed pens. As orderly and neat as the woman herself. He heard a light scratching on the door and Graddon entered.

'I thought you might like some refreshment, sir.' He brought in a tray laden with glasses, decanters and water plus a lighted taper.

'No.' Dominic stopped him after he had touched the taper to only two candles. 'Leave them. And make sure I am not disturbed again!'

His rough tone earned him an affronted look from the butler, but without a word Graddon left the room, closing the door carefully behind him.

Impatiently Dominic pushed his fingers through his hair. It was unreasonable of him to vent his ill humour on a servant, especially one as loyal as Graddon. He unstoppered the brandy and poured himself a generous measure. He would have to beg his pardon, of course, but he could do that tomorrow, when hopefully this black cloud would have lifted from his spirits.

Dominic carried his brandy over to the window, warming the glass between his hands before tasting it. He could get riotously drunk. That would bring him some measure of relief, but he would pay for it in the morning, and so would his guests, if he was surly and uncommunicative. Damn his sense of duty that obliged him to act the perfect host. He put his arm against the window and rested his forehead on his sleeve.

It was that same sense of duty that made him hold back from informing Jasper of Zelah's past. She had told him in confidence and he thought it likely that she would tell Jasper, too—he understood his twin well enough to know that the story of her seduction and the lost baby would elicit nothing but sympathy, but if she chose not to do so, he would not expose her. And what of his own connection with Zelah, the kisses, the passion that had threatened to overwhelm them? Would she tell Jasper of those? He guessed not. She was too honourable, too generous to want to cause a rift between brothers. And if she could put those precious moments behind her, then he could too. He would do nothing to spoil her happiness.

A movement on the drive caught his attention. There were shadows on the lawn, two riders approaching the house. Even in the dim light there was no mistaking them. As he watched they looked up at the tower. Dominic jumped back, cursing. What in hell's name was Jasper doing, bringing Zelah to Rooks Tower? It was late—did he mean to make sure of her tonight? Could he not wait until they had exchanged their vows before he took her to his bed? Dominic dragged the chair over to the side table and threw himself down, reaching for the brandy. Let them do what they wished, Zelah Pentewan was no longer any concern of his.

He leaned back in the chair and stretched out his legs, wondering how soon it would be safe to cross the great hall to his study. He had no wish to see Zelah. Would Jasper take her into the drawing room where family and friends would be gathered now, or would he take her straight to his room?

He shook his head to dispel the unwelcome images that thought brought forth. He heard a soft knock and turned towards the door, snarling, 'Damn you, Graddon, I told you not to come back tonight!'

'I do not recall you doing so.' Zelah stepped into the room, unperturbed by his ill humour. With a smothered oath he jumped to his feet, sending the chair crashing behind him.

'What are you doing here?'

'I saw the light and came to find you.'

'Well, now you have found me you can take yourself off again!'

'You are not very polite, sir.' She came closer, stripping off her gloves.

'I don't feel very polite,' he retorted. 'If you want me to bestow my blessing upon the match, I will do so tomorrow.'

'If you wish.' She pointed to the decanters. 'Is that Madeira? Perhaps I could have a small glass? I have had quite an exhausting day.'

He scowled, but automatically filled a glass for her. 'You should not be here.'

She took the glass from him, her clear eyes upon his face. 'Why should I not? I have quite come to look upon this room as my own.'

He concentrated on refilling his own glass and deliberately avoided looking at her. 'You will soon have much bigger properties than this at your disposal.'

'Ah. You mean when I am Viscountess Markham.'

She moved closer, so near he could have reached out and embraced her. He had to force himself not to do so.

'Jasper is very rich, isn't he?' she said, sipping at her Madeira.

'Exceedingly.'

'Handsome, too, and charming.'

'Yes.' Dominic ground his teeth. Damn him. He took a mouthful of brandy, impatient for the powerful spirit to begin clouding his brain.

'I turned him down.'

Dominic choked. Carefully he put down his glass. Zelah put hers beside it.

'I am very sorry to hear that,' he said cautiously.

'Are you?'

'Of course. He could give you everything your heart desires.'

She shook her head. 'No, that is not possible. You see, I do not love him.'

'If you are still pining for Lerryn, then you are a fool,' he said bluntly.

She waved her hand impatiently. 'No, of course I am not. Oh, Dominic, you are so, so *dull-witted* tonight!'

'Well, I, too, have had a difficult day. Give Jasper time to win your heart. You will come to see that there is not a better man in England—'

'That may be true. Jasper is very charming and I was very sorry to cause him pain, but I am not the woman to make him happy, and he is not the man for me. He is not you.' She stepped up to him and raised her hand to caress his left cheek, her palm cradling the scarred tissue. 'There is only one man who has ever held my heart,' she said softly, her eyes shining into his and filling his soul with light. 'Only one man that I could imagine spending the rest of my life with, and that is you, Dominic.'

There. She had said it.

'And what of Jasper? How did he take your refusal?'

'Like the true gentleman he is. I do not think he is truly heartbroken, but even if that was the case, I could not act differently.'

Zelah waited breathlessly, her eyes fixed on his face. Jasper had guessed her reason for refusing him. He had told her Dominic was very much in love, and all she had to do was to make him admit it. Now, as the minutes ticked by and she could discern nothing in his hard impassive gaze, Zelah wondered if Jasper had been wrong about his twin. Her hand dropped and she turned away, blinking back the hot tears.

'So there it is,' she said lightly. 'I am a hopeless case. I have heard nothing back from the widow in Bath, so I must surmise I was unsuccessful there, too. Do—do you think your sister will write me another ref—'

An iron hand gripped her arm and swung her round. The collision with Dominic's unyielding chest winded her, but the glow she saw in his eyes set her heart pounding.

'You would take me, rather than Jasper?'

'I will take no other,' she answered him solemnly. She saw the desire leap in his eyes, but also uncertainty. She prayed he would not reject her now.

'Are you sure this is not just…pity?' His voice was harsh, the words edged with bitterness.

Summoning all her courage she slipped her hands about his neck. 'No, not pity. Love. I love you, Dominic. Let me show you how much.'

She pulled him down towards her and kissed his mouth. His touch was cool, wary, and she closed her eyes, willing him to respond. She felt rather than heard him growl, or was it a sigh? His arms went round her and he kissed her, working her mouth hungrily beneath his, forcing her lips apart, his tongue invading, demanding. Zelah gave way to her passion.

Her hands scrabbled with his jacket, pushing it off his shoulders. The waistcoat followed, but she had to break away to see how to untie the intricate knot of his neckcloth. Impatiently he pushed her hands aside and ripped off the muslin. He was breathing heavily and the crisp dark hair of his chest was visible at the shirt opening. Her hands shook a little as she tugged his shirt free from his breeches. He was far too tall and she could only gather it up and allow him to pull it off. The sight of his naked chest enthralled her. A dark cloud of hair ran down the centre of his chest and the shadows from the candlelight enhanced the rippling muscle. She leaned forwards to press her lips to the ragged scar that crossed his body, trailing kisses down its length as it passed across his breast and the hard undulations of his ribs to the soft, flat plain of his stomach while her hands unfastened the flap of his breeches, her heart jumping with pleasure and anticipation when she noticed how hard and aroused he was beneath the soft buckskin.

She pushed aside the material and began to kneel, intending to follow that wicked scar its full length, but Dominic stopped her.

'This is unfair,' he muttered, pulling her to her feet. 'Let us take this slowly.'

Her body sang with anticipation as he undressed her, pausing to kiss each new area of skin as he exposed it. She gasped when he reached her breasts. She reached out for him, but he caught her arms, pinning them to her sides while his mouth circled and teased her exposed flesh until she was almost begging him to stop. Only then did he raise his head, a devilish gleam in his eyes.

'Now you know how I feel when you touch me.'

As soon as he released her she threw herself at him, kissing him hungrily, tangling her tongue with his and pressing herself against him. It was not enough. There were too many layers of fabric between their bodies. In silent accord they hurriedly shed the remainder of their clothes until they stood before each other, naked and breathless. The glow in Dominic's eyes burned into Zelah. She felt beautiful, powerful. Glorious.

With a growl he swept her up and carried her to the bed. The silk was cold as he laid her naked body down upon the cover, but only for an instant, and it was soon forgotten as he knelt beside her.

'Now,' he said softly, 'where were we?'

She sat up and reached out to touch him, just below his navel. 'I was about there.'

'Hmm.' He cupped her breasts, which tightened immediately beneath his hands. 'You are a little ahead of me, but I will catch you up.'

She shifted around until she could place her lips on his abdomen, steadying herself by placing her hands on his hips, revelling in the feel of his smooth skin beneath her fingers, her mouth, her senses enhanced by the attention he was giving to her own body. Even as she made him groan with pleasure he was moving lower, his lips burning a trail across her body while his hands, the vanguard of his exquisite assault, caressed her thighs, preparing her for his most intimate kiss.

She wanted to please him, to worship his body as he was worshipping hers, but he was sapping her control. She tried to move her hips away from his pleasuring tongue, but his hands gripped her, holding her firm while he continued his relentless onslaught, rousing her to a bucking, crying frenzy that left her almost sobbing with the pleasure of it.

Dominic gathered her to him and she lay for a few moments in the shelter of his arms. Her senses were still heightened, she could feel his soft breathing, hear the stir of the breeze through the distant trees. The fragrance of lavender from the sheets filled her head, mixed with the musky male scent of the man beside her. The candles had guttered and died and they had only the moonlight now, casting its silver gleam over the tower room. She stirred a little, but when Dominic tried to pull the covers over them she stopped him.

'No, I have not satisfied *you* yet.'

He chuckled. 'There is plenty of time for that.'

Zelah sat up. 'No, let me do this.'

He was still aroused, but she was pleased, and slightly awed, by the way his body reacted to her touch. It excited her and she could feel her body responding again. Dominic groaned and pulled her to him, his mouth seeking hers. His kiss reignited the fire and her body was soon burning with desire.

He rolled over her and she opened for him, tilting her hips, inviting him to enter.

He pushed against her, deep and satisfying. She matched his rhythm as he gradually increased the momentum, each thrust carrying her closer to the uncontrollable excitement that was so alarming and yet so exhilarating. She clung on tightly, digging her fingers into his back, afraid she might faint with sheer pleasure. Then, just when she thought she could stand no more, he cried out. She felt him tense. Her whole body gripped him. He shuddered and her own body answered with a tremor of its own. It was a climax, a tipping point and she clung tightly, as if to let go would plunge her into some black and endless abyss.

Exhausted, they sank down together beneath the covers, Dominic wrapping himself around Zelah in a way that made her feel safe, cherished.

'I hope you are going to marry me after that,' he whispered, nuzzling her neck.

'If that is what you want, Dominic.'

'I have no choice. I love you too much to risk losing you.'

'Oh.' She struggled to sit up. 'Oh, please, say that again.'

'Say what?'

'That you love me.' Suddenly she felt very shy. 'I have wanted you to say that for such a long time.'

'Have you? Then I will say it every day from now on.' He drew her towards him. 'I love you, Zelah, with all my heart. No, you *are* my heart. You are my reason for living.'

He kissed her gently and, smiling, Zelah gave a contented sigh and snuggled down in his arms to sleep.

She awoke the next morning to birdsong. It was not yet dawn, but the lack of curtains or shutters in the tower room gave them no shelter from the grey light. She opened her eyes and found Dominic propped up on his elbow, watching her. The sight of his naked torso was enough to bring memories of the night's activities flooding back. She put her hand up to his cheek and he turned to plant a kiss in the palm.

With a little shiver of pleasure, she slipped her arms around him. 'Oh, I am such a lucky woman!'

He gathered her against him. 'No regrets, then?'

'Not one.' She turned her face up and he obliged her with a long, lingering kiss. 'Mmm.' She snuggled closer. 'I feel quite dizzy. Perhaps I should not have drunk that Madeira last night.'

'You need some water.' He slipped out of bed and

went to the cupboard. Zelah watched him, enjoying the sight of his bare, athletic body moving effortlessly as he crossed the floor.

'How did you know to come back?' he asked her, pouring water into two glasses. 'I thought I had done everything I could to keep you away, damned fool that I was.'

Zelah scrambled off the bed, but she paused to find her chemise from the tumble of clothes on the floor before she joined him, not quite comfortable yet to stand naked before him, except when she was in the grip of passion.

'Jasper told me how angry you were when you thought that he was merely toying with me.' She took the proffered glass. 'He said you wanted me to be happy.' The water was sweet as nectar. 'So I told him what would make me happy. Pray do not frown so, Dominic. I thought if anyone could tell me if there was any hope, it would be your twin.'

'And what did he say?'

'He had guessed you were not…indifferent to me, but we agreed that you were—how did he put it?— *too damned noble for your own good.*'

He scowled at her, his look promising retribution for her mockery. It sent a pleasurable shiver of anticipation down her spine. She continued.

'Jasper consented to bring me back with him, so that I might try to discover how you felt about me.'

'Damned foolishness,' he said explosively. 'What if I had turned you away? Worse, what if I had taken you to my bed and then cast you aside?'

Her stomach tightened in horror at the thought, but she merely shrugged, turning to put down her glass as an old quotation came to her mind. 'Then *I would build me a willow cabin at your gate...*'

'Ah, don't, love!' He pulled her into his arms. 'I don't deserve you,' he muttered, covering her hair and her face with kisses. The now-familiar flame of desire began to burn inside, but she tried to quell it.

'You are right, of course,' she murmured, her head against his chest. 'As I shall endeavour to remind you at every opportunity.'

He put an end to her teasing by forcing her chin up and kissing her ruthlessly.

'When all our visitors have gone,' he growled once he had reduced her to shivering, adoring silence, 'which I hope will be very soon now, I plan to make love to you in every room in Rooks Tower. But for now, we will have to confine ourselves to this one.'

As his mouth covered hers, his arms tightened and he lifted her off the floor, carrying her backwards until she felt the solid edge of the desk against her thighs. The kiss deepened as her lips parted and his tongue invaded her, hinting at the pleasures to come. Her pulse was racing, control slipping away as he pushed her back on the desk. Her wayward body began to sing, straining for his touch. She made one last conscious effort to be rational.

'Dominic, the books!' she muttered against his mouth as he swept everything from the desk and laid her down on its unyielding surface. His mouth ceased the tender exploration of her lips and he raised his head a fraction to gaze down at her. The intense look in his eyes was so dark, so danger-ously seductive that she shivered pleasurably be-neath him.

'Damn the books,' he growled, before lowering his head again and continuing his meticulous inch-by-inch kissing of her body that taught her more about her anatomy than all her reading had ever achieved.

* * * * *